Aftershocks

A. N. WILSON grew up in Staffordshire and was educated at Rugby and New College, Oxford. A Fellow of the Royal Society of Literature, he holds a prominent position in the world of literature and journalism. He is a prolific and award-winning biographer and celebrated novelist. He lives in North London.

ALSO BY A. N. WILSON

AFTERSHOCKS

A. N. WILSON

atlantic·*fiction*

First published in hardback and trade paperback in Great Britain
in 2018 by Atlantic Books, an imprint of Atlantic Books Ltd.

Please see p.277 for permissions details.

10 9 8 7 6 5 4 3 2 1

A CIP catalogue record for this book is available
from the British Library.

Hardback ISBN: 978 1 78649 603 4
Trade paperback ISBN: 978 1 78649 604 1
E-book ISBN: 978 1 78649 606 5

Printed in Great Britain by TJ International, Padstow, Cornwall

Atlantic Books
An Imprint of Atlantic Books Ltd
Ormond House
26–27 Boswell Street
London
WC1N 3JZ

www.atlantic-books.co.uk

Homage to E.R.M.

A NOTE

A NEW ZEALAND FRIEND READ THIS NOVEL AND ASKED – 'WHY not set it in New Zealand? Why call your imaginary country "The Island"?'

The answer is that this is not a novel about New Zealand. It is about a group of people caught up in an earthquake, two of whom fall in love. It is set in an imaginary place, and it is not intended to be a *roman à clef* about Christchurch, which suffered a devastating earthquake in 2011.

I visited Christchurch in May 2017 for three days, and nothing had prepared me for the experience of seeing a city which had been completely laid waste by a quake. It was during my short time there that the seed of this novel was planted in my mind. My imagined city, Aberdeen, is, like Christchurch, a Victorian colonial city which is, likewise, all but wrecked. But I do not know Christchurch, and I did not want to write a novel about its real inhabitants. The mayor, the Bishop and the property developers in my story are, fairly obviously, all invented. So is the Green MP. So are all the characters in the story, except for the blind busker, whom I have named Penny Whistle, and who, throughout my three days in Christchurch, could be heard singing eighteenth-century English songs in a robust baritone, never repeating himself, among the ruins. I hope he will forgive me for putting him in a story. Although the English characters inhabit actual named places (Winchester, and some named Midland towns), these too are fictitious. There is a funeral in Winchester Cathedral. That was because I wanted my heroine Nellie to pause beside the grave of Jane Austen, not because I wanted to depict the actual clergy of Winchester Cathedral.

The invented Island in this book finds itself in the position of several real postcolonial, mixed-race, modern countries. In this respect, it has characteristics in common with New Zealand, with Fiji, with Australia, and with some African countries. To compare great things with small, it bears such a relation to former dominions and colonies as Joseph Conrad's *Nostromo* bears to several countries in South America. I have spent less than three weeks in New Zealand and could not possibly hope to write a book about it, even if that had been my intention.

Part One

CHAPTER ONE

IT WAS ALWAYS THE TWO OF THEM, DIGBY AND ELEANOR. THE inseparables. Then came the Earthquake, and everything changed.

I don't want to swank, but I was the only one in Aberdeen who saw this. An early sign of love, I suppose. True love, the full works, orchestra playing Puccini, blood coursing through your temples, inner certainty that this wasn't some fly-by-night thing, but Destiny in the Person of the Beloved calling us to Newness of Life . . . But this is jumping ahead a bit, people! Sorry about that. Let's go back to the Dyce, where I was wandering around in a bit of a daze that lunchtime, having just broken up with my tutor, Barnaby Farrell.

An art gallery's a good place to go and think, specially if, like the dear old Dyce, it doesn't really have any good pictures. Course, now the paintings in the Dyce have all been destroyed, I miss them, the Alma-Tadema of Aeneas at the court of Queen Dido; the Holman Hunt of 'Caedmon tells St Hilda how he received the gift of song' – in which the cowherd bard had those strange flesh tones which Hunt's figures always have, as if they had been made up for

American TV with loads of orange slap. No one would ever have sat in front of that picture and been lost in rapture, as you would if you saw a Vermeer for the first time. They are the picture-equivalents of background music, those middle-rank Victorian efforts, and so you can just wander round, have a look at them, smile a bit; or have your own thoughts; or spy on the other gallery-goers, who, during lunch hour on a weekday in our city, Aberdeen, tended to be a mixed bunch – some of them like the sad people wandering round parks in Larkin's 'Toads' poem, and some of them there for reasons which a gossipy person, like me, would like to winkle out.

But I'd primarily gone there to think. To ask myself – what did you imagine you were DOING, sleeping with the man who is meant to be teaching you about tragedy? I mean, if I'd been nineteen, you'd have understood it, but I was twenty-seven. I'd been round the park, had a number of not especially satisfying relationships in the recent past, and I did not need to prove anything, to myself, or to him, by sleeping with Barnaby Farrell. Nothing against Barnaby. He's very good-looking, in a classic hunk sort of way – thick curly dark hair, quite muscular, fine-boned face – and a lot of the women in the class fancied him. Well, I did – obviously, but why not just leave it at that? Now it was all going to be just a bit embarrassing, attending the class he ran with Digby. (She did the Greek tragedy stuff, he did Shakespeare and Hardy, it was a fantastic class – I'll tell you more about it in a later chapter.)

He'd been really nice, said he wanted us to continue, said he wanted to see how it would go, but I could see how it would go a mile off – we'd sleep together about twenty more times; then one of us would start thinking they were in love, and the other would be going off the boil; then he'd say he wanted me to move in with him and look after his kid, and, thanks, Barnaby, that wasn't my idea of a life. I'd taken a year off from an acting career which was going really well. But I was finding that when I was faced with a real challenge – like when I was Hedda Gabler at the Redgrave in Carmichael, which has been the high point of my career to date – I just did not *know* enough. Mum said, actors don't need to know, they need to feel. I don't agree. I know what she means, but – well, let's pitch it really high, why be modest – Mrs Siddons or Sarah Bernhardt or Ellen Terry or Sybil Thorndike really knew Shakespeare and the Canon in and out. True, an actor's perspective is different from an academic's, but it is a form of intelligence. I'd rather hear Gielgud or Branagh talking about Shakespeare than read some middle-grade university lecturer on the subject. Barnaby and Digby, though, who gave our seminar jointly, were well above the middle-grade. Their seminar really fizzed. And I'd reached a stage of my career where I needed to think more – about the drama, about what I wanted to do in my theatre life – and I was in the fortunate position of being able to come back to Aberdeen, live at home with my mum, and go out to Banks University a few times a week for seminars and lectures.

I'd said quite firmly, when Barnaby asked why not just let's see how it goes – no, we should stop NOW. Of course, I'd said, 'before we get too fond of one another'. And at least he had not embarrassed me by making any declarations of love or anything like that. But I felt rather foolish all the same and, like I say, I was wondering what on earth a grown woman like me thought she was DOING behaving like that.

I think the answer was that, before I found True Love, I wouldn't ask myself – when the question arose of going to bed with someone – why I should. Instead, I asked why I shouldn't, and quite often I did not see the reason even if it was staring me in the face.

Anyhow, the Barnaby thing was over now, and there I was in the Dyce. I'd had the embarrassing conversation with Barnaby the previous day, and we'd been all very 'civilized' about it, and kissed one another on the cheek and given a little hug after breakfast (I'd been staying over at his place) and then I'd slipped out of the flat before Stig, his kid, woke up.

It was nice, always, that day or two after you'd broken up with a lover. Even if you'd been in love (which Barnaby and I certainly weren't) there was always also this feeling of being free, and wondering what you'd seen in him. (Very unlike NOW, when the thought of splitting up with the one I love would be totally unthinkable, and I'd quite honestly rather die than suffer such a thing. Luckily we both feel the same, and I am sure I have found True Love Forever and Ever Amen.) But this is to leap ahead. That's what this story is about. How an earthquake helped me find True Love. My lover, my East and West, said I should call this book *The Earth Moved for Me – How About You?* But I'm settling for *Aftershocks*.

Anyhow. There's me in the Dyce. And another good thing about wandering around an indoor public place like that is noticing all the other people and speculating on what they are up to. Of course, you get the odd pest, wondering if you are on for it, but as I have told you, I was twenty-seven, a big girl, capable of looking after herself. By big, I do not mean heavy (in spite of someone later in this narrative describing my face as 'fleshy'!), but I mean grown-up. And quite tall. I don't know if that is a disadvantage in my profession. Most theatrical people are smaller than average – Judi Dench, Laurence Olivier, Garrick . . .

It was while I was ambling about idly that I heard her voice.

Maybe before we hear her together, I should explain that when I heard that voice, I never knew if it was Digby's or the Dean's.

Different as they were, they both sounded exactly the same.

I saw more of Digby, 'cause of my course. Already, by this stage, she was coming to fascinate me. I loved her mind. Her grasp. Her sure-footedness. The way she really loved that Greek stuff, knew it backwards, and had not merely mastered it in an academic way, but lived with it. The Dean was a frostier, much less passionate person, or so it seemed to me when I sometimes accompanied Mum to the Cathedral. As I stood there in the Dyce, though, a second or two of listening assured me that it was the Dean's voice I could hear. The Dean's name was Bartlett, Eleanor Bartlett.

—I know we're not supposed to like this sort of thing, but gosh, I DO. Always HAVE ever since I was nine.

—How did you see this picture when you were nine? You were in England, surely.

—I grew up in England, but Mum was a Huia. She taught at St Hilda's here. Science. Came to England one summer to stay with relations. Met Dad.

It would be hard to find a voice which was less 'Huia' than this. It was real old-fashioned English. It put me in mind of the old St Trinian's films. Joyce Grenfell. 'Gossage, Call me sausage.' You hardly ever hear a voice like this on the Island, and I'd guess it is dying out in England. Yet she was only forty. Course, when I heard her dad's voice, all was explained.

The pair were certainly closely absorbed in one another. They did not see me. I wasn't hiding, and I wasn't in disguise, but I was wearing shades. OK, I may as well admit this, as well as being a relief, breaking up always made me a bit red-eyed. I wasn't in love, course I wasn't, but I felt I'd made a fool of myself. Again. I was wondering why I'd got to twenty-seven without getting this love business straight, perhaps no one can get it straight, and . . . well, anyhow, that made me just a little weepy. I was wearing a white tee-shirt, jeans and white Converse with red piping.

Why would pairs be wandering round an art gallery at lunchtime on a weekday? Think about it, and there can only be a few answers. The lonely singletons have a whole variety of reasons, no doubt. Some were like me, still a bit stunned from breaking up. Some might have been bereaved, fearful of going into a café or a pub in case they suddenly found themselves crying. Some were just depressed, drifting about in a daze. Some of them were genuine enthusiasts for second- – no, let's be honest – third-rate painters such as Gilbert Rhys, or for the poorish pictures by good painters like G.F. Watts, which was all the Dyce could muster. If you're European, reading this, you probably are used to going to galleries which have Titians and Rembrandts and Picassos by the score, but don't mock Aberdeen. We did our best, and the Dyce was all we had.

But back to the pairs who went there at lunchtimes . . . I don't mean the pairs of seniors, 'cause they have usually become 'Friends' of the Gallery, partly because they no longer have many real friends of their own, and partly in the hope that they can get free coffee in the Friends' Room, or find reliably clean toilets.

Pairs which are real pairs, though, they wouldn't come to a place like this at 1.40 p.m. on a weekday. They'd wait till they had finished work and meet up for drinks in some bar – there were plenty of good bars in central Aberdeen before the Quake – or go home together. And those who were in the middle of some irresistible adulterous passion – they wouldn't be ambling about the Dyce, they'd be in a hotel or some flat somewhere. The point is, think about it. Only those whose relationship had not started, or was in a state of crisis, would have chosen to come here at this point of the week. So if you sit still and wait, in a place like the Dyce, you'll see a lot of drama.

Aftershocks

The two likeliest dramas are: 'Are we falling in love?' or 'Shall we break up?' And I did not think this pair were about to break up.

It was clear that he was nuts about her. I'll describe her first, though my ways of describing her will change as this book goes on. I'm trying now to recollect exactly what I saw, WHO I saw, that day in the gallery. Tall, like me, taller than me, nearly six foot. Thick dark hair, cut quite short, so you could see the nape of her neck. The swan-like, truly beautiful neck. It was so beautiful that it took my breath away. Deep blue eyes which had not yet seen me. Eyes only for him, seemingly. A short nose. Creamy complexion. Apparently no make-up. That toothy smile, instantaneously beguiling.

He was a bit older. Or maybe being so worried, and so in love, made him look older. Long face with black hair which flopped over his forehead, cut short at back and sides. Raven black eyes. Hollow cheeks and the sort of blueish chin which he'd have had to shave at least twice a day if he wanted to keep it smooth.

By the way, in case you're thinking all the people in this book are going to have dark hair – and there would be no reason why they shouldn't – I have mousey-blondish, very thick hair, quite long, cut with a fringe over my brow; brown eyes, freckles. But back to Charlie.

His voice was Huia, but of the old world – a bit like Mum's. We – my generation – speak with much stronger 'accents' – whereas they sound more English. He was wearing a smart suit and highly polished shoes, but you wouldn't have been surprised to see his lean face sticking out of Victorian costume – an earnest Mr Rochester or Mr Dombey.

The woman was telling him more about the year her mum, a young teacher from Aberdeen, had been to England, stayed with some cousins near Birmingham, and been introduced to her dad who was a young clergyman in a place called Dudley. Mr Dombey's facial expression suggested that this conjunction, of the woman's parents, was the happiest thing which had occurred in the history of the world. I was asking myself how much he'd paid for his shoes. Hundreds of dollars.

—Mum had intended to stay in England for the summer, but she stayed for good! And about a year later I arrived on the scene!

—She bucked the trend. Normally, it is the Huia men who go abroad. Meet an American or an English woman, and stay; whereas Huia women have a homing instinct. So it has now been shown. Hence the Man Drought.

—The Man Drought?

Her question came out as a schoolgirl hoot.

—What on EARTH?

—Surely you knew? The proportion of women to men on the Island is something like sixty to forty. And the gap is widening, among the graduate classes, aged between twenty and fifty.

—What accounts for that, I wonder?

—Some people think it explains our having so many lesbians.

—I hadn't noticed.

I liked that reply. I even more liked the suddenly peremptory tone in which she said it. It's not a word you'll be reading much in this book. I don't know about you, I'm against labels, and find it really bizarre that people want to be categorized as black, white, LGBTQI, etc., rather than being individuals. She did not let him expand on his generalization, but plunged on with the autobiography.

—Anyhow, Mum brought me back three times when I was a child, and we always used to come to the Gallery. I know we aren't supposed to believe in colonies any more – well, of course we don't believe in them – but it does not stop me having a soft spot for this sort of thing. And it is such a lovely pair of pictures. Dear old Gilbert Rhys!

A whoop of schoolgirlish mirth. The Madcap of the Remove.

They were standing in front of Gilbert Rhys's *The Death of George Pattison*.

Since it no longer exists – it was pulverized by the Quake, and was in any case lucky to still be hanging on the walls of a public gallery, given its content – I'll describe it for you, in case you never saw it.

It was one of his most famous landscapes – famous on the Island, that is. It evokes with great love the wooded hillsides which still rise majestically above the western suburban shores of our city. Perhaps it was the sheer topographic accuracy of it which allowed its survival, in spite of the fact that no historians believe in the scene depicted. It was said that Obadiah Fairbrother – the lawyer whose family had grown so rich through wool – attended the death-bed of the greatest Tangata chieftain, Tamihana Huli, from whom he had leased vast tracts of fertile land. 'George Pattison' was the name adopted by this proud tribal chief after he had not merely formed land agreements with the Europeans, but had also been baptized as a member of the Church of England.

Fairbrother allowed it to be known that 'George Pattison', in his dying breath, had not simply given his land to the Europeans, but that he had done so in perpetuity. He is supposed to have gasped out, 'Remain here after I am gone – ake, ake, ake – forever'. Even the most fervent admirers of the Victorians take this story with a pinch of salt.

After the signing of the Treaty in the 1840s, the growth of population following the gold rush, the development of Waikuku Harbour into an industrial port, it was almost inevitable that our colonial forebears should wish to build a city. They climbed over the ridge beyond the site of present-day Pakenham Street to the vast plain which sits behind the harbour. Here, for five hundred years and more, the Tangata had pursued their watery lives, paddling in the wetlands, fishing, and gathering reeds which they used for clothing and artefacts.

When they became aware that the Malahi intended to build their city on the wetlands, the local Tangata chieftain and his advisers had requested a meeting with Fairbrother and the other European worthies who were drawing up plans, arranging loans from European banks, and commissioning English architects to build streets, squares, warehouses, the Guildhall, the Garrick Theatre, the Liddell Library and the churches.

The wetlands, which had been part of the domains of the great 'George Pattison', were an entirely unsuitable place on which to build a pastiche European city. The chieftain's sons told Fairbrother and his companions that it was crazy even to contemplate such a building-scheme. Fairbrother took this as an attempt by the younger Malahi to subvert the Treaty of HuruHuru. Historians now tend to the belief that, though there was an element of resentment in the Tangata, they were, for the most part, trying to give the newcomers some very necessary warnings. These had been wetlands time out of mind. They were not suitable for building edifices of brick and stone. It would not be possible to lay deep foundations in such a terrain. And besides, there was the possibility of earthquake.

When Fairbrother dismissed the younger Tangata's attempts to warn him, they asked for another meeting, bringing with them one of their elder statesmen, the formidable Gee-wara-go. The old chieftain, a Merlin-like figure with an abundant white beard falling from his cheeks, had tried to warn the Europeans by reference to an old folktale which the Tangata people told themselves. The Earth Mother Siyuta was pregnant with her difficult son Mudu. He was still in her womb, but he was kicking and raging to be let out. Every now and again, when this obstreperous foetus kicked the sides of his mother's womb, there was a tremor in the earth. There had been tremors in the wetlands. Many Tangata carried the memories of these moments, when their little skiffs suddenly found themselves overturned by disturbances beneath the waters, or when apparently dry meadowlands suddenly swelled with mud which came from beneath the surface of the earth.

Obadiah Fairbrother, emerging from a conversation with the chieftain on this subject, wrote home that it

> almost beggared belief that the savages, in their avaricious desire to hold on to this land – rightfully ours since the Treaty – should attempt to invoke the authority of their heathen gods to dissuade us from bringing civilization to this territory. I thank the one true God that we shall be able, in spite of their superstitious attempts to frustrate our endeavour, to build a British city in which every mountain shall be laid low, and every valley shall indeed be exalted.

They had moved on to the painting beside it.

—I like this even more, she said. The arrival of the *First Tangata Settlers*.

—It reminds me of the watercolour illustrations to my Bible when I was a kid, said Mr Dombey.

—Harold Copping, was her reply.

—That's right!

How weird is the madness of love! Her casual naming of a

watercolourist was greeted with an enthusiasm which could not have been more excited if she had just offered something improper.

—One would once have called it exotic, she said, but probably even the word *exotic* is pejorative now.

—I'm not sure. I'm one eighth Tangata. I'll allow you to call us exotic.

—You're right, the men on the canoes are comparable to the figures of Pharaoh's daughter and her entourage as she found the infant Moses among the bullrushes.

—Painted about the time Lord Cromer was lording it over the real Egyptians.

In both cases, the 'exotic' 'natives' could have been 'extras' in a contemporary production of Shaw's *Caesar and Cleopatra*, perhaps directed by Harley Granville-Barker. Over their heads, skimpily clad handmaids waved ostrich feathers, and their male companions wore greaves, cuirasses, golden buckles, and kilts which resembled stage costumes. As the pair spoke, so eagerly, I sensed she did not really fancy him as much as he fancied her. On the other hand, she would not have agreed to come for this little tryst if she had not fancied him a bit or at the very least felt flattered by his worship. She was teasing him, perhaps teasing herself? I sensed her holding back, while he was evidently ready to gallop forward into whatever madness his passions led him.

—Eleanor, he said, I've SO enjoyed this!

—Well, it was fun . . .

—Can we . . . can we make it a regular . . . *thing?*

No, evidently, she did not want a 'thing', or not what he called a 'thing', for she looked away and smiled, flattered but troubled.

—I think we've both got jobs to go to, she said.

As they turned, they both saw me. Her creamy pale cheeks

flushed scarlet, and then, with her perfect garden-party manners, she said, 'Hel-LO!' as though I was the person she had most wanted to see in the world. He merely nodded at me, as they walked out of the room together. They were not hand in hand, but I did wonder, had I not been there, whether they might have been. Well, well. The Dean of our Cathedral, Eleanor Bartlett, and Charlie Nicolson, one of the highest-powered lawyers in Aberdeen, both seemingly on the verge of a bit of midsummer madness. But presumably, even the clergy, and even senior lawyers, can fall in love.

Like I say, those two period piece paintings by Gilbert Rhys, and, indeed, the whole of the dear old Dyce, with its big stone stair-case and its portraits of King George V and Queen Mary on the landing, and its air of not having changed all that much since that pair had stirred the loyal feelings of many a Huia sheep-farmer to send out their sons (at their own expense) to be slaughtered in France and Flanders; the Dyce with its Gibson statue of Venus in the cafeteria, where old ladies drank coffee next to giant rampaging cheese-plants, has all been blown off the face of the earth. And here we are in the ruins of Aberdeen. And, yes, 'We've got to live,' as the Lady said, 'no matter how many skies have fallen.' (Or rather, as the man said, before he told us that racy story about the Lady.) With us, it's not just the skies that fall, it's the land that rocks. Who knows what lies ahead?

We're, like, *post*, here on the Island; very post, us; post just about everything, except post-truth. That's not the Huia way, and it's certainly not mine. This book is my journey into Truth – because it is a Journey into Love, which we – my Love and I – believe to be the same thing. But we are very definitely post-much else:

post-Earthquake, that is. Postcolonial. Certainly. In many ways, until the Quake, we were carrying on like the post-war generations. But now all that's behind us, and some of us, well, we're posthumous some of us. Postcards, pretty tourist postcards sent from addresses that have been blown sky high, views of beauty spots that will never be spotted again, that are post-spots. Postal votes in an election for a local Parliament which is just a heap of bricks and concrete. Post-it notes stuck to dead computer screens in roofless office blocks. Posts in the shifting sands, post-hoc; postscripts in history; post-traumatic stressed. Postmen and postwomen with no mail to deliver, no doors to put it through if we had it in our post-sack. Post men, too. Is that what we are, my Love, you and I? Not so much that annoying L word, which, like I say, I'm not planning on using in this book . . . but – well, Post Men?

We can't climb out of our post-seismic, post-structuralist language games. Metaphor is our only home now our material homes have all been demolished by God. (Is He or She a metaphor, by the way?) We only speak scornfully of metaphors as 'obvious' because they are true. (My beloved's dad apparently liked to say, 'Only second rate minds despise the obvious.')

Now – it really is true, we can't trust the ground we tread on.

The tectonic plates which, in their violent convulsions, created our mountain ranges and our green tufty hills are on the move again. They really are on the move, shaking up our idyllic sheep farms; our quaintly retro, smugly happy, Victorian parks really moved. They changed us forever. No wonder we clunk from one metaphor to the next, post-structuralists all. The Kantian hope of being able to describe a thing-in-itself is put on hold. Religion itself can never be quite the same . . . Can it, Nellie? Are we all post-Christians now?

Digby would maybe once have snorted at such language, Digby the single-minded atheist. She preferred to think of herself as pre-Christian, a Euripidean sceptic, or a Stoic of the Senecan breed. But witness the journey of our Dean, Eleanor Bartlett.

It needed no earthquake, of course, to draw forth a stream of clichés from Rex Tone, our go-ahead mayor; their unstoppable lava-flow spouted when he first stood for membership of the Council – no, probably much earlier when he was a student politician at Carmichael University, reading Business Studies.

Rex's emptier sayings got picked up and mocked by Cavan Cliffe, legendary radio voice and host of *Island Breakfast* for quarter of a century, but even she could not escape the metaphor-trap.

Skilled oarswoman she may be, but she found her little skiff adrift in the shallows, her oars clogged with reeds, as she tried to describe the Quake to her listeners, or as she interviewed so many of them afterwards, shellshocked, walking wounded, somnambu-lists, air-raid victims looking for their old lives in the rubble, mix and match your metaphors, they were the only instruments she had, to build pictures for us as we rummaged in the debris for fragments of our old certainties.

Even Cavan, who had built her career on cynicism about the half-truths and false hopes peddled by salespeople, politicians (same thing), charlatans, saw us all needing to find something we'd lost in the ruins. We needed to rebuild our Convention Centre, Rex Tone's pride and joy, our sports stadium, our concert hall, our schools. We needed to find among the wrecked concrete slabs, the spaghetti of twisted cables, the gaping holes in the highways, the buckled tramlines that stood upright like inebriated lamp-posts in the post-streets, that old something which had led our ancestors to settle here in the first place. We needed their optimism, their sense of a future. You'd expect an earthquake to obliterate evidences of the past. What none of us predicted was the way it obliterated our capacity to imagine a future.

The Dean, Eleanor Bartlett, said that here we have no abiding city, and maybe that's about all we can say. Our Island had once been home, and it no longer is. None of us feels at home here, not even the Tangata. Maybe none of us is MEANT to be here. Meant by Nature or the gods. Historically, the Island did not even have mammals on it, never mind human beings, until the thirteenth century. So of course we quite literally aren't at home here.

After all, although they called it – seemingly from their first arrival, depicted by Gilbert Rhys – the Homeland, or *Whenua*, they are immigrants, just as we are, those Indonesian tribespeople who sailed here in cane, masted rafts or paddled in their gigantic canoes to these shores, at about the time, from another region of the planet, that Dante Alighieri was journeying through the infernal, purgatorial and paradisal realms. The early settlers – known now collectively as the Tangata, though they actually came from a variety of Indonesian tribes and families – were, as far as archaeology is able to shed light upon the matter, the first human beings to set foot upon our Island. The Tangata fought many tribal wars with one another before we – the Malahi – arrived. Dutchmen in the seventeenth century were the first Malahi to come, discovering our shores almost by chance, as they made their way to the Indies in pursuit of trade. A century later came the famous English sea captain and his naturalist companion. Later, of course, the waves of Scottish and English soon came to outnumber the Tangata – hugely. By the time they erected the bronze statue of the Imperial Mother in Argyle Square, at whose plinth Penny Whistle busks daily, there were ten Malahi to every one Tangata. There was much interbreeding, of course, so that today the proportions are blurred. The seven per cent Tangata realize that, of the ninety-three per cent Malahi, very many have Tangata great-grandparents. Over the years, there have been many disputes between us, the Malahi and the Tangata, about the rights and wrongs of land-ownership, and about the evils of colonialization. But all of us carry a guilty sense that the arrival of any human beings at all, in such a paradise as ours, was a kind of intrusion, a pollution.

No hominid feet, no primitive ancestor of the human form, ever trod our thickly wooded hillsides. No hairy, hunched figure, on its way to becoming a human being, ever tried to spear or cudgel the multifarious fish in our wetlands. There were no troglodytes in the caves at the foot of our great Southern Alps, whose snow-capped beauty came into being when, millions of years ago, tectonic shifts took place, equal in majesty to those which tower over Switzerland and Italy. Indeed, there were not even any mammals, until the Tangata brought them on their rafts. There were only fish, and birds and insects and reptiles. They buzzed and twittered and trilled about in the pure air of the forests with no marmoset or koala or dog or human eyes to appreciate or to threaten them.

It was the early Tangata who brought dogs to help them hunt. Intentionally or not, they also appear to have brought rats. The Royal Naval vessels of the eighteenth century certainly disgorged ships' rats. Innocent of any of the modern sense of ecology, these bluff folk also gave to the Tangata pigs and sheep. By the close of the nineteenth century, our Island was famous for its sheep-farmers. Little by little the birdlife diminished. Within a few centuries of the human arrivals, there were about half the number of birds. The songs from the brake which had so delighted the visitors of the eighteenth century were stilled.

All of us, then, Tangata and Malahi, bear within us, like some felt folk memory of pollution, a sense that to arrive here was to spoil it. Science in our own day, with its keen sense of ecological balance, told us a Fall Myth which we already carried within our imaginations. The very emblem of our Island, the Huia – our nickname for one another – is an extinct bird, though it wasn't extinct when it was chosen as a national emblem on the first Victorian coins minted in Carmichael. Visitors to our National Museum there will see fine examples of Huia feathers in the cloaks of the Tangata tribesmen. There were also similar examples in the museum here in Aberdeen, though they, among so much else, were destroyed in the Earthquake. When the Dean of our Cathedral was first brought to Aberdeen as a child by her parents, she remembered being shown the feather cloaks by her father, the canon. He pointed out to her that there were two fine specimens of just such Huia cloaks in the Pitt Rivers Museum in Oxford.

When the Victorian anthropologists and collectors had bestowed these intricate examples of tribal workmanship on the various museums, there were still actual Huias – the birds that is, not human beings – trilling their melodious songs from the branches of the eucalyptus trees. Their dazzling plumage, however, was no less tempting to Edwardian milliners than it had been to the Tangata tribespeople of old. Both in our Island, and back home in the Old Country, distinguished and titled ladies swept into luncheons, their necks trimmed with mink, their hats resplendent with Huia feathers. Queen Alexandra was especially fond of them, and there is a charming photograph of her standing beside Sir Dighton Probyn, a Huia boa round her neck which probably required the feathers of two hundred birds to supply.

It only took a few London seasons after the First World War, a few irresistible flourishes by the milliners, as they prepared for another Royal Ascot, another County Ball, another Garden Party in the Governor's Residence in Carmichael, for the voice of the Huia to become silent in our land. And, as I have already said, the only Huia feathers we had left in Aberdeen, those of the ceremonial Tangata cloak in the museum, were lost in the rubble when our museum, with its beautifully preserved Tangata canoes, its dress uniform of Alfred, Duke of Edinburgh (who came twice to our Island when he was in the Royal Navy and who wanted to be our governor – an idea vetoed by his Imperial-imperious mother), its ceramic collections, its Victorian watercolours of our Island landscapes, its education centre, added in the 1990s, with its informative notes on the gold rush and its plausible reconstruction of a Digger's hut, as well as its older military memorabilia, its uniforms and medals, and its photographs of Island regiments in the Dardanelles, in Crete, and at Anzio, were all lost in the Quake, an event which reminded us that human beings are not the only wreckers. That metaphor, God, had something to do with our destruction, surely? Since that disaster, we Huias, anyway the Huias of Aberdeen, have the feeling that we are everlastingly on the threshold of imminent danger. The very homeland beneath our feet had become more explosive than a minefield; only luck could spare us from obliteration of one sort or another, however bright our hopes, or however colourful our extinct feathers.

If this were a play – and it's natural for me to think like that, given what I do for a living – then all this bit of the book would be contained in a prelude spoken by the Chorus.

Nietzsche thought the Greek tragedies started as just the Choruses, and that the idea of *plays* came later. I like that – if I understand him rightly. Some people think that the Choruses in the Greek tragedies either represent the audience of the play, or, in some cases, actually *are* the audience. Digby explored this idea in one of her lectures once – which I attended, when my obsession with her was beginning. (This was a lecture, not one of her classes with Barnaby Farrell.)

Maybe at this stage I'm the (sort of) Chorus of this book – hammering it out on my laptop. Only, I'm about to be a character in the story, so maybe I'm not a Chorus, just a narrator, which is different. Maybe you are the Chorus, interacting with what I have to tell you. Each reader makes her own narrative, after all, as my mum's generation, fed on Roland Barthes, Derrida and co., bla bla bla, all believed. Probably something in it. After all, how you react to mention of the Aberdeen Quake will tremendously depend on who you are. If anyone outside the Island is reading this, she will probably scarcely remember that there WAS a quake in Aberdeen. If she's European, she'll remember the dreadful quakes in Italy; if she's American, California. Our Island isn't even on the radar of most of you. Besides, there have been so many other calamities in the world since then – wars, tsunamis, floods, famines. Why should you remember our earthquake: which in any case, was a little like the proverbial dull newspaper headline, 'Slight earthquake in Chile, not many killed'. We had over two hundred and fifty killed and over a thousand badly injured, but what is that to the numbers killed in the civil wars in Rwanda or Iraq or Syria? Many of you would not be able to find the Island on a world map. We Huias don't blame you. We are a small faraway country of which you know little – but the Quake matters to us. Maybe most of you reading this are Huias. Maybe some of you lived through the Quakes, or lost people in the second one, the big one. Maybe, you are just reading this as a novel, a work of fiction. I can't remember enough of Digby's lecture to remember whether you ever get to know the Chorus in a tragedy, or whether that matters. Are we meant to know who they are? She made us laugh by quoting something her dad once said about the choruses in Sophocles – they were 'Moaning Minnies'. Digby was far and away the best lecturer I ever heard.

In case you are interested, I'm the daughter of Cavan Cliffe, who's quite a well-known journalist in Aberdeen. I've mentioned her already and I'll describe her in more detail later, because she comes into the story. Can't decide whether it's worth mentioning anything else about myself at this stage. Prefer in some ways the narrative voice, the irony of holding back. Prefer to write the story in a dispassionate way, and even in a godlike way, telling you what is passing through Eleanor's mind and stuff. And then again, our perspective shifts. When I was in the fifth form at St Hilda's and Deirdre was my teacher, she was an object of derision. Now, she's a heroine for me. In between, I've had all sorts of complicated thoughts – especially about her and Barnaby. The tectonic plates beneath the earth's surface are not the only things which are constantly on the move. The kaleidoscope is being shaken at irregular intervals, and the patterns are different every time.

You'll get to know me in the course of the following pages. No need for me to go into much detail just now. It's probably worth mentioning, though, before the Earthquake completely destroys our city and we are all changed forever, that I do come from Aberdeen. I was born here. Cavan and Richard Ashe – that's my dad, who now lives in Sydney; he was a journalist too, in those days, but he now works for a photographic library – split up when I was five. I stayed with Mum – with Cavan. Dad left the Island when I was twelve and, although I still see him from time to time, we've never been close. I think Cavan is still quite angry with Dad, at some level – or angry with herself – or both – because of the failure of the marriage.

When this story begins, the Me who was wandering idly round the Dyce Gallery would have said that this is the really great division between my generation and all the ones which went before. Mum's generation expected everything to last forever. In an ideal world, that is. Cavan and Richard and the other baby-boomers, they thought that whatever they started in their youth, they'd still be doing when they were old. Richard changed jobs, but most baby-boomers never even expected to do this. Become a shop assistant aged sixteen and you'd hope to go on working in the same shop for the next forty years, when you might have risen to become assistant manager. Do teacher training, and you'll go on being a teacher until they pension you off. And it was the same with their relationships. They nearly all got married. They'd seen the wartime marriages of their parents, and they'd seen how disastrous most of them were, and they could see, with the rational part of themselves, how utterly unlikely it was that two people, forming a relationship when they were twenty, would still have enough in common to want to stay together ten, twenty years down the line. But off they went, regardless, to the register office or to church, to tie the knot. And then came all the acrimony and sadness of divorces and settlements and lawyers, and everlasting self-questioning. Get Mum with a glass of our Island Riesling inside her, and, as like as not, she will start asking, aloud, why she and Richard did not make a better fist of it. Whereas I, at the age of twenty-seven, had some relationships behind me and thought some of them were mistakes – some of them pretty disastrous mistakes! – but the others? Well, they ran their course. No hard feelings, on my part anyway.

Aftershocks

That was how I was before the Quake. Afterwards – well, how things changed. That feeling which I've just described as so crazy – a belief that I've found love which will last forever and a day – that's what happened to me. I'm Ingrid, by the way. Ingrid Ashe.

One more bit of gossip to get out of the way before I tell this story. I don't want you to think this book is just going to be tittle-tattle. You have already read enough to realize that I am what Mum calls a Nosey Parker. (Who was Parker, I wonder? Being Nosey, he could probably have told you a thing or two about Riley, whose life we are all meant to envy?)

I've told you about Charlie Nicolson and Eleanor Bartlett in the art gallery. Well, not long after I'd clocked that part of the Aberdeen-soap-opera, I had a strange experience in the University. It was all fine between me and Barnaby. A friend of mine says you have to go to bed with someone ten times before there is any danger of breaking your heart, and we'd only done it three times (well, three times in bed and once in his office). We'd got over the thing. I'd even been round to his flat and had a nice high tea with him, Stig and Deirdre Hadley, our Green MP, who sneaked in to see him there whenever she could.

One of the things which this book is all about is Digby and Eleanor. No swanks, but I was the only one to have seen the truth about them, from really quite early on. This was partly because, as I say, Mum goes to the Cathedral and I sometimes go with her, so we had seen quite a lot of Eleanor in her professional capacity, and because I was doing this course on tragedy at Banks. So I'd seen a lot of Digby. Most of the Cathedral Folk (as Eleanor whimsically called us, after the title of one of her favourite Russian novels) were unaware of Digby, and in our seminar at the University, I was the only churchgoer. You certainly wouldn't have got Barnaby into a church, and if you had done, it would not have been an Anglican one. (His parents were very VERY lapsed Irish Catholics.) I was the only person, really, who had clocked Digby and Eleanor. But we'll have more, much more, about this, when the Quake brought out the truth.

Nell Digby, known to readers of the *TLS*, and to the scholarly world, as E.L. Digby, was a leading expert on classical tragedy, especially Euripides. She's very well read in modern literature too, which is what made her class with Barnaby Farrell fizz like it did. One minute, he'd be off telling us about Thomas Hardy – which is his special area of expertise – and she'd cap it with thoughts about Sophocles, Shakespeare, and back he'd come with Primo Levi, Solzhenitsyn, whoever. We were all, the twenty or so graduate students who crowded round that table at Banks, really in their debt. We learnt so, SO much. I'd never read so much as I did during the months of that semester, and every evening, I'd come staggering home with armsful of paperbacks, longing to talk about my latest essay. Mum was brilliant, and because she is really well read too, I think she enjoyed it, and certainly never showed signs of boredom, even when I told her the plot of *Jude the Obscure*, and she said, with a quiet cigarettey chuckle, that she had read it, actually.

Anyhow. I was late handing in an essay to Digby. It was comparing Euripides and Hardy. Mum had helped me with it and therefore said it was the best thing I'd done. Because I was late with the essay, Digby said, no worries, just hand it in some time that week. She actually meant I should put it into her pigeon-hole in the corridors near the front entrance of the Forster Building. But she'd also said she'd lend me a book, so I took the essay to her office.

Aftershocks

I did knock on the door, honest – but I did not wait before I flung it open, and there they were in one another's arms. The funny thing is that, although he looked embarrassed, she almost glowed at being discovered. I did not tell anyone about it – like I say, I'm not the gossiping type. I just have this gift – or I do for the purposes of this narrative – of being *around* when stuff happens. Anyway, there they were, in a clinch, Digby and Barnaby Farrell. I'll tell you in another chapter what I felt when I saw them.

CHAPTER TWO

—WHAT ON EARTH IS THE MAN DROUGHT? ASKED HER DAD, with the light laugh which greeted any subject which might have been considered serious, or any discussion of modernity.

Her dad's face was distorted when they spoke on Skype because he sat too near the screen, and gawped incredulously at it. From the way he peered into the machine at his end – an Acer laptop which had known better days – she felt she knew what it would be like to be a specimen on a slide under the microscope. She by contrast sat well back. So he saw his daughter, with her dark bob of hair, and her natural cherry lips, and her toothy smile, and the large eyes the colour of the midnight sky in summer. She saw his neat silver hair, his gold-rimmed, round spectacles, his pink face so closely shaved that it looked as if it had been polished; but she saw it as if reflected in one of those convex glasses in amusement arcades which are supposed to be so funny, and which make you one minute one of the Ents in Tolkien, long and lagubrious, and the next, a squat Toby Jug.

—It's one of the things that makes life on the Island so distinctive, said his daughter. Mum bucked the trend, marrying an Englishman. Most Huia women come home to breed, but when they get here, after their year off in England or America, or the Far East, they find the Huia men have all gone backpacking in Europe, or taken jobs in banks in New York or Shanghai, where they marry the local girls. So there are far more women than men.

—It sounds like the ideal situation for a musical comedy – *Princess Ida* or something.

When they had laughed, he said, perhaps prompted by the mention of marriage and breeding,

—Any news of . . . um . . .

—Everything's fine, Dad.

When Eleanor and Doug had been married – well, they still were married – but when they had been together, she sometimes used to call him, to his face, 'What's-is-name' or 'Whosit', or 'Nemo', in reference to her father's dislike of the man. Mum had actually been able to get her palate round the single syllable 'Doug', but Dad, usually, would end telephone conversations with – 'Oh, and love to, um . . .'

—So, North Carolina is . . .

Doug had taken the job at Duke when she had come to Aberdeen. Had Mum still been alive, there would have been questions – 'Is your marriage in trouble, hun? Do you want to talk about it? Can we do anything to help?'

But Mum had been dead eight years now (cancer). Dad had retired from parish life and moved to Winchester, where he lived in a small flat with his favourite books, and attended Cathedral services every day. He was a spry seventy-one, and was still 'in demand' – preaching, conducting retreats, and still sitting on ARCIC, the committee of optimists charged with seeing their way to reuniting the Anglican Church with that of Rome.

He had few friends, apart from Lesley Mannock, with whom he had trained for the priesthood at Cuddesdon. Lesley, like Ronald, was a clever man, who could've become, had he chosen, a college chaplain, or similar, followed by a climb up what he called 'the Church of England snakes and ladders board' – Area Dean of Smethwick, Suffragan Bishop of Basingstoke. Instead, Ronald and Lesley had faithfully lived out their adult lives in sad towns, among people with whom they had little in common, apart from their faith. They had followed the bright angels, as Eleanor sometimes thought – her mind, filled as it was, with lines from her favourite poet.

When Eleanor had the chance to come out to Aberdeen as Dean of the Cathedral, she had, naturally enough, asked Ronald's advice. His reply had been 'classic Dad'.

—I've given up having opinions about anything.

—But you must know whether I should take the job or not.

—I'll ask Lesley.

—I'd love to know what Uncle Lesley thinks, Dad; but I'd rather know what YOU think.

—Oh, it's so restful having Lesley. There are so many things nowadays which it does not seem quite sane to have an opinion about, and yet – to judge from all the voices on the radio – it seems more or less obligatory that one should have some view or another.

Cue for the light laugh. And then, one of the stock of quotations with which he peppered his conversation. This one from Hawker of Morwenstowe, the Victorian poet-priest who wrote 'Twenty thousand Cornishmen will know the Reason why'. A bore was pressing him for his views. Hawker took the visitor to his study window and showed him the wild seas of north Cornwall. 'Those are my views. My opinions I keep to myself.'

—Oh, but with Lesley! I do not need to know what to think about anything any more – women priests, gay marriage, Brexit, I simply say, 'I think what Lesley Mannock thinks.' He's always right. He's like the Oracle.

Next time they spoke, guided by his oracle and friend, Dad had weighed all the arguments, for and against, entirely in terms of her professional career. On the one hand, she would surely soon be in the running to become a bishop – if this was what she wanted. Coming to the Island would not commit her to a lifetime of exile. She could always return home. It would be a good thing for her to get out of Oxford for a while. Her academic career need not be seen as 'on hold'. And since you're . . . you know . . . since um . . . North Carolina . . .

Had Dad told Lesley about Doug? Had the two old friends discussed her marriage? Should she, who could not talk of such matters to Dad, have tried to confide in Uncle Lesley, who was a wise old bird, if rather scatty, and was much in demand as a confessor, and spiritual director?

—But my work. My academic work . . . It'll be a wrench, giving up the fellowship . . .

—There are plenty of scholar priests, surely in our Church. Or were. Lesley is one.

—So are you.

—Scarcely. Lesley really has kept up his theological reading. He's read Rahner, Balthasar . . . I rather gave up after ploughing through Barth. I stick to diaries and novels. I've been reread-ing Hensley Henson. They're so funny, his diaries. But *terribly* unkind!

—Well, there aren't so many scholar priests as there were, she had said, to be greeted only with the light laugh.

The laugh reflected his inner commitment, some years ago, to check his natural tendency to compare present with past. Every now and then, the light laugh, which Eleanor had inherited, preceded some uncontrollable value-judgment on a measure in the General Synod, a liturgical infelicity, a particularly ripe fatuity on the part of this or that Bishop of their Church. The words 'donkeys' – more laughter – or 'Ichabod' – had sometimes escaped his cleanly shaven lips. But less and less frequently. The past was the past. There was no recovering it. He and Lesley were determined not to be miserable old gits, though, on the second or third sherry, some degree of satire, when discussing the contemporary Church, was unavoidable. The difficulty was, that in refusing to make pessimistic statements, they were in danger of not making statements at all. Lesley had always been a man of silences. Mum, who read French fiction for fun, used to speak of *Les Silences de Lesley Mannock*. Dad never used to be like that. When Mum was alive they had chattered like sparrows. And Mum would certainly not hold back on the idiocy of the Bishops or the Synod. Eleanor sometimes wondered whether, had she not become a priest herself, her father would have not greeted the ordination of women with the same light laugh which was inspired by the new liturgies or the debates about global warming, as though it made any difference what the synodical busybodies thought about these matters. He was a natural conservative. His ARCIC work was made much more difficult, now that we had gone ahead and ordained priests and bishops of both genders – should that be 'all genders or none', nowadays? – while Rome stood, for the time being, unbudgeable on the issue. He had never, however, breathed a syllable of disapproval of the ordination of any genders.

Uncle Lesley, anyhow, rather to Eleanor's surprise, had always been in favour of the ordination of women, years before it happened. Now that she was a priest – had been for seven years – it made a bond between her and her father. How could it not?

—Have you got the radio on? he asked suddenly.

—No.

—Someone singing in the background.

—It's Penny Whistle. He's started early this morning.

For a short while they paused, and could hear the distant baritone –

> *In tarr-y dress*
> *We reached Stromness*
> *Where we would go a SHORE*
> *With the whalermen so scarce*
> *And the water even less*
> *We'll have to take on MORE!*

Was the bond between father and daughter too close? Did she take the job in Aberdeen, not to escape Doug, who had already gone to North Carolina for a three-year stint, following his successful sabbatical there – but as a breather from the much closer relationship with Ronald? Is that why wise old Uncle Lesley had advised her to accept the offer of the Deanery of Aberdeen – because he could see that she was too close to Dad? She did not feel it as an oppressive relationship. But, once she had left England and come to the Island, she did wonder whether it had been fair on Doug, really. *Why have my sisters husbands if they say they love you all?*

What was this whole ordination thing, her wish to be a priest, if it wasn't in some way a wish to BE Dad, or please Dad, or walk in Dad's shoes? She even looked a bit like Dad had done when he was young, and she had the same voice, which to our Huia ears sounds almost ridiculously posh, almost like the Queen, and the same light laugh.

It was only after she had been married for a couple of years that she realized quite how deeply the two men disliked one another. She was in love with Doug in those days. This was a difficult thing to recognize – *now*. With love had come a total lack of realism about what she had done to both men by marrying Doug. She had condemned the two people she liked best in the world to eating Christmas dinner for the rest of their lives with a person they utterly detested. The month-long holiday together in the Welsh cottage, always one of the high points of the year when it was just the three of them – her, Mum, Dad – had become, now it was another trio – her, Dad, Doug – a torture. For the four or five years that she was in love with Doug, however, optimism blinded her to the emotional reality. She supposed that because they were both clever, well-meaning men, they would grow to like one another. Human kind, as her favourite poet said, cannot bear very much reality.

Doug had known Digby and Eleanor Bartlett of course, but I wonder, did he ever get the hang of them? Did he understand what was going on, as – again, no swanks – I did, almost from the first? Me and the Quake sorted out that pair, made them face up to the truth of things. Maybe, when she got together with Doug, she just wasn't ready for that realization? He loved Digby, that's what I think, and he did not even begin to understand Priest Eleanor. Did she become a priest – partly – as a gesture of defiance, of independence from Doug? I dunno. I never met Doug – though

Aftershocks

I so nearly did, that momentous day in Winchester, England – of which more anon!

We have seen Dean Eleanor Bartlett in the Dyce Gallery, beginning an unwise flirtation with Charles Nicolson. And we've had a glimpse of Digby in the arms of my supervisor (ex-lover) Barnaby Farrell. Maybe it's time to ask whether Doug had ever really engaged, clicked, with Eleanor at all? Wasn't the truth that it was *Digby* he had been in love with all along, Digby he betrayed, Digby who broke his heart, and he hers? While Eleanor Bartlett, of the light laugh, crossed the world as a priest of the Chosen Frozen, Digby had to come with her. There was no choice. But there were far harder choices for Digby than for Eleanor.

When Eleanor was offered the Deanery of our Cathedral, E.L. Digby had taken a post as a research fellow in Classical Literature at our University. The Cathedral staff were scarcely aware of Digby. A room in the tower was assigned to her, where she could work unimpeded on her book, *Euripides and the Masks of God*.

In one of their Skyped conversations, Eleanor's dad had remarked that he would not wish to be immured in that tower if there was another quake, and Eleanor had replied that there wasn't going to be another quake. Dad had answered,

—Lesley is not so sure.

—Since when was Uncle Lesley an expert on seismology?

—He saw a programme about Aquila. It was really too dreadful. And at the end they went through all the other places in the world which had been built on a fault line – San Francisco, and so on. Too dreadful.

The move from England had affected Digby much more than it did Eleanor. Eleanor, for one thing, had her duties and concerns as a priest to numb the culture shock. She was in charge of running the Cathedral, supervising its music and liturgy, discussing its preservation with the fabric committee, performing civic duties, meeting such figures as Rex Tone, the go-ahead mayor who devised a brighter and ever brighter future for us in his tall white concrete tower-block City Hall. Digby, by contrast, had given up the fellowship of an Oxford college, a weekly routine of lectures and tutorials, and regular attendance, at least during vacations, in the Lower Reading Room of the Bodleian Library. All this was now over. True, Banks University in Aberdeen had been extremely welcoming, and, as well as conducting her Tragedy class with Barnaby Farrell, she was supervising a few graduate students who were working on the Greek tragedians. She had given lectures in the faculty. For the time being, however, the formal 'career' was on hold. She was using the time to set in order the book which had engaged her, with different degrees of intensity, for the previous twenty years.

The work had its origin in her DPhil thesis, which had been a commentary on *Trojan Women*, a searingly painful play in which some of the principal figures of the Trojan horror story prepare to go into exile as the sexual slaves of their conquerors who destroyed their city and killed their husbands, sons, brothers. The women of Troy are Hecuba, the widow of Priam and mother of the slain Hector; Cassandra, her crazy daughter, who had predicted the whole disaster, and was now in a state of frenzied hyper-excitement, even relished the prospect of losing her status as a virgin priest and being ravished by Agamemnon, her new master; Andromache, the widow of Hector, who was to be forcibly married to the son of Achilles, the son of the man who murdered her husband; and then, perhaps the most pathetic of all the 'Trojan' women, namely Helen, whose abduction by Paris had started the war a decade previously.

The whole story, as told by Euripides, rippled with ambiguities.

Even more than Homer, his principal source, Euripides empha-
sized the quasi-divine status of many of these characters, or their
involvement with the gods. The human beings were not 'ordinary'
humans, any more than the gods were remotely like the Jewish
'God'. Achilles was the son of a sea-nymph. Helen was the child
of Leda and the Swan (who had been Zeus in disguise) and had
hatched from an egg . . . and so forth.

Digby was fascinated by Greek religion, but partly as a weapon
against the Christian theology which so fascinated Eleanor. Indeed,
the chief difference between them was in the matter of religion.
Eleanor was a tribal Anglican who had been ordained as a priest.
Every day in the Cathedral, she took part in prayers, sometimes the
traditional ones in the old Prayer Book, and sometimes the newer
liturgies, devised by our Island Synod – for we are an independent,
autocephalous Church, with our own primate, Yvonne, the Archbishop of Carmichael, and our own hierarchies.

Digby has nothing to do with any of this. To judge from the draft
chapters of *The Masks of God*, she would appear to be a complete
atheist. Terrible events happen. The gods are projections of the
pitilessness of things, of natural forces or uncontrollable passions
over which the human characters in the Euripidean dramas have no
control. Prayer has no effect on them. Yet, Digby sometimes seems
to suggest, Euripides is not undermining the pagan mythology so
much as making use of it. He is saying – yes, this is the way things
are: wars break out, plagues, earthquakes, famines. Why? Because
'the gods' decree these things. What matters is how you respond
to these things as human beings. Do you do so with cowardice?
Do you submit blindly to fate? Or do you, as in some of Euripides'
greatest lyrics and choruses, do you question the nature of things,
do you assert the dignity of human beings in their suffering? Do

you lament the degradation of women by war, and by the nature of society? Nothing, exactly speaking, happens in *Trojan Women*. The four chief protagonists have to stand there while history and war and nature and *men* hurl misfortunes at them. That is the nature of things . . . no? No incantation in a shrine, no incense-offering, is going to help them.

It was a potential embarrassment that Eleanor and Digby were so bonded. Yet without one the other would have died. When Eleanor was offered the Deanery of our Cathedral in Aberdeen, Digby had been part of the deal. Digby would come too. The two were, after all, inseparable. In the event, the Cathedral staff were scarcely aware of Digby. Like I say, a room in the tower was assigned to her, which had once been used by the early twentieth-century church historian, Archdeacon Otway. This learned cleric, an expert on the Christian Platonists of Alexandria, whose editions of Clement and Origen are still indispensable (apparently!), had a considerable library. Well over three thousand of his books were moved from the solid Arts and Crafts oak shelves (designed by the architect of our Cathedral, Oswald Fish) and replaced by Digby's own extensive classical library.

Digby's passionate interest in these books was not shared either by the small Cathedral Chapter or by Bishop Dionne who, such was the way Church matters were conducted on the Islands, had the ultimate say in any such question. The Bishop probably did not know what incunabula were, let alone whether Erasmus's own copy of Origen's *Contra Celsum*, printed in Antwerp in 1512, was of interest or value. Since the Bishop (as far as Digby could make out) was something of a fundamentalist (when it came to the story of the Resurrection, for example), it was unlikely she would have found Origen's writings to her taste – for that Platonist of Alexandria had held it completely unimportant whether Bible stories were literally 'true', reading them as allegories of truth, stories about what was going on inside our heads, myths which contained inner kernels of truth rather than improbable histories which asked readers to contort or massacre their intellect.

Eleanor, who had to work with Bishop Dionne and the rest of the chapter on a weekly basis, did not allow herself to have uncharitable thoughts. Digby, however, found the Bishop's simplicities excruciating, and worried that the wrong decision would be made about the precious remnant of the Otway library. It would have been so much better to make a start on the restoration of the really interesting volumes – there were about a hundred books which came into this distinguished category – and their value, according to Jill Varley, an antiquarian dealer friend of Digby's with whom she had been in touch about the books, was in the hundreds of thousands of dollars, possibly millions.

Having sorted the Otway collection, Digby had been enabled to use the old shelves to house her own modern scholar's library. Unpacking the cases had been an experience which brought conflicting emotions. To see them arranged in their new, well-dusted home – the greens and reds of the Loeb editions, the dark blues of the Oxford Classical Texts, and the very many books, still in their dust-wrappers, from modern university presses – was to be reunited with old friends. At the same time, to see them in Aberdeen was to be reminded of just what a move had been made – not only a move to the other side of the world, but also a decisive change of status. For the first time, the balance had shifted.

Hitherto, Digby's career had been predominant, and Eleanor's decision to be a priest had been subservient to that. Now it was different. Eleanor's priestly role was the reason for Digby's career having been, if not brought to an end, then suspended. There was a certain quiet relief in this decision, but its felt finality was quite worrying. Immured in her tower with the Book, she was free to 'get on with it'. Yet there were some days when this very freedom – the absence of tutorials, Governing Body, lectures, and the absence of the whole world of Oxford which had been her habitat for almost a quarter of a century – had a paralysing effect on the writing, and she sometimes found herself sitting quietly at her laptop waiting for words which did not come.

Today, she had put slightly more time than was necessary into the preparation of her pot of green tea from an electric kettle in the corner of the room. Nor had she settled at once to the chapter she was writing on, yet again, *Trojan Women*, but she had, rather, stood at the casement of her tower window. It was a latticed, Victorian window, with stained glass – the coat of arms of the first Bishop, Bishop Gladstone – a distant cousin of the Prime Minister – with its punning heraldic motto, *Laetatus sum*.

Outside the window, the hot summer sun of a February day fell on Digby's face like a blessing. Beneath her, fantails sang and fluttered in the branches of the old eucalyptus tree. She could see beyond the tree, to Prince of Wales Parade, and beyond that, the city, with its streets and squares, its winding river, its creamy white stone Public Library, its redbrick and ashlar Albert Hall, its arterial roads stretching towards wooded suburbs of clapboard houses, and beyond, in another direction, the docks, with their cranes, ships and many masts of yachts and dinghies. Beyond, at sea, she could discern the white sails of those who were taking a day out in their dinghies. It was a scene of peculiar innocence and happiness. She found in this quiet moment an intensity of joy. The uncertainties of her professional career were quite suspended. There was no homesickness; only a sense of life being brimful of possibilities and potential joys. Beneath, so immediately beneath the tower as to be invincible, the blind busker must have been standing, as he stood every day. She could hear his words blending with those of the birds in the eucalyptus tree.

> *From broadside to broadside, our cannon balls did fly,*
> *Like hailstones the small shot around our deck did lie.*
> *Our masts and rigging was shot away*
> *Besides some thousands on that day,*
> *Were killed and wounded in the fray*
> *On board a man o' war.*

Doug did not believe either. One of the things he had in common with Digby. When Eleanor had told him she wanted to be a priest, he had not stood in her way. They were too distant, perhaps, by then for either of them to stand in one another's way about anything. She had not stood in his way when he was offered a sabbatical in America – it was, as it happens, the year she was made deacon – the preliminary ordination, which takes place a year before you become a priest. She had known, when Duke made Doug the offer of that year as a visiting professor, that she would not accompany him, and that he did not want her to do so. She had known that, when her husband went away for what was the best part of a year, he would not miss her, and she would not miss him. It was a sabbatical from marriage every bit as much as a respite in Doug's academic routines. They had both felt a burden lift, from the moment his aeroplane took off. They both knew this, but neither of them would have expressed the thought. She had inherited from Ronald the ability to avoid directness. Doug and she had never discussed their marriage with one another. She had married him when he was forty-one, and she was twenty-three. She was a virgin when they met. She had been flattered by the attention of an older man, she had, initially, enjoyed the sex, and she had liked the fact that, as Doug's wife, she had a more interesting range of grown-up friends than were provided by her contemporary graduate students.

Only later did she decide, with resignation which gave her no pleasure, that he was unfeeling, and unfaithful. As the sex withered, she became aware of the other women, about whom she did not choose to inquire. And with the coming of computers, she suspected a pornography habit – a suspicion confirmed during that first American year, when Doug emailed her in agitation to send him a file left behind on his old computer. Lecture notes on nineteenth-century fiction. (Doug was a Dickensian. They used to have fun, in their earlier days, with the ambiguity of this sentence, seeing him, with his Pickwickian bespectacled face, as a character in the Master's oeuvre, as much as its critic.)

She had had no difficulty in finding the file, DICKENS AND THE ART OF POPULAR FICTION, and dispatched it within minutes. In doing so, and without any desire to snoop, she had found the porn. Simply by clicking – in search of the Dickens notes – on 'recent items'. Apart from a wave of sadness, she had stabs of anger. There was so much of it. He had accumulated a whole library of the demeaning, horrible stuff. Some of the images, she regretted to admit, were unforgettable. Five years after she had seen them, when she sometimes had difficulty in recalling Doug's face, she could still remember this *stuff* – which was, presumably, a part of his mind. Why would anyone WANT their head to be full of this tawdry, disgusting . . . *stuff*? Though filthy, it was the reverse of what she would have considered erotic. And it was – was this part and parcel of being a Dickensian? – it was so crude.

Never so strongly, when she had switched off his laptop that evening in Oxford, and sat, numbed, at the thought of all that . . . that horrible stuff, as it were in their house, *What? In OUR house?* . . . had she felt so particularly angry with Doug. Was it because of her childlessness? She had been in her mid-thirties when she discovered the porn. By then, he had long ago tricked her into being his wife. It wasn't too late to have a baby with someone else. That is what a secular woman would have done. But how could she? She, with her silvery-haired father, with Wood in the Fridge and the Scripture moveth us in sundry places?

—We don't want to go in for all that, do we? had been Doug's way of telling her that children were out of the question. That was before they had married – on the third time she had ever slept with him. She had said they must be careful if he did not want her to become pregnant, and he had made it into their rule of life. 'We don't want to go in for all that.'

—Can't stand nippers, he'd said on another occasion when a colleague had brought her two, rather charming, children to tea. Eleanor had noted the cruel glint in Doug's eye when his remark had made her blue-black eyes well up.

Perhaps Doug, who sometimes accompanied her to church, but who had shown no sign on any occasion of being religious, was pleased by her choice to be ordained. Something to keep the woman occupied, take her mind off babies? The absence of a child gnawed at Eleanor. Sometimes, here in Aberdeen – especially if she had spent the day visiting a school, or talking to the choirboys in the Cathedral – she would find herself lying in the dark weeping copiously. Rachel weeping for her children . . . and would not be comforted, because they are not.

It wasn't so difficult, was it? It wasn't so BLOODY difficult, having a baby? Just one? Three quarters of the women she met had children. Even Bishop Dionne had Charlene, a veterinary nurse, doing so brilliantly at one of the best practices in Car-michael . . . Sometimes, Eleanor felt she was in danger of driving herself crazy from thinking about it. One of the most dangerous thoughts was if she met a kid of, say, thirteen or fourteen, and she'd think, if Doug had not set his face against my having any babies, my first kid would be *your age. Bloody Doug.* And, even though it was now the last thing in the world, literally, that she wanted to do, Fuck Doug. But she tried not to give way to hate. *O Lord, who hast taught us that all our doings without charity are nothing worth: Send thy Holy Ghost, and pour into our hearts that most excellent gift of charity, the very bond of peace and of all virtue . . .*

Whereas, Digby's unbelief was a way of feeling at home in her own skin as a classicist. No external being from outside could come to her and pour charity, or any other quality, into her heart. She had in common with another brilliant classicist, Friedrich Nietzsche, the sense that the Greeks, especially in their early literature – in Homer and the tragedies of Aeschylus and Sophocles – had an unrivalled ability to respond intelligently and imaginatively to the world. Tragedy was the highest expression of human intelligence, the acme of literary achievement – because it told the truth about our condition.

Morality was human. That was the central, Nietzschean, truth for Digby. What Homer, Aeschylus and Sophocles all showed us were, on the one hand, the pitiless gods, raining down disaster on the human race; and on the other, the tragic heroes who respond, not by simply howling, but by asserting human virtue in the face of scarcely endurable experience. Nietzsche thought that Philosophy, the other great gift of the Greeks to the world, then came along and spoiled this imaginative way of viewing the world. Socrates persuaded his young followers that the 'gods' were not real, and his disciple Plato took this further by making 'The Good', a sort of abstract 'God' or 'Absolute' something outside and beyond ourselves. Thereby had begun a confused and confusing story which the human race had been telling itself ever since – never more confused, perhaps, than when Christianity arrived, and formed a melange of Platonic ethics with Jewish religious laws. Jehovah, the Jewish One God, and Plato's The Good formed a merger, and the Christian religion was born.

But no such Being as this God could ever 'exist'. It made sense, imaginatively at least, when you (if you were Phaedra) fell in love painfully and disastrously (let us say with your stepson Hippolytus) to blame Aphrodite. The end of the tragic war in Troy could be attributed to the malice of Athene, still smarting because Paris, in his notorious Judgment, so beloved by the Renaissance painters, had deemed Aphrodite more desirable, Helen more beautiful. The gods were agents of pain and malice, and you, as a dignified person had to learn to lead a good life in spite of them. This was the beginning of human ethics, a purely social agreement. The Good is what we agree to be Good – hence the fact that in some human societies, fourth-century BC Athens for example, it is 'good' to be gay, and in others (twenty-first-century Lagos) it is supposedly 'bad'.

Christianity tied itself up in knots even further, though. As well as asserting that God was all-good, it asserted that He was all-loving, and, at the same time, all-powerful. Once you feed these requirements into a definition of 'God', you will come up with a completely impossible contradiction. The Gospels show that Jesus, believed by Christians to be God Incarnate, was capable of reversing Nature. He could still storms on the lake. He could cure the blind and the lame. So God is capable, if He wishes, of preventing human beings from suffering the calamities which befall them on every day of history? He does not do so. All the plagues, famines, floods and – yes – earthquakes – which had devastated human lives came about through the will of a God whom Christianity asserts to be loving.

Digby could see why Eleanor loved the benign version of Christianity which is embodied in musical settings of Evensong, and in Victorian Gothic architecture. Nevertheless, she was suspicious of Christianity, even in this gentle form. Perhaps especially suspicious of it in these beautiful clothes. When it comes at you, nakedly aggressive, telling you that God wants gay people to go to hell, or that God has given Palestine to the Jews, no questions asked – or, come to that, that Allah wants to kill all the harmless teenagers in a disco because they were wearing jeggings or miniskirts – you can see religion for what it really is. Could Eleanor Bartlett really be quite sure that, deep down in her 'benign' Anglicanism, there did not lurk some sick distrust of the human body, some sublimation to very male concepts of 'control'? Why did she put up, for so long, with that scumbag husband? And why did she still hesitate about divorcing him – because the 'laws' of the Church for so long forbade such a thing? Because Dad would disapprove? Even in her devoted Skype-conversations with the old canon, is she quite sure she is not – in a very gentle, Chosen-Frozen sort of way – betraying the sisterhood, subverting her nature to stereotypes required of her by patriarchal values? Are those patriarchal values any less ugly because they are set to beautiful music by S.S. Wesley or C.V. Stanford? How does she feel about being a priest in a Church about a third of whose members do not believe in her priesthood, solely on the grounds of her gender? As for the English branch of her Church, how does she feel about it having waited twenty years, after ordaining the first woman, before it would agree to have a female bishop? What sort of primitive, misogynistic, nasty impulses were guiding it, as it processed gently up the aisle in scarlet cassocks and white surplices, as the candlelight flickered on pretty little boys' faces, and as they sang to the Patriarchal God, and could only revere the Mother of Jesus if they persuaded themselves of the nonsensical myth that she was an everlasting virgin?

For these reasons, and many more which I won't bore you with, Digby kept her distance from Eleanor Bartlett over the religious question. For these reasons, when Eleanor Bartlett was offered the Deanery of Aberdeen, Digby had worries about abandoning her Oxford fellowship, and moving her classical library to the Deanery. There was no question, she had to come too. Where Eleanor went, she went. But Eleanor could not accept the Deanery until Digby was able to secure a research fellowship, and the chance of a little teaching and graduate supervision, at Banks. To deafen her ears to the oh-so-beguiling Anglican mood music, its Psalm settings by Purcell, its Communion Service in C by Darke, or 'Wood in the Phrygian Mode' (known always as Wood in the Fridge), Digby strained for an older music, a more Dionysian wisdom; she retreated to the Greeks. When she surfaced from her ever-stimulating engagement with them, it was to face, not church congregations, staring up at a pulpit, but engaged graduates and colleagues round the seminar table, responding in a modern way, untrammelled by religion, to the challenges of literature. I was lucky enough to be one of those grad students – that was how I met her, first saw her beautiful head and began to contemplate the mystery in the blue-black eyes. You see, when I saw her in Barnaby's arms that day in her office at Banks – I did not think, Barnaby, you bastard! I thought, Barnaby, you *lucky* bastard.

CHAPTER THREE

COME WITH ME FOR A WALK IN THE FOOTHILLS OF THE
Southern Alps. 'Cause it's just possible some of you aren't Huias,
and don't know Aberdeen, have never been to the Island, even. Let's
have a tourist interval. Breathe in the pure air. Look westward over
the bright blue Pacific, eastward towards the mountains, north to
the busy, undulating valleys which end in our chief mining districts
and industrial heartlands, and south to the plain where our forebears built the city of Aberdeen – we're named, by the way, not for
the Scottish granite city, but for the Prime Minister. Our Charter,
proclaiming us a Dominion of our Sovereign Lady Queen Victoria,
was signed and sealed when Lord Aberdeen was Foreign Secretary.

Come with me into the city before the Quake and see the River
Windrush weaving through half-timbered or clapboarded suburbs to
the city centre. Past warehouses and two breweries, we will come to
the two big flint-knapped Gothic Victorian schools – St Augustine's
for the boys and St Hilda's (my old school) for the girls. Come further in, and find our Victorian city.

Visitors liked to say it was more English than England, but it wasn't. For one thing, it was all built in one go. You don't get cities in England which are only of one date – or hardly ever. I know there's cohesive eighteenth-century Bath, and there was the City of London rebuilt after the fire in 1666. But even in these cases, there is a patina of after-generations. Our city centre was all built in one go: the little cast-iron bridges and spindly lamp-posts all came in a job lot from the same Birmingham (UK) iron foundry. The art gallery – where I've already taken you, and we saw the Dean with Charles Nicolson – the old City Hall (before Rex Tone moved out of it into his tower-block 'baby' ten years before the Quake), the Botanic Gardens with their pavilion and their bandstand are of a piece – or were. And towering above us all was the great Gothic spire of Holy Trinity Cathedral, the most splendid building on our Island, and a symbol, for many of us, of the Church of England's peculiar dominance in our Island's history.

Just a little guide-book stuff, because the Cathedral will be mentioned a lot. You'll all have seen the building, with its spire jutting up into the sky. It's the first thing to catch any pilot's eye as she lands a plane at Aberdeen airport. The architect chosen to design our Cathedral was Oswald Fish, better known for his flamboyant Arts and Crafts designs in metalwork than for his buildings. His only complete church in Britain, St Aidan's, Purgstall Heath, was a fine piece of Gothic revival, demolished by the developers in Margaret Thatcher's time, but still missed by the locals in that now diverse region of Britain's second city. (To us on the Island, it is a district, if we have heard of it at all, known as the scene of multiple arrests after the terrorist atrocity in Birmingham last year.)

St Aidan's was a much-loved church, but it was not one of the great nineteenth-century buildings. The architectural historians who know about that era, however, place the Cathedral which Oswald Fish designed for us here in an altogether different category. Some compare it with Sedding's Holy Trinity, Sloane Street in London (where Fish's beaten copper reliefs of angels are a memorable feature). Whereas the Sloane Street church is a work of pure Arts and Crafts, Aberdeen's Holy Trinity Cathedral is a masterpiece of eclecticism, combining – its exterior – the medieval wonders of grey Gothic with the exuberance of its interior. The late Sir John Betjeman – Cavan interviewed him once on *Island Breakfast* – wrote that it was 'worth flying round the world' just to see Oswald Fish's masterpiece. Dr Gavin Stamp, who made the Haj to Aberdeen and gave us a marvellous lecture on Fish, called it 'the most surprising, and also the most impressive work of English Gothic in any of the Victorian Dominions'.

This is not just a church. It is a psycho-drama which you entered as soon as you pushed open the heavy cast-iron doors, modelled on the Baptistery doors in Florence, but containing reliefs of virgin martyrs and also, if you looked carefully, figures who were probably not so virginal. Bishop Suter, who dedicated the building, was short-sighted, but some observers could see that the nymph, or virgin martyr, in the panel which he struck with his crozier, as the choir intoned *Lift up your heads, O ye gates* by S.S. Wesley, was revealing an unmistakable tuft of pubic hair as her shift parted at the waist.

Now come inside. Most visitors gasped on their first sight of the huge cast-iron rood screen which divided the choir from the nave, constructed in the Fish family works in Birmingham. The beaten copper reliefs in the panels of this screen, at its base and to its sides, were recognized as among the finest things made in the 1890s. The candour with which they represented the female form still had the capacity to shock, even in our generation. The nymphs hurtled sideways through space, the diaphanous folds of their angelic garments parting to reveal the breasts which panted with an ardour more profane than spiritual. None was more beautiful than the one on the left of the screen, which the architect himself nicknamed 'Atalanta in Calydon'. Her bare chest undulates, rather than protrudes, but nothing is more feminine, nothing more sensuous. You can imagine nestling there and believing yourself in paradise, between the curves of her breasts and the firmness of her nipples. The windows, which many visitors supposed at first glance to be by Burne-Jones, were likewise filled with female forms who were thought, even by the earliest congregations in our city, to owe more to classical mythology, as interpreted by the headier poets of the decadence, than to the Christian scriptures.

No visitor, either in the lifetime of Fish, or in our own day, however, could step into our Cathedral and remain indifferent. It was a building – must I speak of it in the past tense? Well, you must decide – which seized your heart. It pulsated. It was passionate. Bishop Suter, when he became aware of some of the details in Fish's designs, expressed himself as outraged; but he was wrong, surely, for Fish, as well as celebrating the beauty of the female body, was clearly a man tormented by a divided nature. Think of the window depicting the Magdalene. Her abundant hair falls over the feet of the Saviour, her tears anoint him; but he, a young man of clearly Victorian and Caucasian origin, gazes downwards at her with mournful passion. His long hand is stretched out to touch her hair-cloaked shoulders. The mingling of piety and concupiscence which was a part of the architect's own character seemed embodied in its bricks and stones. The young females in the windows, offering their censers of fuming love to a lamb upon the throne, could have been angels; they could equally have been young Huia women of 1897, grateful for the boost given by that animal to our Island economy, and, to this day, one of our most celebrated exports. And it was impossible not to admire the way in which Fish played with light and dark. Walk into the Cathedral at first light, with sunshine streaming through the green dresses and white flesh of the feminine angels, and you entered a glory of morning brightness. But even at this time, the side-aisles were shadowy. Every church, Oswald Fish used to say, needed secret corners 'where the soul could shudder at its own unworthiness, or where the heart could bleed'. There was much heartbreak, as well as exuberance, in this interior. The great hanging lamps, made at the Fish and Co. works in Birmingham, were Oswald's signature design feature. You see them in all the churches he restored, such as Carlisle Cathedral. He is said to have taken inspiration from the gigantic censer which swings across the aisle of the Cathedral at Santiago de Compostela. No more magnificent Fish lamps were ever seen than the copper ones in Aberdeen Cathedral.

In the days when it was still fashionable to mock the late Victorians, Fish was held in scorn, never more so than by the brutalists. No one, however, can doubt his technical competence. Unlike some of the Victorian architects (John Loughborough Pearson, for example, who roughed out designs for the Cathedral at Carmichael, but never actually came here) who were commissioned to adorn our Island with their work, and who merely sent out juniors from their offices in Britain with a sheaf of drawings, Oswald Fish came in person to oversee the laying of the foundations. He had not, in his youth, been primarily an ecclesiastical craftsman. Those who appreciate his work enjoy not merely the twists and flourishes of his Arts and Crafts metalwork, but also his contributions to industrial and civic design in his native Birmingham – a Venetian warehouse, loosely Gothic gasworks and various industrial buildings along the Birmingham canal betraying, to the cognoscenti, the master's hand. (The Venetian warehouse, with its playful allusions to the Ca' Rezzonico, now boasts the addition of a minaret.) They are all sturdy constructions, whatever you think of their design, and he knew his craft. After only a few weeks in Aberdeen – we pass over the complaints made by the manageress of the George and Dragon Hotel and the claim, which Fish said was unsubstantiated, that he had lured a chambermaid into an unsuitable liaison – he had surveyed the land in what became Argyle Square, and listened to the advice not only of his Church employers, but also to some of the Tangata inhabitants. Having done so, he had questioned the suitability of constructing so large an edifice with a stone frame as his patron, our first Bishop, had required. A wooden-framed building, Fish urged, would withstand the vagaries of the Pacific climate.

Earlier in the century, indeed, the Tangata inhabitants, whose forebears had first settled the wetlands on which the city was now instructed, seven hundred years before the arrival of the British, had questioned the wisdom of building a city there at all. Their ancestors, centuries before a tall ship arrived in the sound and changed their destinies forever, disgorging men in the uniform of King George III's Royal Navy, together with a naturalist – eager to dig up botanical specimens for shipment back to Kew Gardens – and an astronomer with instruments, and a cartographer, the Tangata headmen had found the wetlands rich in reeds, useful as building materials and for fabrics. They had caught fish there. And drifting on their rafts, gazing across Oka-kiri-sawa – what became Castlereagh Sound – its stupendous Pacific skies, its pink waters at sunset, its pale-fringed shore, they had sung their songs and invoked their deities. Here the Earth Mother Siyuta had felt the kickings of the angry foetus Mudu in her womb.

Since time out of mind, he had lain in her womb beneath the still waters of Oka-kiri-sawa. As she carried him, from Gooara-wey-wo in the north, with its snow-capped peaks, to the great granite gulfs of Hi-tula; from the fertile north-western plains of Bangi-fortu to the southerly silver sands of Mara-giwi, lapped by the Pacific, the Tangata had known that Mudu was disconcertingly stirring in his mother's womb. From time to time, he kicked, and struggled to be born, though she wanted him to remain inside her, tied to her umbilical cord. It was said by those who composed the songs of old time, that from time to time, Mudu's stirrings could be felt, however, and that Siyuta the Earth Mother cried out in pain, or even felt the pains of birth to be close at hand. The waters gushed in the warm geysers, near the great swampy moorland near the fjord-like headlands of Sama, and sometimes the earth itself shook.

Oswald Fish had known little or nothing of these things, though it is possible he had learnt them from Belinda, the tall, narrow-footed, springy-haired young Tangata woman with whom he so scandalously and openly took lodgings after the attachment to the chambermaid in the hotel caused him to pack his bags. They claimed they had gone north for a weekend and married, by special licence, in Carmichael. No one exactly believed this. He had, however, read not only the poems of Swinburne, which our Bishop, at the time, considered a quite unsuitable indulgence for a church architect, but also Sir Charles Lyell's *Geology*. The Bishop, and the other clergy, found this knowledge on the architect's part if possible even more offensive than his taste in verse, suggesting, as it did, scepticism about the processes of Creation itself, as described in the Book of Genesis. Fish knew, and did not hesitate to tell the

Bishop, that to have built an entire city in the former wetlands was an act of incalculable hubris. He had written formally to his Church patrons to warn them that the Cathedral of the Most Holy and Undivided Trinity would be safer with a wooden structure. In the event of a tremor, this would allow the stone-built structure around the wooden frame some room to sway.

The trustees who were supervising, and costing, the new building allowed themselves to be guided, not by the architect, but by the Bishop. He was a man of a self-confidence which his contemporaries had considered admirable. As a young man, he had been a master at Rugby School, going on, while still in his thirties, to become a headmaster himself, albeit of a less distinguished character than his old hero Dr Thomas Arnold, at a newly founded boarding school, where the boys endured team games, corporal punishment and very little in the way of intellectual stimulation beyond what could be found in the Latin histories. Even as a bishop, his reading, when he found time for it, would have been in the manly histories of Livy and Macaulay, rather than in the seedy incense-drowned imagination of Algernon Charles Swinburne which so entranced Oswald Fish.

When minerals were discovered in our Island during the 1840s, the large Pacific island had changed its character entirely, and it was now regarded, by the politicians and merchants of the Old Country, in an entirely different light. No longer merely a beautiful adornment to the British Empire, a fern-fringed Eden in the South Seas, doubling as a minor penal colony, as well as a place to which enterprising Britons could go to establish farms, it was now a source of wealth. There was copper, and there was gold. Although these were never, as it transpired, to be discovered in anything like the quantities which were later found in Nigeria or the Transvaal, there was an acceptance of the feeling that our Island must no longer be a place where the British farmers and their families could be expected to worship in charming wooden churches on the edge of their villages. Our Island was becoming a land of towns and cities. In Cambridge, the town furthest south in our Island, the Roman Catholics had built a church for their Irish navvies, Our Lady, Star of the Sea, the flamboyance of which amounted, in Bishop Suter's eyes, to impertinence. In the small town of Blandford, which had been settled by people from Ulster, the Presbyterians had a chapel which was almost bigger than the Anglican church. Aberdeen had been an Anglican city since its earliest settlers. We have, to this day, the largest Anglican private schools – St Michael's, the school for juniors, and St Augustine's and St Hilda's. There were six Anglican churches in our town before the Cathedral was built. The people of Aberdeen counted themselves lucky that the Catholics had made little inroad by the 1890s, but the Presbies were threatening an edifice as grandiosely ugly as the monster they'd built in Blandford. It was essential to show the flag, and neither the manly Bishop nor the trustees were having any truck with the decadent architect's idea of a wooden-framed building.

Everyone knew about 'Atalanta'. The Anglicans could not wait for their architect to leave them, and return to his dissipations in the Old Country. It disgusted them that he had chosen not merely to fornicate, but to do so with a young woman who did not even have the decency to be English. None of them believed for one second in the marriage certificate. The man was a dissolute monster, the woman no better than she ought to have been. Oswald Fish's suggestion of wooden frames was rejected with the same manly vigour with which the Bishop would have defended the Thirty-Nine Articles, or the custom of beginning each day with immersion in a cold tub. To Fish's idea that the new Cathedral be framed with pliable material, the Bishop was able to reply that other foundation had never man laid but Jesus Christ, the chief corner-stone. As for the architect's ludicrous suggestion that an edifice built to God's Glory, and to the honour of the Church's supreme Governor, Queen Victoria, should be threatened by tremors – who ever heard such nonsense? It was faith that was required, not wooden frames. As for the suggestion that our Island had come into being as a result of the clashing of tectonic plates – some notion culled by Fish from Lyell's *Geology* – the Bishop considered that, had it not verged on the blasphemous, it would have been laughable. The Cathedral was therefore built of stone.

The Bishop, moreover, had been reconsidering the design which Fish had submitted. True, the grey Gothic of the exterior was admirable, but was it not too restrained? Did not the city require a symbol of the supremacy of the Church by law established, a finger raised aloft to admonish the faithless and the nonconformists, in short, a tower surmounted in true medieval glory with a spire?

Fish did his best to resist the notion, but in the end, it is the customer who gets what his money demands. Fish warned them that such a structure would be unable to withstand any more shifts of those tectonic plates. They told him they were paying for a building, not for advice. The spire which he drew was indeed a glorious one, as was the tower beneath. The bells were commissioned from the foundry in Aldgate East in London, though it was some years after Fish left us that they were ready to be shipped out to the Island, blessed and hung in the tower. Belinda, the beautiful Tangata woman, was by then in her twenties. She was married. Her name was Mrs Wheeler. She had five children. She affected a dignified indifference to those gossips who claimed to see a resemblance between her firstborn and the by now absent English architect.

Aftershocks

When she first heard the changes rung from the tower, she had wept, just as her heart always swelled a little, when she entered the sacred edifice, to see the Atalanta-like running nymph in the left-hand panel of the rood screen, an immortalization of a happy time, one which she considered beautiful, whatever the puritans and spoilsports might say. There are still old people in Aberdeen who met 'Atalanta', a tall old lady with a frizz of white hair and a jaunty felt hat, sometimes dangling with cherries or blossom. She continued to attend the Cathedral well into her nineties, dying in 1962.

Like I say, I used to go to the Cathedral with my mum, and like many Huias, I was brought up Anglican, but I've never been too sure what I actually believe. Nevertheless, there's a kind of borderland in the mind between things we think as matters of fact, and things we experience as episodes of imagination. This is the borderland where Art flourishes. One of the things I really REALLY envy Digby is that she once met Iris Murdoch at Oxford. Murdoch did not believe in a personal God, but she believed we were living in something called the Time of the Angels, that there were, as it were, angelic presences, hanging over from the old days when the Christian religion was as solid and safe as earth before it was all shook up.

I like this idea. And I like the idea of Presences from the past, coming to haunt us, help us, inspire us. Is this what is going on in *Four Quartets*? I think so. Anyhow, I really like the idea of Oswald Fish, the architect of our beloved Cathedral. In my fantasy-life – and this is just from looking at the carvings and modelling and windows – I feel he was one of those really rare males, one who understood about women.

Liked them, for a start, which is an advantage not enjoyed by all the men I've ever known. You see, take Barnaby. OK, he's a bit spoilt, because he has been the lover of Deirdre Hadley, our Green MP, and she is still in love with him, and I'm sure she's told him he's the best lover in the world, and for HER, he may have been. But my Love and I have talked about this, not in a nasty way, but with smiling, amused knowledge, and we are agreed. We think Barnaby's idea of being a good lover is to make it last a long time. By 'it', he is simply referring to the simple tantric THING – just the shagging part, if one is being crude. He has not said this, but we both know. He thinks of all the rest of lovemaking as 'foreplay', and he probably thinks it is just something a bloke does out of politeness to get us in the mood. He does not realize that the whole THING is making love – the looking into one another's eyes, the holding hands over the table, as we drink our last glass of wine, the embraces, the undressing, the stroking, the dancing, the kissing and tasting, all of it is making love. There are some people who think that when you go to church, you should banish all these thoughts. Apparently, Eleanor's father Ronald was not one of them, and his daughter once told me about his wedding sermons in the fogbound West Midland towns. He would tell his parishioners – some of whom – she suspected – did not have her father's love for the medieval Italian poet – about Dante Alighieri finding the love of God through the love of woman. He would sometimes tell them about the Albigensian Crusades. Cruel, desperately cruel, they had been, with such slaughter, all over the South of France, of the Cathars, who believed that the human body was wicked and that we are all spirit, and you get to the truth by denying the flesh. And however cruel the Church was in persecuting the Cathars, Ronald would say, they were right to attack the Cathars' ideas, because Christianity taught that God had become human, and thereby sanctified the body. And in the marriage service, we were reminded of this, where it says Christ 'adorned and beautified' the marriage feast at Cana by his presence. 'And,' Ronald would say to his parishioners, 'he adorns and beautifies your marriage with his presence, as you say to one another – *With my body I thee worship*.' St Dominic was right to dispute with the Cathars. The body is sacred. By your bodily worship of one another, in sex, you make human souls.

Lesley Mannock used to say, 'I don't HAVE a body, I AM a body.' And he and Ronald used to say the reason the Anglican Communion is tearing itself apart about homosexuality is because it has not understood the true Christian theology of sexuality of any kind. 'With my body I thee worship.' And all the distrust of the body, and fear of sex, and division of flesh and spirit, this was Gnosticism, not Christianity. And quite what the congregations made of it in the fogbound West Midlands, we do not know.

The trouble with this is it is very very difficult to believe. It is easy to say, but in practice, it is much easier either to be a pure materialist and think (whatever this would mean) that the body and the material are all that there is; or to be a Gnostic and to think that flesh and spirit are always at war. Most forms of Christianity, even those practised by St Dominic (who had so opposed the Gnostic Cathars), encouraged austerity, chastity and a distrust of the physical.

Perhaps this was true of Eleanor Bartlett, our Dean. Although, when conducting wedding services, she tried to reproduce her father's theology – encouraging the couples to rejoice in their physical union, and to worship one another with their bodies – she actually shrank from the physical. True, she was married, and Charlie Nicolson was married. But even if this was not the case, she would have shrunk from a full sexual relationship with him. Indeed, the very fact that they couldn't 'go the whole way' was presumably what made the flirtation a possibility in the first place.

Digby's attitude to sex was harder to read. There she was, in Barnaby Farrell's arms, but – she held back from what D.H. Lawrence calls this ridiculous dancing of the buttocks. But then, Digby and Eleanor were very different. Had to be. Their survival depended, in some ways, on their apartness. So, Digby, inside her, with a large part of herself, resented being in Aberdeen and wanted to become the Regius Professor of Greek at Oxford, or some such, whereas Eleanor was in love with Dad, and revered his life of ministry in obscure and fogbound places, and wanted to be like him, and regarded it as a privilege to be the Dean of a cathedral. There were so many other points of difference too. Eleanor fought uncharitable thoughts as soon as they arose; Digby did not check judgment. Winced, for example, at the way that Dionne Lillicrap, our Bishop, spoke; thought she was a waste of space, and allowed herself the reflection (privately, of course) that this was quite a lot of space. Eleanor was happy to be here, it made her think of her visits with her Huia mum; Digby sometimes looked out of her tower window and longed for old Europe, simply anything old, a Georgian drainpipe would do, whereas Eleanor? You know what? It was actually a relief to her not to be bothered by the clang and peal of bells from Oxford's dreaming what's their names.

Eleanor the tribal Anglican was sincere when she sang, *O Lord open thou our lips*. She thought that Plato was right, there was a world of value out there, a world of value and truth bigger than ourselves which religion helps us to contemplate. She did not believe it was possible that Bach or Hildegard of Bingen or T.S. Eliot were listening to nothing; she deemed their experience, translated into music and poetry, to be something real. Whereas Digby. She was a cynic about religion. She told that Tragedy class over and over again that tragedy is based on the contingency of value. Morality, or Ethics, are something we human beings make up for largely utilitarian reasons. We do so to make order for ourselves in a dis-orderly hostile universe. God, the gods, the Fates, the Furies, etc. are ways of describing the capriciousness of things. Tragedy is a way of giving a dignified response to the indignities thrown at us by Nature. Anyhow, that's them – Digby and Eleanor Bartlett, and I was the only person who had quite seen this.

But I wonder whether they did not both respond, as I did, to Oswald Fish's 'angels' in the Cathedral, to the Atalanta figure ever running, ever about to lose her diaphanous drapery; to the obviously feminine angels in the windows, to the Swinburnian paganism of the Cathedral's décor. Maybe Atalanta, and the female angels, in this Time of the Angels, were guiding us all in ways we could not see. Guiding you and me, my Love, to Love and to Truth?

CHAPTER FOUR

WE NOW KNOW THAT DEIRDRE HADLEY, OUR MUCH-RESPECTED Green MP, had thrown herself into public life with especial vigour when her heart was broken. Broken by none other than Barnaby Farrell. But if you don't mind, I'll tell you about that a bit later. When I say that Deirdre is much respected, I really mean it. Even those who are in a different place politically recognize her courage, her total integrity, her intelligence. And she has been a wonderful MP since the Quake, helping her constituents in innumerable ways, like, for example, persuading local businesses temporarily to empty their warehouses on the edge of town and make the space available for performance-space, for schools, and so on; like chivvying to get central Government grants to speed up rebuilding of the hospital. She has also been a very practical helper – every spare hour has been spent dispensing tea and food in the temporary refuges which, for years after the big Quake, are still needed. This is not to mention her tireless, detailed work with lawyers pursuing the insurance companies who have been mean, or slow, in paying up to allow householders to rebuild or repair their properties; and, more exacting, and more dangerous, pursuing some of the dodgier property developers in their attempts to cover up their secret deals with Rex Tone, and, as we now know, with Dionne our Pontiff. So, the more I admire her now, the more I repent of how little I used to revere her when she was my English teacher at St Hilda's. That isn't to say she was a good teacher!

Hers was the only voice in our public discourse which consistently warned us about the dangers of a possible quake. Everywhere else on the Island people had been imagining for years that they would be affected by a quake on the scale of the disasters which have befallen San Francisco or Italy or New Zealand in the past. Hadley was the only person to argue that Aberdeen, because of where it was built, on the wetlands, was a prime site for a catastrophe.

None of us took her seriously. One reason was that, although Aberdeen is a city of getting on for half a million people – or it was before the Quake – it is – or was – in atmosphere more of a village really. It feels as if we all know one another, and it is rare, when two Aberdonians meet, for them not to discover some acquaintance in common. So an awful lot of us could remember her lessons at St Hilda's. And even those Aberdonians who had never been taught by her had known people who were.

As I say, I'm afraid I had been NOT taking her seriously since I was sixteen, when I found myself in her English set. I used to keep a diary of her sad attempts to interest a roomful of unruly adolescents in the rarefied, beautiful mind of Mrs Woolf.

English with Badley Dreary. Hair grips in the woolly mop she calls her hair. Bright green granny-cardie. Jumble-sale floral dress. Grey knee socks. Crocs (also green). 'This morning, we're going to look at the way that . . . no . . . no, PLEASE . . . You must switch off your mobiles. Your phones, you must switch them OFF. Fiona – Jan – Rachael – PLEASE. Rachael, if you won't put that phone away, I shall have to . . . I shall have to . . . Rachael, please, if you could put the phone away and tell us what we know about Mr Ramsay from the opening chapters which you will . . . QUIET EVERYONE! . . . you will surely have read by now . . . Well, after three weeks, I should have thought you could read a few short chapters. QUIET! Rachael, I did not catch that. [Roars of laughter] Say it again, Rachael . . . Well, now.' Her sunburnt face freezes into a brave smile and yet the cheeks are pink with embarrassment and indignation. *'I can't imagine how you can draw that inference about Mr Ramsay. Well, it is true that Virginia Woolf knew some homosexuals . . . THERE IS NOTHING WRONG WITH BEING A HOMOSEXUAL, Jenny, but I fail to see how you could think that Mr RAMSAY . . . No indeed. And we should never EVER use that word to describe such people . . . Because it's . . . because . . . Steph, what is so funny? I think if you have found something to amuse you, you should share it with the rest of us . . . There are some words which intelligent people do not use, that's why, Jan Kirkby.*

Though we all spoke, and I wrote, about her as if she were a granny, she was miles younger than Mum. She was only in her thirties when I meanly transcribed her Virginia classes. I didn't know then that she shared her house with George Eliot, a grey parrot whom she was trying to teach to recite, and a young graduate student working on Thomas Hardy called Barnaby Farrell. And . . . Hey, I thought I was meant to be the gossipy one, and here you are, wondering. The answer is yes. He told me when he and I were in bed together. Not only had she been his lover, they still were – very occasionally. If you'd told me that when we were all yelling our heads off during her *To the Lighthouse* class, I'd have thought it was grotesque, but once I'd grown up I could see her heartbroken hippy charm.

On her very first Sunday as Dean, Eleanor had spotted Deirdre Hadley in the Cathedral. Thin, almost worryingly thin, with blonde-greyish hair and a smile which appeared to conceal something. Deirdre, as I say, is one of our local members of Parliament. When she's not on the campaign trail, or sitting at home teaching George Eliot to recite, you'll often see her, walking in a kind of dream, in our beautiful Victorian Botanic Gardens in Gladstone Park. One of the things which made me so cruel about her when I was a kid was embarrassment. She lived quite near us in Harrow, a riverside suburb which, when Mum and Dad bought our little house, was really run-down but which little by little 'rose'.

Even when we were giving Deirdre hell in the classroom, we recognized that, if you got her off the subject of that ruddy lighthouse and Mrs W's stream of consciousness, she appeared to know every exotic tree and shrub, and to treasure them rather more than she did her perhaps too comfortable pupils.

Eleanor, being a principled person herself, was principled in a more subdued style. Her principles were clothed in politeness. So, she liked Deirdre while fearing an intensity, and held her therefore, from the first, at arm's length. Eleanor's dad often mused, during their Skype-colloquies, on the unpredictability of church congregations. What made some people attend on a regular basis, and made others into 'occasional' attenders? Deirdre's whimsical blue eyes and her thin-lipped smile made her seem a dreamy child. If she had worn make-up, you would have felt disturbed, as can be the case when a little girl plays with her mother's lip gloss or eyeshadow. The jumble-sale clothes, however, and the usually bare, slightly downy stick legs ending in crocs or Birkenstocks were old ladyish. When they appeared to be moving from the position of acquaintanceship towards something which might become a friendship, Eleanor had invited her to supper at the Deanery. The invitation, meant as a gesture of kindness, but borne also of a certain loneliness herself, and a feeling that they might have things in common – books at least – had caused flurry, not pleasure. After a number of unconvincing claims that the dates proposed were unsuitable, Deirdre had begun to mention dietary restrictions – Eleanor was not altogether surprised, Deirdre being one of those regular members of the Cathedral congregation who opted for gluten-free Communion wafers. But after a while, Eleanor began to draw the conclusion that she did not eat or drink anything, perhaps lived on air.

> *Hollow of cheek as though it drank the wind*
> *And took a mess of shadows for its meat.*

The dinner idea was dropped, though the pair had enjoyed a couple of walks along the banks of the Windrush, and after one of these Deirdre had consented to come back to the Deanery for refreshment in the kitchen. Tea and coffee having been refused, she opted for lemonade, and Eleanor had almost offered her a straw. She had sipped it very cautiously at first, in the way that children do who are afraid of an unfamiliar taste.

It was after she left teaching, and after Barnaby began his compensation for the Man Drought by taking on the conquest of the women of Aberdeen single-handed, that Deirdre's interest in Animal Rights, and green issues generally, had come to the fore.

She was not afraid. Even as a kid, I'd noticed her courage. While we were all taking the piss during her Woolf classes, she'd been unable to control us; but she had never shown fear. Now that she was a Friend of the Earth, and an activist, she had great boldness. Eleanor first noticed it after Deirdre had met Shadrach, Meshach and Abednego, Bishop Dionne's three pugs. The Bishop had brought them to the Cathedral for the Animal Blessing Service which was held on the nearest October Sunday to the Feast of St Francis of Assisi.

Deirdre strode up to the Bishop and asked,

—Did you know that these pugs are in-bred?

—You're beautiful, aren't you? was Bishop Dionne's response. If she had been addressing Deirdre, her words would have been true. The Pontiff, however, was cooing into Abednego's ear (maybe Shadrach's, who could be sure?).

—Brachycephalic dogs always are prone to breathing difficulties.

—Do you have reading difficulties, darling?

Dionne's wit, like the Bishop herself, was on the heavy side.

—It is inhumane to breed brachycephalic dogs, and then to in-breed and in-breed so that they have flatter and flatter faces. They can't BREATHE properly! When you think they are snorting and snoring in a charming way, they are gasping for BREATH!

Those who overheard the exchange began to realize that Deirdre was furious. She never raised her voice, though. From the educated, modulated tone, she could have been just talking to the Bishop about the flower rota.

Dionne gave her the brush-off. Suddenly showed a deep interest in a guinea pig that one of the choirgirls had brought along. The sight of the guinea pig made Shadrach, Meshach and Abednego splutter uncontrollably. Their protuberant eyes fixed on Fudge, the guinea pig, suggesting they would have liked to tear him apart, if they were able to open their jaws widely enough. All over their black, smooth, slobbery mouths and their sparse, black whiskers there were skeins of spittle. Those animal services for the kiddiz certainly brought out the red in tooth and claw side of Nature – more than they made one think of all things bright and b. or St Francis preaching to the song-birds – which, come to think of it, being Italian, stood a higher chance than most European birds of being netted, shot or ending their days encased in pastry. He might as well have preached to a crowd of sausage rolls.

Next day, and every day for a week, Deirdre stood outside the Bishop's house with a placard. It was inscribed in gigantic italic letters, written with two fluorescent highlighters, one green one black.

PUGS ARE BRED TO CHOKE

She stayed there until Cavan Cliffe saw that a 'story' had been created. Then Deirdre came on Cavan's radio show – *Island Breakfast* – and poured out all the stats: pugs and French bulldogs being bred as lapdogs for 'SELFISH humans'. Her beautifully modulated voice, which we'd drowned out at St Hilda's when she'd tried to read aloud from *To the Lighthouse*, now rang bell-like over every breakfast table in the Island.

—The Island is full of stray dogs, unwanted dogs, dogs in rescue homes. Why not ADOPT one of these dogs, who need your love, rather than wasting HUNDREDS of dollars breeding dogs artificially? Nature never MEANT SUCH CREATURES TO EXIST. They are human creations. The humans who do this think it is charming when their pugs snore – do they not realize that these creatures are gasping for BREATH? And we have a BISHOP, who is supposed to be a Christian, who has spent three hundred dollars EACH for these pathetic animals. The Bishop should surely be setting an example. To have brought those creatures to the Cathedral, on the Feast of St Francis of Assisi, was tantamount to blasphemy!

Dionne was asked on Cavan Cliffe's show to provide an answer. It wasn't very sensible of her to have accepted the invitation. Her interview was a car-crash. She came over as smug, and blinkered. Everyone thought – you've got to hand it to Hadley: even when you don't agree with her, she makes you think. Trouble is, she did not make us think hard enough. And even if we had, what would we have done? Evacuated the city before the Quake, and just left it to fall down empty, and without us? If we're Trojan Women, she was certainly our Cassandra.

Later, we all came to know one another much better, and I realized she was one of those people who took up public causes because of private heartbreak. For most of the three years that Barnaby had been her lodger, he had also been her lover. Deirdre says that at first, they were really wonderful together, he was in love with her just as much as she with him, or seemed to be. The age difference is not that great – she is twelve years older than he is. In her quiet, strange way, she was always very matter-of-fact in the way she spoke of it. Said it was unrealistic to suppose that sexual intensity would last forever, but she would have been perfectly happy if this had evolved into quiet tenderness, the shared bed, the walk beside the Windrush, hand in hot, passionate hand. She deeply wanted his child. When his rampage through the female population of Aberdeen began, her heart cracked, but she could not be surprised. He was immature. He was vain. By all conventional standards he was beautiful, whereas her ethereal beauty was something which crept up quietly on you. Then you saw it and you could not forget it, in rather the way that Turner's watercolours, when you have begun to see the world through his eyes, enable you to see beauty in supposedly bad weather – sun struggling to come through mists, grey clouds, yellow sun shimmering in morning fog. Deirdre's beauty was like that, inseparable from 'the eternal note of sadness'.

Eleanor often spoke about Deirdre to her father.

—Lesley Mannock thinks, if only she could get the young man to marry her!

—But, Dad, there's Bar now, and the little boy.

Her father sighed.

—Lesley says, love will find a way.

—But Deirdre can't MAKE him marry her.

—Well, we should pray for her.

There was an awkward little silence.

—I said . . .

—I know, Dad. I heard what you said.

Working alongside Bishop Dionne was undoubtedly the chief drawback of Eleanor's job, but, unlike Digby, she suppressed feelings, swallowed contempt, and only 'let off steam' during her Skyped conversations with the canon. Dad always referred to Dionne as 'the Pontiff' and this helped a lot. She knew that if you were an Anglican, there had to be Bishops. They came with the territory. Whatever the drawbacks of Dionne, and of Brian, her Australian, golfing, businessman husband, they were not capable of blotting out in their entirety the benefits of the long Anglican tradition.

—*Who alone workest great marvels* . . . Dad would laugh, recalling how he had been 'helped' – a very Ronald verb – when he was in parochial life, by reciting the collect for the Clergy and People in the Prayer Book. *Almighty and everlasting God, who alone work-est great marvels: send down upon our Bishops and curates, and all congregations committed to their charge, the healthful Spirit of thy grace . . .*

The author of the Prayer Book knew that it would indeed be a marvel if the Bishops and Curates could be so blessed, but it was something after which to aspire.

The great difference between Eleanor and Digby was that Eleanor accepted, as did her father, the possibility of divine help. She believed in God, whereas Digby did not. (Digby liked the joke, How do you define a religious maniac? Answer – Someone who believes in God. Another one she liked, she had seen printed on tee-shirts one day in the street market in Howley Street – 'Too stupid to understand science? Try Religion'. Of course she did not share these jokes with Dean Eleanor Bartlett's parishioners, such as the home-less to whom Eleanor took soup and comfort in the refuge centre she had opened in the Crypt – long before the Quake.) Most of those who saw much of Dean Bartlett, in or around the Cathedral, were either unaware of Digby, or only passingly aware of her. Most of the academics who enjoyed Digby's seminars and lectures at the University, or who read her articles in the *TLS*, were what Eleanor's father called 'modern agnogs', with no interest in religion one way or the other. The world is becoming more and more secular. The religious outlook is something most of us, especially my generation, simply do not begin to grasp. Eleanor was in this respect anomalous and Digby was normal. Apart from the religious divide, Digby and Eleanor held most stuff gently and ironically in common: a nostalgia for an England which no longer existed; exasperation with, but affection for, Oxford; a growing love of our Island, where they felt more and more at home; a love of the old canon, left behind in his modest flat. I was one of the few who saw them both – Digby in her world, Eleanor in hers.

The old Oswald Fish Cathedral, with its spire, and its stained-glass windows, and its choir in ruffs and surplices, twice daily singing their way through the repertoire of Prayer Book settings, from Merbecke to Howells, was a glorious thing in Tribal Eleanor's eyes, an embodiment of what was best in the world. She saw that building for the first time when she came to Aberdeen with her Huia mother to meet her Huia granny. Both women had been teachers. Both had been baptized in the Cathedral. Ever afterwards in England, when Eleanor sang the evening hymn, she had thought of our Cathedral in Aberdeen.

> *The sun which bids us rest is waking*
> *Our brethren 'neath the Western sky*
> *And hour by hour fresh lips are making*
> *Thy wondrous doings heard on high.*

The hymn, with its tear-jerking tune, made her think of the mysterious time changes which steal upon the traveller as she flies from Europe to our Island, mysterious because somehow or another you do not merely fly into a different time zone – you actually seem to lose a day. She thought of the Anglican Communion spread all over the globe, a much-derided group of men, women and children, but forty million of them, trying, so far as she could see, to do good and to spread sweetness and light. The nickname for Anglicans in America was 'The Chosen Frozen'. Eleanor happily identified with this. She was happy to be frozen, rather than responding to life with the often hollow expressions of emotion which were heard at Oscar ceremonies, in political speeches, in 'misery memoirs' and in broadcast interviews with 'slebs' who wanted to share their pain with the rest of the world. Behind the frozen exterior of dignified liturgy, seventeenth-century language, formal music and apparent unwillingness to be too dogmatic in religious definitions, there was a heart. Hearts which were exposed ceased to beat. The Chosen Frozen yet believed in the ragamuffin anarchy of the Gospels, the most revolutionary texts ever written, in which human beings are enjoined to die in order to live, in which human hierarchies are completely upturned, in which the meek inherit the earth, the mighty are put down from their seats, the poor have Good News preached to them and the rich go empty away. Who but God could have delivered such utterly life-changing messages to the planet? It was Trevor Huddleston, the monk who had challenged apartheid in South Africa with such wonderful consequence, who used to say that no more revolutionary text than the Gospel could be conceived.

It was so easy to mock Anglican wishy-washiness – did they or didn't they . . . provide your own shopping list: believe in divorce; accept gay rights; believe in the Bible? Perhaps all the esoteric matters which threatened to 'tear apart' (the usual metaphor) this benign conglomeration of Churches – sexual morality of one sort or another being the one which caught the imagination of secular headline writers – really derived from different ways of reading the Bible?

Eleanor had never supposed that – for example – the words of St Paul were infallible, or that they could not be understood as coming from their own time and place. Those fellow Christians who took seriously his injunction that women should not be allowed to open their mouths in church (always assuming that Paul actually wrote the part of the letter in which this appears) seemed to be approaching the Scriptures in a way which – Eleanor believed – was simply wrong. So, she was not troubled by what St Paul or the Book of Leviticus said about same-sex relationships any more than she worried about the Jewish dietary laws with which much of the Bible was concerned.

The Bible, that prodigious library of poems, legends, history, moral teaching, internalized myth, challenge, was, in any case, only one of the wonderful things which Christianity had handed down from generation to generation through the centuries, together with the writings of the Church Fathers and the mystics, the example of the martyrs and saints, and, when Christianity came to be the religion of the Roman Empire, the wealth of Christian art, mosaic, architecture, music. At the core of it was a real experience, the experience of millions of human lives who, in the Gospels and the Christian tradition, had known God. Somewhere in first-century Palestine, a group of women and men had an experience of an individual whom they believed lived in the breaking of bread. And from this had sprung Christianity – a nobler, cleaner, kinder creed, in Eleanor's opinion, than the gimcrack paganism of ancient Rome. There used to be corners in the imperial city of Rome where women dumped unwanted babies, the way we dump garbage for recycling. Overnight, when Constantine declared the Empire to be Christian, orphanages opened in Rome. It was because, overnight, the human individual was seen as sacred. And this, for Eleanor, was what made the incarnation of Christ the central event of human history, however unlikely it was that his birth had come about as a result of a virginal conception, or was heralded by a choir of angels.

When she was trying to explain this feeling of hers once, an antagonist said, 'Yes, but that's just do-gooding. You are reducing theology to do-gooding.'

And she'd wanted to reply, but did not think of it until a few days later – IS there anything deeper than doing good? Revering the Good? Contemplating the Good? Isn't our capacity to do good one of the things which distinguishes us, not only from all the bad PEOPLE of history but from the pagan gods, who heartlessly tormented their adepts? Is not one of the strangest, and most beautiful, facts of history, that in the darkest places of history – in the Gulag, or the Concentration Camps – we find examples of outstanding forbearance, self-sacrifice, gentleness? Is not Christianity's claim one of the most outrageous and extraordinary imaginable? Namely that God discarded Omnipotence and went about doing good, and died the death of a slave? Lesley Mannock used to quote something from Evelyn Underhill's book on Mysticism – words to the effect that prayer could not work unless you were also actively engaged in acts of charity to other people; it would fizzle. Faith in the incarnation could not be detached, either from contemplation or from deeds of good.

Eleanor knew that Christianity had done terrible things, in its blood-spattered history of heresy-hunts, crusades, burnings and tortures, and its sinister capacity both to suppress sexual impulse and to turn a blind eye to the consequences of that repression – in depressions and suicides and child-molestings.

Anglicanism had been a brutal religion to the puritans of the seventeenth century, true. Prynne lost his ears. The Pilgrim Fathers had been forced to sail to an unknown land to worship without the Prayer Book she loved, and they hated. Exclusion Acts made it impossible for nonconformists to worship according to their conscience. Even in those days, however, Eleanor maintained that what the Church of England was looking for was a Common Prayer – a religion which was inclusive of all.

Historians would dispute that, she knew. She did not consider it her duty to wring her hands in guilt about the past. She knew that she was happy with the Chosen Frozen. When doubts assailed her, as they assail any intelligent being, she still knew herself, in all her instinctual responses to life, to belong to this tradition. For most of the time, she quietly, but not smugly, rejoiced, in belonging to the Church which had nurtured George Herbert, Samuel Johnson, Jane Austen, Charlotte Mary Yonge, Charles Kingsley, T.S. Eliot, Rose Macaulay . . . This was where Eleanor was at home. More at home than she would have been with, say, Nietzsche, Wagner, Shaw, Bertrand Russell, Samuel Beckett, clever as they were.

It was literally home. Anglicanism was the creed of her parents. When she doubted, or when the idiotic utterances of some senior cleric made her wince, she remembered her father, a clever man who could easily have opted for an easy life. He had a first class degree from the University, and it was assumed that he would go on to become a Professor of Theology. Instead, like Lesley Mannock, he had been a clergyman in poor parishes, only at the end of his life accepting a Cathedral canonry. He had lived his life among the poor, as had his Island-born wife Gwen, and their only daughter. They had found Jesus Christ in the poor. The day had begun with her parents reading Prayer Book Matins together. On Thursdays and Sundays, her father had celebrated the early Service, and to the few who attended that rite, he had dispensed the Body of Christ. Later in the Sunday morning, at the Sung Eucharist, his congregations – initially all speaking with West Midland accents, but in more recent times, West Indian and Africans predominating – had sung the words of Cranmer to the music of Merbecke. Christ was there. That was why Eleanor believed. That was the setting in which her religious impulses moved, and were moved. The still small voice spoke to her in the early Communion services celebrated by her father in bleak Midland towns, churches with no beauty, churches and parishes with no glamour. One of her theology teachers once said to her that the only phrase in the Creed which he believed was 'Suffered under Pontius Pilate'. Well, maybe. On a bad day, maybe. But set the creed to Merbecke's music, and sing it with the congregations in those damp fogbound towns, the thirty-five or so faithful, the Jamaican nurses and their gawky sons, the old women in woollen hats, the inevitable awkward bachelor who had never found a friend, standing there in his anorak, and it became something other. It became like an anthem, a rallying cry. The music had been composed in the reign of Edward VI to accompany the new Prayer Book of 1549, and we had been singing it ever since. There was something more, though. There was a something which could not be defined, but which could be heard, experienced.

There was a something. It was unnecessary to be dramatic about it or to put it into words, there was a something. The still small voice, which spoke to her in the context of the Anglican liturgy, the Anglican worship. It was both quietly mystic and at the same time radical.

In her grown-up life, and especially since she had chosen to become a priest, there was more than this. There was an awareness of the whole Anglican Communion throughout the world. When she still lived in England, she often heard church-people say, 'Why not let these bigots go their own way?' – when, for example, the Nigerian Church condemned gay people Eleanor knew this could very well happen – such was the gulf in sympathy between, say, the Church in our Island, or in the USA, and the Churches in other parts of the world. Since coming to be the Dean of Aberdeen, though, she really wanted the Anglican Communion to stay together – not because she thought it was possible for its disparate views ever to be reconciled, but because she thought, *au fond*, that they all had something profound in common. That something was not an ideology, but the unnameable something, the . . . Unspeakable . . . The unforgettable THING she had experienced when her father said Mass in the light of dawn in those fogbound West Midland towns of her childhood.

> *O Christ whom now beneath a veil we see,*
> *May what we thirst for soon our portion be.*

It was not often palpable, as it had been in her pious adolescence; but sometimes, it was. Sometimes, as she walked about the Cathedral in Aberdeen, she could sense it – the Presence. Even if these feelings only came occasionally, that was enough.

—I thought Deirdre did really well on *Island Breakfast*.

Digby had only lately discovered, on the grapevine, that he was, or had been, Deirdre Hadley's lover. He, of course, had never mentioned it to her. She looked across the restaurant table at him.

—Good old Deirdre.

The broadcast to which Digby referred was a debate with Rex Tone about climate change.

—She had a go at the Bishop the other week. That tirade against pekingese. Did you hear it?

They laughed. Her pedantic need to correct error made the words 'Pugs, not pekes – PUGS' come to mind, but she managed not to say them. She stared at him, wondering which would be worse: to extract from him a confession about Deirdre, which would have made her (she realized) jealous, or NOT to receive a confession and to feel he was trying somehow or other to pull wool over her eyes.

They were eating in a nice Vietnamese place where they had been a couple of times before. It was in Manners-Sutton Street. They'd started with some deep-fried spring rolls – Cha Gio – and some salad rolls – Goi Cuon – and then shared a dish of Chicken with Vermicelli – Bun Ga Nuong. He was drinking more than she was of the delicious bottle of Riesling.

—For some reason, she said, I love the Island Riesling. I can't stand German wine in Europe, but here, it's . . .

—Light, he said, picking up her hand with the casualness with which one might pick up a fork or a napkin. She allowed this to happen.

They had talked about the success of their course, and discussed what they were going to say in their next – which would be the one about *King Lear*. She made no resistance as their knees touched under the table. Suddenly he said,

—Why don't we go back to my place?

She wanted to, but she said,

—What about your little boy? What about Stig?

—He'll be asleep.

—But, the baby-sitter . . .

—She won't be asleep. Or anyway, I hope not.

She laughed.

—You know what I mean. She'll know. She'll know I've come back with you. She stroked the back of his hand with her index finger.

—Well, it's up to you.

She was thinking, 'Stig! I would give everything, everything, to have a Stig in my life.' She was not even, specifically, thinking, 'Bloody Doug!', though it could have been said, at this stage of her experience, that her whole life was an expression of those three syllables. Deep, deep within her, the longing for a child, and for lovemaking, and for the fulfilment both uniquely brought, flooded over her, as she looked into his eyes, aware that he could, within an hour at his place, have made all these things possible, and connected her to the planet.

He went home alone, shortly afterwards, and she remained one of the childless, the disconnected ones. They'd had no more than a little cuddle before he strode away, his Man Bag, containing a good recent biography of Seneca which she had lent him, bouncing on his shoulder, and somehow telling her that he was cross. Later, alone in bed at home, Digby so regretted her decision.

CHAPTER FIVE

THEY WERE APPROACHING THE HOTHOUSES OF THE BOTANIC
Gardens, Eleanor and Charles. It was a winter day in June, so they
would be glad of the warmth. Very light flecks of snow were falling
on the grass. All the same, Eleanor felt it had been unwise. Unwise
to say she would come for this lunchtime walk with Charles, so soon
after that concert. Unwise to come to the Botanic Gardens. Unwise
to enter the ferny tropical steam of the glass house. They made a
handsome pair – he in a tweed cap over his Mr Rochester locks, and
a long tailored black overcoat; she, too, in a black coat, but with a
little pink woollen hat. The trouble was, as she noted, seeing their
reflections in the glass doors of the hothouse, not so much that they
made a handsome pair, as that they made a pair at all. A pair was
most decidedly what they were not, and never could be or should
be. And yet – she could not help noticing it in that reflected glimpse
as he swung the door open and held it for her – they did look like
a pair, and she wondered in some way which was both shocking
and worrying whether, over the last year or so of these meetings,
whether they had become a pair.

It was when they had reached the carnivorous plants – *Sarracenia flava* – that his manner changed, and she became swoopingly aware that the conversation was going to lurch into territories where frankness was demanded. Hitherto, what had characterized all their meetings, whether they sat beside one another at concerts, shook hands at the Cathedral door, in the company of his family, or walked together, as they were doing today, in gardens or galleries, was the absence of anything too sharply defined or too crudely spelt out. It was a flirtation, and could still remain that way; but they were inches away from the border being crossed into a different land, when all sorts of complications which had hitherto been unmentionable would become explicit. She needed, wanted, to backtrack. She even considered a feigned illness, and then, immediately, there came before her mind, as she painted the scene to herself, that he would then be entitled to place a hand on her arm, her shoulder, her waist. That way led the Land of Chaos. A giant tree fern soared above their heads. He leaned against the twisted wrought-iron of the spiral staircase which led to the gallery above their heads. Then it all blurted out.

—Pamela and I aren't happy. She's never made me happy.

—Charles – Charles . . .

—She can't listen. She literally can't hear me when I speak. I try to speak to her – when I've tried . . . It's not like the conversations you and I have . . . Eleanor.

They walked for a while in silence. The thing – it no longer had its inverted commas when she thought of it – had now become a nightmare. She had never realized before that she was vain. It was her vanity to which Charles had appealed. He wanted to lay all his misery, all his neediness, at her feet, like a puppy, abjectly bringing a chewed slipper to its mistress. At first, there had been something almost comic about it all. She had mistaken his crush for gallantry. She had ignored Pamela's glares, when she had gushed, 'It's very NICE of you to lend me your husband for the evening. He says you don't like Poulenc, so I HOPE that's true!'

She had ignored nearly all the emails, deleted many of them as soon as they arrived. She had never in her life exposed her feelings in this way to another person. During adolescence – the agony of loving Miss Firebrace, her history teacher! And later, at Oxford, there were the few short-lived crushes on male undergraduates. And then Doug, which had begun with the banter and shared jokes of two fellows in the same college. One read about abject love such as Charles's, and it was, of course, the stuff of opera or cheap novels. There was surely something absurd about it? Later, talking about it in circumstances which made such talk easy, she realized how close she had been, in the hothouse, to behaviour which would have been, well, catastrophic; realized that it was her vanity which had saved her, for, had he been positive, not negative, had he simply spoken of his love for her, rather than his hate for his wife, had he said he wanted to take her away that moment and make wild love, well . . . who knows what might have happened?

But now he was making more than an ass of himself. He was involving her in the pain of an unhappy marriage. That was surely unpardonable, and she was jolted into irritation.

—Charles, if your marriage is in difficulties, maybe you should BOTH look for some help. But I can't . . . I'm not the person to . . .

—You know I am not coming to you for help, damn it. You know that. You know Pamela. You have seen us together . . .

—I've met Pamela, said Eleanor quietly, carefully. I've met your children, Charles. Josh is in the Cathedral choir, of course I have met you all.

—Then you know what a farce the marriage is.

—I know nothing of the kind. It isn't a farce. Imagine what Josh would think if he heard you speaking. Sometimes I look across at his face in the choir during the Sung Eucharist, and I think how lucky you are to have children. You have him, you have Ella. And if Pamela and you are going through a . . . Through a difficult time . . .

—We're not going through anything. Don't you see that? We should never have married!

—Never had your children? Never had Josh, whom you love so much? Never had Ella, clever little Ell? If you knew what it was like not to . . . Charles, if you thought, just thought, what a privilege it is to have children . . .

—You are being deliberately obtuse. You know they have nothing to do with what I am saying.

—They have everything to do with it. Imagine what Josh would think if he heard us now.

—I don't want to.

—Well, you should.

—Hundreds of children watch their parents' marriages dissolve.

—My dear . . . I hate your being so unhappy, but this is making it worse.

—What is?

—These meetings, these walks, these conversations in which we appear to be saying something and not saying anything . . .

The sentence died on her half-open lips. There were many who had been melted by that half-open mouth, and by the row of teeth which so slightly stuck out. When she had pulled back from him, she knew that she had not done so quickly enough. She had felt the lapels of his heavy black winter overcoat pressing against her breasts. The roughness of his chin against her face was exciting rather than unpleasant. The wildness of the kiss, its passionate intensity . . . Doug had never kissed her like that, or if he had, she had forgotten it.

—Charles, we can't do this.

—We just have.

They walked on in silence for about half an hour. Nor, at the end of the walk, did she say what she should have said – that they must stop meeting at lunchtime, that their occasional attendance at evening concerts must, obviously, stop at once, that she must consider her position – as a dean, as a married woman, and that they must not cause a scandal. She was in a turmoil of confusion.

After the half-hour of silence, he said,

—There's no turning back now.

—I don't know what you mean.

—Just now. Your kiss . . . it spoke.

She wanted to say that it had not spoken, that if it had done so, there would have been nothing for it to say. She wanted to say that she should not have allowed him to kiss her, that they must stop, stop, stop.

—I'm going to tell Pamela.

—Tell her what?

—Tell her that we have fallen in love.

That's where Eleanor was at. And then, there was Digby and her seminars, and her relationship with Barnaby. This is a difficult one to write. Dramatic irony's the one where the audience knows more than the characters on the stage. We can all cope with that. Just about. Sitting there and wondering – Oedipus, how can you be such a prize banana as not to realize that you have just slept with your MOTHER, for God's sake?

But then there's narrative – so different from drama – and here am I, knowing so much more than you all do about what Digby was going through that day of the Thomas Hardy class, when we were going to discuss whether *The Mayor of Casterbridge* was a tragedy in the same way, or the same sense, as, say, *Oedipus Tyrannus*. And by now I am so much more than a Chorus, I'm in this story, or at least, I so much want to be in it, because . . .

Well, because I am starting to realize that I am falling in love, falling in a way I had never done before, not with anyone else.

These classes had been a tremendous success – I think I've already told you that. Looking back, I wonder whether half the reason for this was that we were all genuinely stimulated by Digby and Barnaby's brilliance – their range, their depth, their cleverness. Partly, though, for at least some of the class – I'd say most of us – the interest of the hour was hugely quickened by speculation on the theme of themes. How far had they gone? What stage had the relationship between them reached?

Funnily enough, although some of the gossips and matchmakers were so obsessed by this question, they actually knew remarkably little about either of the two protagonists of the drama which was playing inside their heads. Many of them, for example, were amazed, quite a bit later than the day I am describing, when they found out about Stig – Barnaby's little kid, aged six. And I can't actually remember when I found out all the details. But I'll set some of them down now, so you don't turn round and say that this narrative has been arranged to trick you, like Nabokov's *Pale Fire*. You are going to say that in a minute, I know, and then you go flicking back asking yourself how you could have been so dumb, and realizing that the narrative is UNRELIABLE. Mine isn't – honest – except in so far as a human being can't know everything, and clearly, she can't tell you all she knows all at once. That's why I just want to get some of this Barnaby/Bar/Stig stuff out of the way. So you know. He told me some of it himself – during the month when we had our 'thing'. But some of it I don't think I knew at this stage – found it out later.

He and Stig's mother, a woman called Bar Melville, had been the reason he had broken up with Deirdre Hadley. He had liked living with Deirdre. I think I've said that. They were good together. Deirdre is quite a bit older than Barnaby, but that wasn't – was it? – the reason he was unfaithful to her? He liked to think he was less vulgar than that. I like to think so, too. He told me once, when we were lying there together and having one of those conversations you have when you haven't got any clothes on and you have just slept with someone, he sometimes wished he had been to a therapist. During his twenties, it had seemed normal to sleep with any woman who made herself available. And plenty did. Then, while he was still finishing his PhD, and lodging at Deirdre's house in Harrow, he had started sleeping with her. It had been really nice. He was happy in a way he could not quite have imagined before it all started.

They had found that they were a couple. It had gone on two or three years. Then he'd met Bar at a Christmas party for graduates at the University. Barbara and Barnaby. They'd made jokes about one another's names. Poor little sheep who had lost their way, Baa, baa, baa. She had long red hair, and lips like Swinburne's Dolores (*the cruel/Red mouth like a venomous flower*). A few drinks did the rest. He felt guilty about it, but he began a clandestine affair. She'd become pregnant. They both decided it would be madness to try to live together. They had nothing in common. She had been doing a Master's in Business Studies and wanted to do something or other in IT. He'd never actually listened to what it was she wanted to do with her life, but it was the sort of thing he could not even imagine, let alone take an interest in. Something grown-up and lucrative. They did the decent thing, he and Bar, and agreed to bring up their son as best they may, posting him to and fro every week or so. Poor little chap. It worked, for as long as Bar was in Aberdeen, but when she left and got an even more lucrative, even more boring job in IT in Carmichael, she had more or less abandoned Stig to live with Barnaby most of the time. They never exactly quarrelled about money, though there were a number of acid telephone calls from Bar when she considered she'd paid more than her whack for clothes, new trainers, holidays for the little fella.

Deirdre had been very much wounded. Devastated, in fact. But, being Deirdre, she had soldiered on. Bar and Barnaby (it was ridiculous, their names) stopped sleeping together months before Stig was even born. Deirdre would have been perfectly happy to welcome Stig into her home, and bring him up, with Barnaby. In many ways it would have been the ideal solution, especially in the last two years when Bar had moved back to Carmichael. But Bar was having none of it. She made a kind of enemy of Deirdre, demonized her, said it wasn't a suitable environment for her son to be brought up in. No one really knew what she meant by this, but Barnaby rather weakly capitulated. He moved out of Deirdre's house in Harrow. Got an apartment near the centre of town. Looked after Stig more often than the boy's mother did, especially after Bar got married to a man who lived in Carmichael and who already had two kids of his own and who she'd been two-timing with Barnaby. In fact, it was several months since Stig had seen his mother.

Deirdre still loved Barnaby, and they still met from time to time. Deirdre had been a celibate since Barnaby moved out. There had been no substitute. How could there be a substitute for love? That was her view. He'd taken a different line – well, men would. There had been a queue of women ever since, including me. Our love life – sex life would be a more accurate term – had been, well, mechanical. Once, though, afterwards, when we were lying back together, we'd told each other the story of our earlier bedroom experiences – which is how I know about him and Deirdre, him and Bar. Funnily enough, although I was so much more closely involved with Barnaby than most of the other students in the class, it was the thought of Deirdre which really consumed me at that point. It was really weird, lying there with no clothes on, all those years after being taught Woolf by her, and finally understanding that Badley Dreary was a Woman, someone with feelings. I felt such a little baby, realizing how much I was still happy keeping most people as stereotypes in my mind – former teachers and older people especially.

It's actually a mistake, that lying back with no clothes on and blabbing about former lovers. It's the way half the secrets of the world get told, but it is not a kind way, and we learn and disclose things that way which we shouldn't have. Better to be a bit mysterious and not tell the current lover about her or his predecessors. Even I, who had not the smallest intention of having a serious relationship with Barnaby, felt a bit jealous of the fact that he clearly regarded the thing with Deirdre as the most serious relationship in his life. I could see why Bar could not cope with this. The others knew nothing of this, and I did not enlighten them. They wanted to jabber about Barnaby and Digby. And I did not want to join in with that either, because of the feelings which, so SO surprisingly, were creeping up on me. I'd never felt like this about a woman. I'd never felt this way about another human being. I supposed it was what all the poems and operas were about. I'd thought they were describing things which I had already experienced, only exaggerating the feeling for effect.

Anyway – back to that day when we had all come to Banks clutching our paperbacks of *The Mayor of Casterbridge*. I'll step back now, become a Chorus again, or the impersonal voice of the novelist, and just narrate – as if I knew what was going on inside Digby's head. Maybe even a little bit of what was going on in some of the other heads in the class. We'll see.

Banks, as some of you will know, is a couple of miles out of town. Digby had taken the bus to the suburb of Cheltenham and done the rest on foot. She intended to go back to town in the college shuttle, a minibus which did the journey every few hours. On her way, she was efficiently ticking off, inside her head, the themes which had already been covered in the Tragedy seminar. She liked the way this semester's group were progressing, and the way that she and Barnaby hopped about from theme to theme. At the same time, as an experienced university teacher, she was aware that some members of the class were really engaged, some were lazy and just cruising, and others – these were the ones who caused concern – could be getting so much more out of the course, if she and Barnaby just slowed down a bit and maybe recapped at the beginning of each seminar, asked some of the basic questions which, for the previous twenty years of her life, she had been trying to answer, in her book, in her articles, and in her many reviews, tutorials and lectures.

Is it helpful to define a tragic hero? Is there any mileage in Nietzsche's distinction, in *The Birth of Tragedy*, between Dionysian and Apollonian? Is tragedy essentially religious? Essentially irreligious? Barnaby would tend to supply answers to these questions by drawing upon the tragedies of Shakespeare, though he also made plentiful allusions to Racine, to Seneca, to the Greeks. Digby was not bound to Euripides but her brief was to answer the bigger, broader questions with reference to particular Euripidean plays. She was pleased that it was a lively, popular seminar, sometimes becoming almost too large to be manageable. And it worried her that Barnaby was too flip, too easy in his responses. It had always been a principle of Digby's, both in academic and in personal life, to leave some questions unanswered, and, more, to discover that some questions, which had always seemed perfectly simple, to be, for that reason, unanswerable.

Barnaby was wearing an open-necked blue shirt and jeans. Digby wore a white shirt, a navy blue jumper, a simple blue denim skirt, thick black tights and grey Converse. (Sorry, I know I am meant to be the impersonal narrator here, and not barging in, but I'd never noticed before how amazingly, meltingly, erotic thick, slightly woolly tights can look on a pair of someone else's legs which you are simply longing to have wrapped round your own waist.) Barnaby kicked off the class with an overview of Hardy's Pessimism. Since none of us had read *The Dynasts*, he told us about this long 'drama' about the Napoleonic wars – a play so long that it was never meant to be performed except inside our heads, and whose hero or antihero, in a way, is Providence. The odds are stacked up against human beings in Hardy. And then Digby bounced in with the old jibe that Hardy was the Village Atheist brooding over the Village Idiot. She went on to apply to Hardy what Wordsworth had said of Goethe's poetry – that it was not inevitable enough. The odds were stacked up against the characters in a really artificial way. One of us then demonstrated this by giving a (pretty plodding) account of the plot of the novel – how Michael Henchard the hay-trusser sold his wife to a sailor for five guineas, and then, in his penitence, foreswore drink, went on to become rich, only to lose everything again. Thanks to the nature of things, or thanks to the plot which Hardy had artificially created?

Then the discussion broadened out again, and one of the students returned to the theme which had been the theme of Digby's first class: namely that tragedy, by its nature, undermines conventional views of morality. It makes us think that moral conventions are contingent. It forces us to ask questions about the nature of Good and Evil, where we get them from, whether Laws, civic laws and conventions, reflect some big external general law – the will of God?

—That's right, Digby was saying, and it's very hard to argue against Nietzsche's view that all these tragic figures – whether in Shakespeare or in the Greek canon or in Wagner – are overturning conventional morality.

—There's the passage, said Melanie, a young woman with long bunches and very bright red lipstick, where Nietzsche says that, watching *Macbeth*, we are not horrified by his murdering his way to power, we exult in it. *Tristan* isn't a morality play designed to put you off committing adultery, it exults in adultery.

—In *Daybreak*, said Digby, for the benefit of those who had not read the Penguin *Nietzsche Reader*, which was, she suspected, about as far as Barnaby had ever got in exploring the mind of the tormented visionary of Basle.

—That's right, said Barnaby, with perhaps rather more emphasis than he would have given his response had the observation been made by one of the men in the class. Digby's eye took in Melanie's skinny jeans and tight sweater. I could see from his expression, and from Melanie's, the way they were both thinking.

—*Tristan und Isolde* is a good example of what we've all been trying to establish is the nature of tragedy, said Digby. It deals with the absolute insanity, the arbitrariness of love. This comes upon

Tristan and Isolde out of the blue, just as it casts a spell over Phaedra in *Hippolytus*. In all three cases – Tristan, Isolde, Phaedra – the figures who are overcome by Aphrodite or the Love-drug cannot help themselves´. . .

We all noticed that she was no longer addressing the class, so much as making a speech to Barnaby. Or that was how it seemed. She was staring at him, almost singing an aria at him. Or that was how it looked to me – but then, I was by then singing an aria to HER inside my tousled mousey head. I was, like, on the verge of actually coming out and saying it: *Look, people. Can we just stop for a moment, stop talking about Wagner, Hardy, the gods, whatever, and ask ourselves – have we ever known the swirling danger, the wild music, the total insanity of true love ourselves, 'cause, I thought it was all a sort of fiction, and now I'm feeling it, like I never felt it before, and you all think it's a kind of joke, wondering whether Digby will get off with Barnaby or the other way round, but for me this stuff has become really, REALLY serious and I think my heart is about to break.*

Sorry, reader! I promised that this was meant to be a bit of impersonal narrative here, and I'm stepping on stage before my cue. Won't happen again. Not in this chapter, anyhow.

—The tragic poet will not take sides against life – it is an adventure to live! Barnaby/Tristan further exclaimed. They might as well have been singing it to one another at full Wagnerian belt.

'Cause she – Digby – went really, really red. It was almost funny, actually. The matchmakers would undoubtedly, over coffee afterwards, have subjected this wonderful exchange between their two tutors to a full post-mortem analysis over coffee in paper cups.

That is, had it not been for the fact that in that precise moment, the seminar room shuddered. There's a big bookcase at the end of the room, with bound copies of literary periodicals – the *PMLA*, the *MLR*, *Scrutiny*, and so forth. The back wall suddenly began to throw these lumpy volumes across the floor. I narrowly dodged a bound *Modern Language Review*, for the years 1982–6, the size of a big dictionary, which was hurtling towards my head. It was as if an invisible giant had got into the room and started roughing it up.

There had been a great rumbling BANG. Students on one side of the long table, round which their discussion took place, were thrown backwards, and on the other side, forward. About a dozen of them were on the floor. Several had wet themselves and more than one was screaming.

There was no time, no opportunity, for self-control. Their bodies were being thrown. Digby's diaphragm would be badly bruised for weeks, as she was hurled against the sharp table edge, but instinct made her stretch, stretch across the table as she was thrown towards it. Barnaby, opposite, had been thrown out of reach; but it was towards him that she was reaching. Nothing like an earthquake for sorting out your priorities. Digby was thinking something quite simple – *I do not want to die before I have had the chance to make love to you.*

And as I looked at her, I was thinking exactly the same. Not about Barnaby! Not about Barnaby who, as I've already told you, was a nice chap and a good shag as shags go. But I wanted more than shagging, I wanted to *make love*. It's different. Maybe Euripides and Digby were right and it is those capricious gods who make us love. But we are the ones who *make love*. And I wanted to make love to lovely Digby, the beautiful, the beloved. I wanted to kiss the white nape of her neck, and stroke her back and shoulders, and . . . Oh, my dear, I wanted it all so much. So much.

*

Aftershocks

That WAS the minor one, back in the winter – 7.5 that one was. Quakes of that magnitude had wiped out entire Italian cities. For reasons which the geologists are still puzzling out, the shift in the tectonic plates, some forty miles away from our city, only caused relatively minor damage. In the University, for example, the Forster Building – housing the Modern Language and Literature department – a big grey brutalist structure built of rough-hewn concrete and plate glass – was the only building to suffer truly severe structural damage. One of the heavier concrete door-lintels collapsed in the atrium. It would have caused fatality had anyone been underneath, and the structural engineers were doubtful, after the Quake and the aftershocks had subsided, whether the building would survive. It had been evacuated, and the library of the Modern Language and Literature department was now being housed temporarily in the Longden Building, a flint-knapped neo-Gothic Victorian quadrangle which had completely withstood the Quake.

All over our city, however, the Quake had done its damage. Winchester and Devon were the worst-affected of the suburbs. We were relatively lucky in Harrow. Some of our windows were broken, but the house was still standing when Mum and I got back that evening. No one in the entire city of Aberdeen had been killed, but many had been forced to move out of their homes. Thousands of houses would have to be demolished, or to undergo such substantial repair work that it was touch and go whether a rebuild would not, in the long term, be the more economic option.

Many roads had cracks in them. Many of the buildings in the centre of town were now windowless, and it took us all days to sweep up the broken glass.

There had been a great upsurge of good, civic behaviour. Students on social media had tweeted and facebooked up an army of volunteers within minutes, literally, of the first rumble, and every badly affected area soon had its band of young people in shorts, shovelling the liquefaction, helping the infirm out of their damaged properties, and, in the surviving local buildings – church halls, and the like – making tea, wrapping blankets round poor bony old shoulders, and generally being good. And there were no deaths. And for some people, that was an occasion to thank the Management.

Eleanor Bartlett, professionally, was committed to this belief. She sat in the decanal stall in the Cathedral, wearing her cassock, surplice, scarf and Oxford MA hood. Above her head, carved Victorian angels, evidently women fancied by Oswald Fish, did the dance of the seven veils.

Stately, plump Bishop Dionne Lillicrap was in the pulpit.

The Earthquake was 7.5 on the Richter scale, said Dionne with some emphasis.

If you dressed up Shadrach, Meshach or Abednego in bishop's rig and shoved a pair of specs on what breeding had allowed him in the way of a nose, there would have been a distinct resemblance between pet and owner. But Eleanor, who thought all our doings without charity are nothing worth, never allowed herself to think that way. It was something which Digby once said to me.

7.5. Just think about it. Just think about the scale of damage that has caused in some other parts of the world – in California, or in Aquila, or nearer at home here in the Pacific. We have been spared. We have been . . .

A long pause. Another difficulty, when it came to colleagues, was to restrain involuntary considerations of their appearance. Would it be possible to take Bishop Dionne's utterances more seriously if she went on a diet? Yet, like the stones of Oxford in Auden's poem,

Dionne seemed utterly satisfied with her own weight – and indeed with everything else about herself.

It was a Civic Service of Thanksgiving. Rex Tone was there, wearing his mayoral chain of office over the collar of his shiny dark blue suit. The leaders of the other parties in our local Council were there. Deirdre Hadley was treating the Bishop's sermon as if it was a party political, which in a way it was, and shook her blonde-grey hair in disbelief at what was being claimed. When she returned to the Parliament Building in Carmichael, Deirdre expressed the view that Bishop Dionne was seeking Divine Sanction for the interference in our economy by unaccountable property speculators and billionaires from South-East Asia. It got huge coverage in *The Press*. Many of us Aberdonians felt that Deirdre should have been more loyal to her native city; should have shared in the general optimism after our miraculous deliverance from utter destruction. You did not need to have done a course on Greek tragedy to see she was the Cassandra of the set-up.

Rex would respond testily to Deirdre's remarks that this inference was 'entirely unacceptable', and that the Green Party was discredited by such a piece of unsubstantiated mud-slinging. They were just playing politics with people's fears. But the Greens stood by Deirdre's words.

. . . *spared*, said Bishop Dionne. *We have been spared. Spared for a purpose. For make no mistake – that is what we are here in this Cathedral today to do. To thank God. To thank God that our beloved city has been saved. And to ask God – what next? What is Your plan for the future? For Aberdeen?*

We could so easily have been wiped out. But that wasn't God's plan for us.

It fascinated, but also horrified Eleanor, that Bishop Dionne had been granted these insights into the Divine Mind. Could not Dionne see that, if there were another quake, and if it were more destructive than this, we should have to come to terms with what the Deity had meant by it? Was Dionne suggesting that the people of Aquila, who had been killed in some numbers in their quake, and whose entire medieval city, a place of much greater beauty than Aberdeen, had deserved to be wiped out? And if they did not deserve it, why had God done this to them?

But, you know something?

Dionne had changed gear into her chummier, confiding tone. The high Pontiff had become everyone's favourite agony aunt.

God doesn't want us, in our Thanksgiving, to just be looking backwards. That's not the Christian way of saying thank you to God. Not AT ALL. The world thinks saying thank you is saying thank you for something that's already happened in the past. Something that's OVER.

Eleanor tried to stop herself thinking that this would seem fairly logical on the world's part. The Pontiff had paused in a way which recalled the rhetoric of primary-school teachers. She looked around, and it would not have been surprising had she asked the listeners to raise a hand and tell her if they knew what 'over' meant.

No. Not for us Christians. For us, thanksgiving is looking forward. What am I always saying? I make no apology for repeating it today. We are a Community of Outreach. Where are we reaching out to, now, after this deliverance? What does God want of us – not yesterday – but tomorrow? Does He want this city to be forward-looking or backward-looking? Does He want this city to seek new ways of reaching out to people in the Chinese community, for example? Or does He want us to put up the barriers? Is that what God wants? Does He want us to retreat into a little parochial world all of our own, very cosy, very comfortable? Or does He . . .

Aftershocks

Eleanor tried not to remember Deirdre's placard about Shadrach, Meshach and Abednego being bred to choke. She also tried not to remember that sentence of Goethe, a favourite of Digby's, of the danger of choking, through the repeated chewing of moral and religious absurdities. Eleanor always felt that Goethe was maybe a bit dangerous. You should go easy on the Germans if you are trying to preserve Christian belief. Digby was nowhere to be seen, of course, during the service. She never made her presence felt in church.

Eventually, Dionne stopped, and Eleanor was able to check the flow of her thoughts. The choir, in particularly good voice, sang one of Stanford's finest settings of the *Te Deum*. The calm Apollonian harmony of the Chosen Frozen at prayer soothed, numbed, obliterated some of the aftershock of Dionne's infelicitous words. Josh Nicolson's angelic, piercing treble reached the top C as he trilled:

All the earth doth worship thee, the Father Everlasting.

When it stopped, and the minor canon began the prayers, everyone in the Cathedral could hear Penny Whistle, singing his songs outside in Argyle Square. One of the pleasant features of attending services at the Cathedral was that, in all the quiet bits, you could always hear Penny Whistle, with his huge repertoire of lyrics.

We focus our minds, said Bob, the minor canon, *in gratitude to God*. Bob's voice, even when amplified through the mike, is reedy and weak. Penny Whistle's voice is a powerful bass baritone. If he had been trained, and had a different set of chances, he could easily have ended up as the definitive Wotan . . . I wasn't listening to Bob's prayers. Penny Whistle spoke, or sang, for me:

A. N. Wilson

Now when we're out a-sailing,
And you are far behind.
Fine letters will I write to you
With the secrets of my mind.
The secrets of my mind, my girl,
You're the girl that I adore,
And still I live in hope to see
The Holy Ground once more.

CHAPTER SIX

UNUSUALLY, ABERDEEN WAS COVERED IN SNOW NOT LONG after that first quake. We tend to have mild winters on the Island by European standards, but that one was really freezing, for two or three weeks, which made it a total pain for those whose electricity and heating was up the spout, and whose shitty insurance companies weren't coughing up. Winter did NOT keep us warm, whatever my darling's favourite poet may have thought. But eventually, winter faded. The lovely Island spring came, and the Bougainvilleas were drooping their wonderful cascades all over Prince Alfred Parade; and our little garden in Harrow was a Samuel Palmer, frothing apple blossom. Then came the hot summer of February. We were a hardened, post-Quake people now. We did not believe Rex Tone's bullshit about it never happening to us. Some of us – even the Dean, but we mustn't jump ahead of ourselves here with the story – were not even too sure that the Creator – who had, after all, sat back when the good people of Aquila were totally zapped – had a specially soft spot for Aberdonians. What kind of Mad Inventor-Creator would that be when he's at home? We'd all come to believe Deirdre's warnings that another one was inevitable; that it was not a question of IF but of WHEN. A quake of 7.5 was huge, and we'd survived it without fatalities. There had been earthquakes in other parts of the Island ever since it was settled. But now we, in Aberdeen, had been close to an epicentre of a quake which, if it had been any closer, could have wiped us off the map.

During and after the first Quake, we all drew together, no question. Within an hour of it happening, like I said, students had organized, via social media, working parties to come and clear the mud and liquefaction out of people's paths and driveways. Those whose houses had been badly damaged were offered accommodation, often by their neighbours. There was a real feeling of the Second World War and everyone pulling together. And none of us believed Bishop Dionne that God had singled us out for special blessing, not one of us, but we were grateful nonetheless that we had been spared.

Island Breakfast kept us informed. As always, Cavan Cliffe, far more than the Bishop (or the Dean), started each day for us, focused our thoughts, helped us get a perspective on things. It was our umbilical cord, tying us to mother truth.

Cavan Cliffe, five foot in her socks, and on the chunky side, took her exercise whenever possible by rowing herself to work in the middle of town. Cavan's face, clever and lived-in, looks at you very directly, and often laughs. If you are one of the very many people she likes, and who like her, this is what makes her an instantaneously attractive person. If you are a politician, or a poseur of some other kind, and you are trying to pull the wool over the eyes of the public, Cavan's laugh is destructive – destructive of pretension. That's why over a million people, over a quarter of us, tune in to *Island Breakfast*.

Aftershocks

On that show, she has been talking straight, relaxed, jolly, clever, just as she would talk to you across the breakfast table, for the last thirty years. When she started doing it, she was a young cub reporter on *The Press* and the radio work was a sideline. She still writes for *The Press*, but the radio work has now taken over very largely. She's an institution.

I know I'm biased, but I'd say that Cavan represents everything that is good about Huias. There's no side to her, but she isn't brash or coarse. She's a subtle person. In spite of her very heavy schedule of work, she keeps up her reading. She's the best-read person I know. She never interviews a politician without really doing her homework – so, for example, if you were trying to bamboozle the listeners about some environmental issue, or with some question of farming, you would find that this short, plump, completely urban woman knew as much about genetically modified crops or soil erosion as many of the experts. When she interviews poets or novelists, she shows a sensitive awareness of what they are up to. She's done a lot to silence the philistines in discussions about modern art, drama, experimental theatre, music.

That morning, the blossom on Mum's apple trees had gone, and the Aberdeen Permains, still as small as walnuts, had appeared on the boughs of her orchard. When Mum and Dad moved to Harrow, they fell in love with the little house with its wooden verandah-porch. What's more, they could afford the rent, and most people rented in those days. (After they divorced, Mum bought the house.) Harrow in those days was a run-down neighbourhood, with a lot of Irish working-class families, and houses with outside toilets. By a kind of economic inevitability, however, young couples like my parents gravitated towards this place. They were the baby-boomers, they'd not been alive to see their dads and uncles leaving the Island on ships, some of them with their horses, to fight for the Empire. (Dad lost two uncles in the Second World War, one in Italy, the other in Africa; Mum lost three of her uncles, and her dad. From 1945 onwards, her family had been nearly all women.) All that was in the past, and they were the new, post-war generation, more laid-back, less convention-bound than their parents, not especially religious (though still overwhelmingly Anglican), readier to accept a loosening of the orthodoxies. Nothing too dramatic. That's not the Huia way. We're a small-c conservative bunch. But long before the so-called Sexual Revolution had actually been announced, Mum's generation did not think the skies were going to fall in if you got divorced, or if you were gay, or if you had an abortion. And they were easier about class. All four of my Huia grandparents would have shuddered at the idea of living in Harrow. My dear! Irish! But the house Mum and Dad fell in love with was pretty, as was the whole rackety neighbourhood. The small houses, some of them wooden, some stone, but with clapboard facing, had river- or meadow-frontage. The school buses passed along the main road – Adelaide Highway – which is only a ten minute walk from our front gate. After a few such families had come to live here, it became 'desirable'; and after five or ten years, it became so desirable that the property speculators moved in.

Those who had not been lucky enough to get divorced and buy their own home found that their landlords had subtly changed. They found that instead of their house being owned by Miss Jones or Mr Smith, it was owned by something called Galt Investments.

Galt owned one of the bigger properties, not far from us, as it happened. It had a swanky two-car garage, a tennis lawn and big herbaceous borders. It must have been built before the other houses – in the 1890s, say – and belonged to a prosperous sheep-farmer who had decided he needed a city property, or maybe the owner of one of the bigger stores in Balfour Street. Anyhow. Eventually, Galt's tenants all got letters which were in effect notices to quit.

Enter stage left my much-mocked English teacher Deirdre Hadley, with her stick legs and her little denim sunhats adorned with CND and Friends of the Whale badges. It was Badley Dreary, and her lodger, a young man called Barnaby Farrell, who got us all organized. They were the ones who had been down to the planning office and found out that Galt Investments had obtained permission to build a big hotel on the riverbank. They were aiming to demolish about twenty of our neighbours' houses, and the small wooden church, St Luke's, where I was baptized. Our garden would have abutted the back wall of the hotel, so we'd have got all the cooking smells from the kitchen, and the exhaust fumes of 'parking facilities for up to 100 cars'. (I quote from the glossy brochure which Galt Investments had printed at the time.) It would have ruined our neighbourhood completely, and driven all the young families away into the further suburbs, far from schools, and shops and other amenities.

It was a long battle, with endless late nights with lawyers, giving their advice cheap or for free; endless hearings of planning committees and public inquiries. Galt Investments had all the big guns, businessmen and lawyers from Carmichael, on their side. Deirdre and Barnaby just had guts, determination and patience – and most of the population of Harrow. They won. We owe it to them that we have our little house, with the porch that Cavan and my dad fell in love with six years before I was born, with the apple trees (Aberdeen Permain are juicier but crisp like a Cox). We've let the tufty grass grow into a sort of meadow, which slopes down to the banks of the Windrush where Cavan keeps her little rowing dinghy. I'm at my bedroom window waving to her. It's not quite six in the morning. The light is just coming up, a lovely hazy yellow light which catches the dew on the lichen; the drops on the apple twigs reflect the light of dawn, shimmer like jewels. From the branches of the trees, grey and white Island robins, and tomtits, and little silvereyes are twittering. In the wet grass, almost metallic in that morning light, you can see the dark green footprints of Cavan's trainers. She wears a white tee-shirt, black and white check trousers, and a baseball cap. With her right oar, she pushes away from the jetty, which she and I built ourselves, and her little skiff goes into town.

Now I've waved her goodbye, and I'm offstage for the rest of this scene, I'll go into the past tense.

With decisive, strong strokes, she passed hundreds of back gardens, saw old men smoking as they gazed at the water, through upstairs windows, routine matutinal scenes – men shaving, schoolkids brushing their teeth, impatient brothers, clutching towels or washbags, shouting at their sisters through bathroom doors for being too long in front of the mirror, through downstairs windows, families having their hurried breakfasts before work and school, mother putting packed lunches into plastic containers and yelling at their teenaged sons for losing the car keys. These are all the worlds we leave behind before we go to work, the worlds which go on inside us all, even when they've vanished; the world where the kitchen table exists because we scrub it. Down the towpath stretched the long redbrick walls of Fenton's Brewery, then on the opposite bank, the cemetery, and the tower of St Hugh of Lincoln. (Eleanor had great fun Skyping her father about the 'goings on' in St Hugh, which had been taken over by fervent evangelicals. They had dug a small swimming pool in the back of the nave where they baptized converts by total immersion. As far as could be discovered there was no liturgy, as Eleanor and her father would have understood the term, of any kind, though they had something called Toddlers' Praise and Messy Church on Tuesdays.) Many of the buildings Cavan had passed so far were marked down by the God of Earthquakes for a shake-up. From now on, the buildings she saw were those actually doomed: the garages on the distant ring road, the wide expanse of Prince Alfred Parade, the Winter Gardens, with their elaborately glazed roofs and ornate orangery, the lumpy neo-classical art gallery, the even lumpier Presbyterian church, the dome of the RCs, the white-and-plate-glass geometry of Rex Tone's Convention Centre and the almost identical Civic Centre (what the rest of us still want to call the City Hall), all these the God of Earthquakes had marked down for complete destruction.

Beyond the large, ugly car park on the edge of Leicester Square, the Windrush snaked beneath pretty cast-iron bridges, where the Victorian lamp-posts had recently automatically switched off with the coming of day. To her left was the great Arch of Remembrance, inscribed with all the campaigns where Huias had lost their lives in the two world wars – MESOPOTAMIA, EGYPT, BURMA . . . And here too were the names of battles – DARDANELLES, PASSCHENDAELE, MONS, TOBRUK, ANZIO – where boys from hilltop sheep farms, and grizzled seamen from the many whaling stations which lined our coasts in those days, had been sent out to fight other people's battles, to fight with amazing bravery, and never to come back. Beyond the grandiose memorial, the river twisted. Some parents were already waiting for the big public school to open – what had been the High School but which had been renamed by Rex Tone Opportunity Two. (Opportunity One was what had been the primary school, further into town up the West-minster Highway.) Past the school, and now, on one side of the river, were the buildings of Banks University's Law Faculty, and opposite this complex of buildings was the four-storey white-stuccoed 1950s nondescript building which housed Island Radio. Cavan stood up, wobbled a little, as was inevitable when getting her bearings in a small boat, humped her knapsack over her sturdy shoulders, and tied the boat, which had *Little Ingrid* painted on its prow, in its usual place.

Being a consummate professional, she had been through the outline of the programme the night before online with her producer. She nonetheless had left herself half an hour this morning before she needed to go on air. They could go through any news stories which had broken in the night. But this day was just one of those quiet Island days in which, it seemed, nothing very interesting was going to happen. Deirdre Hadley was scheduled to appear at ten past eight, after the news, with one of her frequent tirades against Rex Tone.

Half an hour later, at one minute to eight, Islanders from all over heard the voice they knew so well – '*Good morning, this is* Island Breakfast *and I'm Cavan Cliffe*' . . . And there was then a snatch of music and Cavan said, '*This morning's news is read by Jenny Bredin.*'

The Dean came into the Cathedral at 7.55. It was so hot that she wore simply a black clerical shirt and a light grey pleated skirt. Bob, who was in the whole rig of choir robes – cassock, surplice, scarf and hood (BA Marsh College, Dundee) – was visibly sweltering, poor lad. There were four others in the Gallipoli Chapel – Abel, the sacristan, a sad-faced, tall man of huge dignity, Tangata, very devout. He was wearing a black gown over his white trousers and sleeveless striped shirt. Eleanor often lost her place in the office book through staring at Abel's face: not out of lust, or not exactly, but out of wonder. There seemed to be so much going on behind that face. She wondered if he was a mystic (whatever that is, exactly); he seemed to be quietly in touch with that something she only glimpsed occasionally, which Eliot wrote about in *Four Quartets*, and she suspected it was the same mysterious something as had made those early-morning Masses of her dad's so meaningful in the fogbound West Midland towns of twenty-five years ago. Bob, that very pleasant, not especially intelligent clergyman, was sitting at the back of the chapel with the office book open. Abel had already lit the two candles on the altar. The frayed banners of the two Huia regiments which had suffered the worst casualties in Gallipoli hung limply over their heads. The light of the two altar candles glimmered in the beaten copper of the reredos. They looked as if they were sweating as much as Bob, as the wax dripped. Behind them, moulded brass Fish maidens danced across the relief, amid a cluster of leaves and birds. They held aloft a banner which was adorned in Gothic lettering with the words 'PANIS ANGELORUM'. One of them appeared to be slightly sucking the tip of her finger.

The two others present were Miss Price, a small woman who even on this blazing summer morning was wearing a woollen beret, and holding a shopping basket. She attended most mornings, as did Penny Whistle, who made the responses in a very loud, conversational tone, slightly out of kilter with the other four voices. So, when Bob said, 'The Lord be with you', and the others replied, 'And with thy spirit', Penny Whistle was several beats ahead of them, and he stressed the word 'spirit' as if he had been long searching for the *mot juste* and was mighty pleased with himself for having selected it at last; his tone implied that, although he was wishing the Lord to be with Bob's spirit, he had weighed the possibility of the Lord being with some other part, or attribute, or relative of Bob – with his mother, for example (with whom Bob lived).

The seemly forms of Morning Prayer were followed, as they were being followed in college chapels, churches and cathedrals every hour of the twenty-four, o'er every continent and island. On our Island, it was the thirteenth morning – though in England it was the previous evening. They recited the 68th Psalm antiphonally. '*O God, when thou wentest forth before the people* – PAUSE – *when thou wentest through the wilderness.*' The Dean, Abel, Penny Whistle and Miss Price followed with, '*The earth shook, and the heavens dropped at the presence of God* – PAUSE – *even as Sinai also was moved at the presence of God, who is the God of Israel.*'

By the time Bob was reading the first chapter of Ecclesiastes, '*Is there any thing whereof it may be said, See, this is new? It hath been already of old time, which was before us . . .* ' Jill had finished reading the radio news, and Sophie Richards was giving the Islanders an update on the weather.

'*It's going to be another lovely day, clear skies, and temperatures well up in the thirties,*' said Sophie's bright tones.

She spoke through the packets of breakfast cereal and the mounds of papers, which included household bills and the vast number of communications sent by the children's two schools – Opportunity One, where Ella was in Year One, and St Augustine's, where Josh was in Year Eight – on the Nicolsons' peninsular kitchen unit. The documents related to details of concerts, sports days, permission-forms for the children to go for outings to the Botanic Gardens, a message from the medical officer about nits and how to comb them out of your kids' hair. Ten minutes of fairly noisy breakfast ensued – Josh was a passable spin bowler, and was talking to his father about an approaching match against a rival school, while Pamela was trying to get her husband to go through the desk-diary which they kept on their kitchen unit, to make sure they were all up to speed on Arrangements – who was driving Josh back from the match against Loretto. On Wednesday, Ella had a dental appointment, but she would need to go directly to this from her oboe lesson, and Pamela would not be back in time to supervise this, so could Charlie? And Charlie was doing that thing of putting his hand through his hair and looking down, which really annoyed his wife, because she read the gesture as meaning – 'Do you realize just how busy I am and how important my job is, and you are asking me to interest myself in all these TRIVIAL little things?'

Instead, he said,

—We really need a full-time PA to manage our diaries.

—That would be very helpful, said Pamela. There was a dreadful coldness in the polite phrase. When she adopted this attitude she could freeze a fry-up with five words.

—No, no, said Charlie, sensing a squabble, I can get back in time for your oboe, Ellie, course I can.

He knew that by addressing the child, rather than replying to his wife, he was irritating Pamela still further.

Her irritation burst forth with,

—It's not the oboe lesson. Don't you listen? She has to go FROM the oboe lesson TO the dentist?

None of them were paying much attention to the Cassandra-like warnings of Deirdre Hadley, who, the news being over, was now haranguing Rex Tone behind the Nicolsons' Family Size pack of Shreddies through the speaker of their small digital radio.

— . . . No . . . no, you can't talk through me, you have taken contracts.

—You don't know that, dear—

—I do know it and I am NOT your dear.

—Rex, Rex [Cavan's voice] – let her finish.

—You have held talks with Wong Developments. They are almost certainly going to win the contract to rebuild the sports stadium—

—Almost certainly isn't the same as drawn up a contract. Who said anything about a contract?

—Let me finish. You rebuilt the City Hall. That was also built by Chinese contractors. We don't know—

—No you don't, do you, you don't know, but that doesn't stop you having opinions about every subject under the blessed sun. Strewth!

—Rex! I'm warning you [Cavan].

—You've given no assurances about whether that twenty-storey building – twenty storeys, Mr Tone – has been quake-proofed. You cannot give us any reassurances whether the new building of the primary school—

—Opportunity One [Rex's voice].

—Opportunity to be flattened under a heap of concrete.

—I don't know what you're talking about – YOU don't know what—

—Last autumn . . . let me finish – last autumn, there was a quake which was 7.5 on the Richter scale. SEVEN POINT FIVE. It was a mira—

—Let me finish.

Pamela suddenly switched from the everlasting marital war to ask,

—You don't think she's right, do you? That Ella's school . . .

Pamela Nicolson was an elegant, serious woman, with a very

pale face, hair which she wore up and whose colour was so non-descript as to be colourless, pale lips and pale eyes. Her colleagues at Minchin and Buss wondered why she did not dye it, or at least add some highlights, but there was a reason. When Charlie (which was how she thought of him when she loved him) Nicolson, five years older, had fallen in love with her – she was working at the time, as she still did, for a rival law firm in the city – he had considered all these muted shades made her 'ethereal'. She knew that he was no longer in love with her and guessed, accurately, that he found her appearance quietly boring. Those who wondered why she did not wear lipstick were unaware that she did so, but wore a shade so discreet that if anything it muted the natural pink of her mouth.

Her feelings towards her husband vacillated. Sometimes she was so angry with him that she wished to commit physical violence. Sometimes, however, she still deferred to him – in matters of taste. She always let him choose the wine when they were entertaining. In political views, she either shared his, mildly conservative, opinions, or silently acquiesced in them. She did not underestimate her own skills as a (company) lawyer, but she knew that he was outstanding, and even when she was hating him, she admired his legal brain.

Of course, although he had made all these declarations to the Dean of our Cathedral, and told Eleanor he was going to announce to his wife that he was now in love with Eleanor, he had not acted on his words. She was nonetheless completely aware of his infatuation, and tried not to think that he had transferred his love entirely from her to Dean Bartlett. One of the things she had once loved about him was his romanticism. Charles (which was how she thought of him when she was upset with him) had never really been at one with her in musical taste. She did not mind music in the background – for example, when they were having dinner together. She actually enjoyed choral music, and rejoiced that Josh had got into the Cathedral choir. She found it excruciatingly boring, however, to sit through concerts, and his fondness for twentieth-century French music – Poulenc, Messiaen, even Boulez – was something at which she drew the line.

Her ways of being independent of him took quieter paths. There was her Book Group, a circle of friends who met each month to discuss, usually a novel, very occasionally another sort of book. There were a number of people with whom she had lunches, usually legal colleagues, but a few old school friends, for, like me, Pamela was born and bred an Aberdonian. Why should Charles not attend concerts with those who liked that sort of thing? Yet, since he had begun to go to concerts with Eleanor Bartlett, things had changed. For one thing, he went much more often than he had ever been in the past. For another, she sensed that there was something 'going on' between them. It was unthinkable – wasn't it – that a senior cleric would actually consider committing adultery? In some senses, this made the situation more dangerous. If he was smitten with a merely Platonic passion, if he and the Dean did not even hold hands . . . might it be turning into a mania inside his head? Much of the time, when he was at home, he did not seem to be with them at all. He was somewhere else, with That Woman.

—She's bonkers, isn't she? Charles asked, in reply to his wife's question. This was the generally held opinion of Deirdre Hadley.

—Did you see her hat on Sunday? Pamela asked. That blue denim hat she wears. In the Cathedral. And all those badges. 'Vegans for World Peace'. But you know she is right about City Hall. You told me yourself. Rex Tone has sold us down the river to the Chinese. Wong Developments, or whatever they're called, DO now actually own the Aberdeen City Hall, and Deirdre Hadley knows that.

—Like I said. Bonkers. Come on, junior.

—Why is it bonkers to want world peace? Ella asked. When no one answered, she said,

—Anyway, we are going to the ZOO.

—Zoos, said Josh, are for babies.

—Packed lunch?

The question was Charlie's. If he had asked the question of his daughter, Pamela would not have found it so annoying, but he asked it of HER – thereby showing, first, that he had not read the school's letter about the zoo outing ('Packed lunches will be provided') and, secondly, that he somehow expected, had a packed lunch been required, that she would have been the one to prepare it – which of course she always was when that sort of thing was needed. So she took a breath and waited for Ella to say,

—The school's providing them, Dad.

—Are you going to make history and choose something other than plain ham sandwiches?

—I like ham.

On the other side of town, in the cool of the Lady Chapel, Bob was saying, *'Defend us in the same with thy mighty power; and grant that this day we fall into no sin, neither run into any kind of danger.'*

The zoo outing was also a subject of domestic consideration in Barnaby Farrell's kitchen, where, through a different set of speakers, Deirdre's contest with Rex Tone was rising in passion.

—If the Quake was 7.5, said Rex, and Opportunity One was still standing, I don't know what makes you say that—

—Because the epicentre of the Quake, as you very well know, was forty miles way. But if it moved. If the next one happens—

—There isn't going to BE a next one, DEAR, said Rex. This is just the doom-merchants of the Green Party, whipping up people's irrational fears. It's 'cause we're streaks ahead of you in the polls—

—What does that have to do with anything?

— . . . ahead of you in the polls, and you need, no, sorry, the listeners have got to realize this, you need to whip up irrational fears. No one's gonna vote for your lot of yoghurt-eating, sandal-wearing prigs unless they are scared into doing so. You just peddle scare stories, which are, as I say, completely irrational—

—What's irrational about the scientific evidence that our city was built on a fault line? That last winter, there was a quake which was SEVEN POINT FIVE? What's irrational?

—OK, said Rex, let's look at a worst case scenario here, let's say there's another one – on 5, 6, 7.5, whatever—

—How can you sit there and just SAY this when—

—Let him finish. [Cavan]

—Then we're prepared. We're ready for it. 24/7, we've been preparing. Rebuilt our infrastructure, reinforced buildings at risk—

—You expect us to BELIEVE this? Where's the evidence you have rebuilt our infrastructure?

—I think most of your listeners will have seen Bus Interchange, and consider it is an important—

—That's not INFRASTRUCTURE. That is yet more concrete building. Heavy concrete slabs which could fall on whole busloads of—

—Let him finish.

— . . . most of the listeners will have seen Bus Interchange-Aberdeen and consider it a considerable improvement on the old clapped-out Bus Exchange, which was built, would you believe, in 1948.

—Many of us liked it. There was nothing wrong with the bus station. Now it has been replaced by heavy concrete – the last thing we want WHEN, WHEN note, not IF – WHEN the next quake comes. And it was not the old bus station we did not like, it was the lousy public transport system we objected to, which forces people to drive their cars when they could—

—Most people seem happy enough with the state of the art facilities we've installed in Bus Interchange-Aberdeen, which is the most up-to-date bus interchange ON THE PLANET. We've got free wi-fi there, we've got a rolling news channel from Island TV showing 24/7 in the waiting-rooms—

—The worst bus service in the world, that's what we've got, and we are still burning fossil fuels on all those buses, rather than encouraging people to ride bikes to work, rather than looking at ways to reduce fossil fuel emissions, rather than—

Cavan said,

—Well, I rowed to work this morning, so I did not use fossil fuels, but I'm going to have to stop you there.

Barnaby meditatively prodded his egg with a stainless steel spoon. He sat opposite Stig, wishing he was with Deirdre. At home, as he still thought of her house.

Stig said,

—Dad, you remember we are going to the zoo?

Barnaby said,

—Course.

Stig said,

—Dad, did you remember?

He had completely forgotten. He had been planning to spend a morning in the library preparing for the next seminar – the big one, both he and Digby agreed, with the title *King Lear and the Gods*. As flies to wanton boys are we to the gods. They kill us for their sport. Now he'd have to take Stig to the zoo? When had he promised that?

—A school trip, Dad. A school trip to the zoo.

—Am I coming?

Stig laughed.

—Strewth, Dad. Course not.

Waves of relief spread through Barnaby. He loved his little boy, while finding almost every aspect of life with him – going to the playground, going to the swimming baths, reading aloud the crappy books people wrote nowadays for children – almost intolerably boring.

While he listened to her on the radio, Barnaby was meditating on the fact that she still loved him. She did not need to tell him this. She'd found no new man as a substitute. How could there be a substitute for love? He thought – it was all right when they made love, which, just sometimes, he did with her. It was fine. Why not be content with that, and stop chasing round after other women, and tell Bar to go screw herself?

He was wistful that morning, as he heard Deirdre's voice on the radio. Being loved was nice. Fuck Bar. (Only he did not and did not want to and she did not want to fuck him now she had a rich husband in Carmichael.) He still loved Deirdre (sort of) and he would always tremendously admire her. Bar's lawyers had persuaded the Family Division Courts that it would be injurious if Barnaby took Stig to live with Deirdre. He told himself this was heartbreaking. At the same time, he was one of those men whose mind is always thinking about the next woman, almost in the way you might think of the next project, in work, or laying out a garden, or travelling to a new part of the world you'd never seen before. And the present project was undoubtedly Digby. He wondered why things had not gone further with her. Since they had agreed to do the seminar on tragedy together, he had felt a real empathy between them. Something growing.

He'd never had dates like this before. Normally, they were gagging for it. There had been kissing, but, in spite of his reputation among some of the students as a bit of a stud, he was shy about pressing women further than they appeared to be ready to go. And he definitely had the sense that there was a borderline, which this one was not going to cross.

He had come really to fancy her. He knew she fancied him. When they kissed, it was with intensity. He was sort of obsessed by her breasts, which she allowed him to feel through her shirt, but which he had not seen.

He loved the feel of those breasts against his. And she seemed to allow him to touch them – didn't stop him doing so, anyway. Then there was a moment, in the middle of it, just when it was beginning to be really nice, that she withdrew, and said she thought she ought to be going. He thought of her big dark blue eyes, which were so intelligent, and the sexiness of the smile, which never took anything quite seriously, and the tightness with which she held him when they kissed, her clawing, almost desperate tightness on his shoulder blades.

On the other side of the town, Bob was saying, *'From battle, and murder, and from sudden death,'* and Miss Price and the Dean were saying, *'Good Lord, deliver us.'* They were not quite in time to beat Penny Whistle, however, who had dived in slightly before Bob was finished, with *'Good Lord, deliver . . .'* and then, with overemphasis, as if the Lord might have wandered off to deliver someone else from sudden death for a change if Penny Whistle had not kept Him on His toes – 'US.'

Back in Barnaby's kitchen, Stig said,

    —Dad, if we don't go, I'll miss the bus. Mrs Chambers said, if we're late, we don't get to go to the zoo. Simple as that.

    Simple as that.

PART TWO

CHAPTER SEVEN

THE NICOLSON FAMILY HAD GONE THEIR WAYS. THE CHILDREN
had gone to school – Josh was doing mathematics, rather well. After
a short morning, because he was in the First XI, he was heading
down to the nets for cricket practice.

His sister Ella was arriving at the zoo, watching with some
contempt as Mr Pollard failed to keep order. All the other children at Opportunity One, from the Reception class up to Year Six,
remained behind in the gleaming new school buildings. The air-con
hummed in the bright learning centres, as the classrooms were
now called. The three-storey structure, built of breeze-blocks, with
heavily reinforced concrete beams underpinning each floor and
weight-bearing wall, cooked in the morning sun.

Pamela had arrived at her office in King Street, an elegant Victorian terrace where several of the city's better-established law
firms, accountants, estate agents and dentists had premises.

Charles had gone into his office in Dalston Street. The firm of
which he was the senior partner had three main branches which

specialized in property law, company law and insurance law. Charles's in-tray at the moment contained a number of claims that the Council had been abusing its authority. Chinese speculators were buying up more and more property in town, and the Green Party were not alone in suspecting that Rex Tone, in order to pay for some of his more extravagant ventures, was putting pressure on the Planning Office to allow schemes to go through which sailed near the wind. It was also general knowledge that many of the apparently different purchasers of property in the middle of town – companies with names such as Enterprise Associates Inc., NewBuild Ltd, Homes Are Us, and the homelier sounding J.F. Gould and Co., Varley and Sons and various other firms – were all one and the same: they were Ricky Wong, a Shanghai entrepreneur who now owned about a tenth of the real estate in the city. Ricky was not a criminal – not exactly, anyway. However, he liked to cover his traces. Charles had a whole file on the number of defunct companies, shells, which Ricky had bought, so that he could present himself to the Council in different guises as he built up his portfolio.

One of the biggest cases on which Charles's firm was engaged concerned the huge white City Hall, plate glass and pale concrete, gigantically out of scale with the Dyce Gallery and the Public Library opposite it. Since this was supposedly a public building, in which all the administration of the city, and indeed of the state, was conducted, it should have been a matter of public knowledge who actually owned the building. The Green Party, which had opposed the demolition of the perfectly adequate old City Hall – a redbrick and Portland Stone structure which had stood the test of a hundred years – asked who actually owned the new one. The Greens had opposed the extravagance of the enterprise. Deirdre Hadley and friends had staged an occupation of the site and been carried away by the police before the bulldozers moved in to destroy the old City Hall. She had persisted, however, in asking the awkward questions in Parliament: why did a City Hall need, in addition to its state of the art Council Chamber in the round, a large white concrete and glass atrium, tall enough to contain a tree? Why did they think the tree would flourish indoors rather than being where it belonged in the Botanic Gardens? (It was, to the absolute outrage of Deirdre's colleagues, an actual tree uprooted from the Botanic Gardens.) But in Parliament, and at the reconvened Council Chamber, where there were now many Green members, Rex had some tough grilling, and not just from the Greens, but from the mainstream opponents too. They had been through the many complicated documents which helped to obfuscate who had actually paid for the new City Hall, which building contractors had been hired, and so on. Murphy and Co., the reassuring-sounding chief building contractor, Deirdre Hadley's office had discovered, had been a company which went defunct, on the death of the last old Mr Murphy, in 2001. It had been bought by something called NewBuild Ltd, which was registered in Dubai. This company, it turned out, had two directors, a Stanley Weinberger of whom no one seemed to know anything, and Ricky Wong. Weinberger cropped up again – though as far as anyone knew he had never set foot in the Island, no Islander I knew had even met him – as a director of two other companies with which Ricky had to do. Moreover, it seemed more and more likely that Rex Tone had given misinformation to the Planning Committee; that the primary site of the old City Hall had not been adequate for the grandiose building which was erected in its place; so, it had been necessary to demolish some buildings behind it, including some which contained social housing, a car park which was owned by something called Hong Kong Knights, and a whole street, Nelson

Street, with the popular Lord Nelson pub and surrounding houses. It turned out that the Lord Nelson pub had, some time before, been taken over by a chain of wine bars and drinking joints called Chinese Whispers, CEO – Ricky Wong. Although the car park, street and houses had all been owned by apparently separate individuals, and the social housing tenements were owned by the Council, the purchase of the whole site had been by a compulsory purchase order. The price for each sale had been passed in the Council, at each stage questioned by the Treasurer of the Greens, Mary Stetson, and the answers which Rex Tone had given now turned out to be false. The compulsory purchases had been for sums agreed by the Council, but it turned out that, in the audit of their end of year accounts, only published in Shanghai, Chinese Whispers had disclosed the purchase of the site for fifteen million Island Dollars less than the sum which appeared in the Council's documents. Someone – it was assumed Rex – had allowed Chinese Whispers to have the site cheap in exchange, presumably, for a bribe.

It now turned out that the Council had not purchased the freehold of the new property, and that, because the new City Hall had been built on part of a car park once belonging to NewBuild Ltd and part of a pub owned by Chinese Whispers . . . that the City Hall which Rex believed to be the city's proudest achievement did not actually belong to the people of Aberdeen at all. It was leased to them by Ricky Wong. And it was in order to get to the bottom of this, to test its truth and its legality, that Charles had been engaged by the Greens for the last three years.

He knew that he had work to do that morning, but before he began, he decided to cross the square. He went into the outer office where Arlene O'Hear, his junior colleague, who was a very sharp cookie indeed, and had found out a ton of damaging information about Rex Tone, sat with Harriet LeStrange, a charming, married Katanga woman, who was their PA. Beyond some glass doors was the reception desk, manned by Cheryl Thomson.

—I'll be ten minutes, he told them, and, when he had gone, they all exchanged glances, because they knew why.

Charlie's head of dark hair was now flecked with grey. His thin intelligent face, raven eyes and lantern jaw were turned downwards. He walked as one lost in crazy, fanatical love.

Dear Eleanor, I sent an email – well, three emails actually (!) – wondering if you were free for Tosca at the Albert Hall. It is on the 4th. It promises to be quite a good production. But, as I said when I first suggested it, I realized that histrionics are not your style.

Even if you are not free that evening, I wonder if we could have one of our walks . . .

Since the clinch in the hothouses during the winter, Eleanor had been avoiding Charles. He had not acted upon his mad threat or promise or whatever it was, to tell his wife that he and Eleanor were in love. He still had a functioning brain, and this enabled him to see that she did not wish to pursue their relationship, whatever it was.

He could not, however, be rational about her. He had fallen in love with her during their first, completely unplanned encounter, three years before, shortly after she had arrived in Aberdeen. They had met walking in the Botanic Gardens, and fallen into chat. Then his boy Josh had got into the Cathedral choir. His wife Pamela was a keen pillar of the Cathedral, so he had recognized her at once. He had been to England often, and she was at that stage homesick. He had talked to her of cricket in the Parks at Oxford, productions of Shakespeare at Stratford, chamber concerts at the Wigmore Hall.

They had walked up and down the allées, explored the hot-houses, and gone for a cup of tea in the Pavilion Café of the Winter Gardens. That was when he had fallen in love with her. Although she was forty, she was schoolgirlish, full of laughter. In his imagination, she was about sixteen, leading him into the pages of the Malory Towers stories which his sister used to read when they were children. She had used expressions like 'oh Lor' and 'Crikey'. He did not know then that she was married. He knew nothing about her, except that she was the new Dean. When he had found out there was a husband she'd left behind it had increased his ardour, rather than the reverse, since – fairly obviously – if she were happily married, she would not have left her husband, apparently indefinitely. Obsessive Googling had revealed that she was married to Professor Douglas Bartlett, now a visiting professor at Duke. He had written a book called *Dickens and the Art of Popular Fiction*. Haileybury and Manchester University, but had later got an Oxford fellowship. About a year later, Eleanor had agreed to meet Charles for a repeat of the walk, and she had subsequently been with him to a number of concerts.

He had never been in love like this, certainly not with Pamela. His relationship with his wife was almost like a business partnership. Or so he now told himself, somehow allowing himself to blot out the deep bond caused by their having children together.

He knew that Eleanor Bartlett did not want an affair with him. Yet she had allowed him to pursue her, there was no doubt about that. And he knew that she had allowed him to kiss her. It was more than that. She had kissed him back. Her tongue had been in his mouth, as well as his in hers. It was something more than just going to concerts together.

Aftershocks

Since the episode in the hothouses in winter, the passionate embrace, the awkward parting, she had ignored or turned down any more invitations to go to concerts with him. His obsession with her had only grown. Because his wife still attended the Cathedral, and Josh sang in the choir, he had continued to go, week by week, to hear Wood in the Fridge, Stanford in C, and Merbecke.

The truth was, he had gone mad. The expressions – crazy about someone, mad about the girl – they were true. He was in a state of insanity, in which he could not get through more than a few hours without either seeing her, addressing emails to her, or wandering about in a dreamy daze, thinking about her. And now a development had occurred in his life. And because he was mad, he HAD to include her in this development, even though it was quite obvious – from her deliberate distancing of herself from him – that she did not want to be included.

In his pocket was the letter.

Something has happened in my life . . .

He was an experienced letter-writer. He knew this was deliberate teasing. He knew that the sentence was crying out, yearning to continue – *You are my sun and stars, my life, I cannot live without you.* He said this to her inside his head a hundred times a day.

But of course, he was not going to write such a letter. In a way, however, what he did write was almost more disloyal to Pamela than a declaration of love.

. . . rather to my surprise – and, obviously, this is completely a secret, I have been asked to become a High Court Judge. There are pros and cons. The pro – it is a great honour not least to my

firm, and a part of myself has always wanted this, ever since I was
a young lawyer. The con – it would mean moving to Carmichael.
And there is much work here in Aberdeen which we have to
complete. Some of this is known to you! . . .

For, before the indiscreet kiss in the hothouses, he had spent
hours of extremely indiscreet conversation with Eleanor about Rex
Tone's shady dealings.

I would very much value your thoughts. Incidentally, I have not
mentioned it to Pamela. No one knows of it. I wanted you to be
the first to know, and you to be the one who helped me decide.

You couldn't put 'love' at the end of a letter like that, so he had
merely put the initial C.

The letter was in his pocket now as he entered Argyle Square,
looked up at the statue of the Queen Empress, and crossed towards
the front door of the Deanery, a fine villa with well-planted gardens
which stood in the corner of the square, and which contained the
Cathedral Offices on the ground floor. Eleanor, he knew, lived in
the upper storey of this building, but he had never actually been
asked there, except with Pamela for a Christmas party. He tried
not to think of this fact, for if he thought of it too much, the essentially fantastical nature of his 'love' would become clear – Eleanor
did not want his attentions. At the Christmas party, Eleanor had
shaken Pamela's hand and said, a boisterous Madcap of the Remove
more than a Vamp, 'I hope you don't mind your husband taking
me to concerts now and again?' And Pamela had repeated, 'You're
welcome to him!' And they had all laughed as if it was the merriest
thing in the world.

Aftershocks

Penny Whistle's eighteenth-century voice now filled the hot, twenty-first-century morning air.

There were three men come out o' the west their fortunes for
    to try.
And these three men made a solemn vow, John Barleycorn
    must die.
They ploughed, they sowed, they harrowed him in, throwed
    clods upon his head
Till these three men were satisfied, John Barleycorn was dead.

Charlie wondered if Eleanor was in the Cathedral Offices, whether her deep blue eyes, surmounted by those triangular eyebrows, were looking out at him. The fact that she had not answered his last three emails, or had any personal dealings with him for weeks – months – presumably told their own story. He could not, however, resist the pain which it gave him to approach her door, and to post the envelope through the burnished brass of the letter flap. There had been the kiss. That surely spoke louder than anything. And might she not, one day, change, melt, admit . . .

It was with the trembling fingers of a lovestruck adolescent that the eminent lawyer pushed the letter through the Dean's front door.

The letter from the Federal Justice Department lay on his desk. He had discussed it with no one. It would undoubtedly shed lustre on his firm and his practice if he were to take the position. On the other hand, were he to do so, he would take a substantial cut in salary.

In the first two decades of Charlie Nicolson's professional life, he would have guessed that, were the offer to become a judge ever made to him, it would have dominated all his thoughts. In some ways, it was the crown of a career, though he knew perfectly well that many law colleagues eschewed the bench, either because they could not live on the measly money, or because they genuinely felt their talents were better exercised at the bar. But, as it happens, this tremendous offer only penetrated Charlie's consciousness as an object which he could use in his pathetic attempts to get Eleanor's attention.

Then something very peculiar happened. The heat of the day perhaps in part explained it. He was tired. The workload of the Rex Tone cases and other matters filled a good twelve hours of his working life. And the frozen state of his marriage caused him, when he did eventually go to bed with Pamela, to lie awake for hours, wondering if she too was awake, and whether they should talk to one another, and if they did, whether it would heal or destroy their marriage. He knew how unhappy Pamela was, and he longed, if only for his own peace of mind, that she should become happy again. And they had two lovely kids . . . And yet, this private madness . . . He did not merely love Eleanor. He was in love with being in love, in love with the unhappiness. It was like being the hero of a film.

Charles decided, before he went back to the office, to sit down in his dark suit on a bench near the statue of Queen Victoria, and to hear a few more of Penny Whistle's songs. When the old sailor began on

> *As I walked down a London Street*
> *A Press Gang I did chance to meet,*
> *They asked me if I'd join the Fleet*
> *Aboard a Man o' War . . .*

Aftershocks

Charles fell suddenly deeply asleep. By this stage of the morning, his son Josh was finishing the last quadratic equation. Within the next hour, he would have changed into whites, and gone down to the cricket pavilion. Ella, at the zoo, would be about to witness the terror of the animals as their cages were ripped apart by the mad invisible giant.

There was assembly – the children sang 'Morning has Broken'. Then the three Year One classes collected their packed lunches, little yoghurt pots and triangular cream cheese or ham sandwiches, and an apple or banana depending on luck of the draw, and lined up to climb into two hired Macnaughton's coaches. The drivers of both these vehicles sat, a little slumped, behind the wheel. This was partly because the glorious February sunshine was already hot. It was also because there was nothing they disliked more than these school trips. The best thing was Scenic Seniors, driving oldies to beauty spots, listening to their yacketty-yak all the way down towards the mountains, or the sea; pausing with the other drivers in the car park of a wayside boozer or eaterie; and then driving them back, full of our best Island Riesling, or sherries, beers, gin and tonic, and hearing the comforting susurrus of their unconscious breath, the reassuring honks of the louder snorers. Rugby fans could be difficult, course they could, and they were loud. Driving them back from an International in Carmichael's Callaghan Park could be hairy – the repetitive, coarse songs, the lager tins rattling down the aisle of the bus.

Relatively few of them, however, actually puked. Whereas on these school trips, puking was the norm. Both drivers laid some of the blame on the teachers, who – they thought – put it into the heads of the suggestible children that they might throw up.

—Stig, let Karyl sit in the front.

—But I was here first, Mrs Chambers.

—That's not the point, Stig. You know Karyl gets motion sickness.

Why tell her? That was what the drivers wanted to know. Why tell kids like Karyl that they might puke? Some of the kids threw up almost as soon as you turned the ignition key. And if they'd been on outings which involved a packed lunch, fizzy drinks, and – worst of all – time in a playground, where they'd been whizzed round and round on carousels, or whooshed up and down in the swings, then the aisles of the bus were full of that stench. Some of the coaches in the Macnaughton's fleet were never quite free of it. Nothing more nauseating than nausea. Even on the rare occasions when the nippers did not actually throw, there was the noise of their tinny voices, which went on *all the time*. No post-prandial Zizz for them. The cockatoo chatter never stopped, often acrimonious, and needing the intervention of a teacher. Some of the drivers had approached the foreman at Macnaughton's about the possibility of demanding extra pay when driving school parties, but the company was not having any of it.

—Now when we get to the zoo, Mr Pollard was yelling down the bus at his lot . . .

And Mrs Chambers, who was one of the lucky grown-ups who somehow could get children to be quiet, was saying,

—What is it we all do when we get to the zoo?

And her lot, in one of those sing-sing collective replies, were chanting,

—Stand-in-a-LINE, Miss-Iz-Chaym-Buzz.

—That's RIGHT, stand in a LINE. And what do we NEVER EVER DO?

—Push-our-fin-guzzz-thru-the-BARS, Miss-Iz-Chaym-Buzz.

—Because we are all fellow creatures, we all share this planet, don't we?

They seemed to accept this on Mrs Chambers's bus, whereas Mr Pollard's lot, closer in their writhings, attempts to stand up on their seats to pull funny faces at those sitting behind, or to lean forwards, and pull or, better still, glue to the safety-belts, with wodges of chewing gum, the plaits of the little girls immediately in front of them, seemed closer to their simian cousins. Unlike Mrs Chambers, who transformed all her announcements into Q and A, Mr Pollard was trying to issue injunctions – no feeding of the animals, no going away from the crowd, you're to stay in pairs, remember, stay in PAIRS – but could scarcely make his voice heard as the bus lurched out of the school gates into Prince Alfred Parade. By the time he was trying to issue two orders at once – NO, You CAN'T EAT YOUR PACKED LUNCHES until we get there, and remember, Don't WHATEVER YOU DO put your fingers through the BARS – some voices at the back were calling,

—Sir, Sir, Emma-Jane says she's going to throw, Sir.

—I think it would be better, Ella Nicolson informed Mr Pollard, if Emma-Jane sits nearer the front of the bus on the way home.

—She wasn't actually ill, was she, Ella?

—She felt ill. She might have been sick.

Ella's intense bespectacled little pale face appeared to be correcting her teacher. Her mum and dad had a thing about false gentilities. Being ill and being sick were different in their English, though not in Mr Pollard's.

—We are NOT GOING IN THE SHOP, bellowed Mr Pollard

to the rest of the class. Their actions belied his words. They were stampeding towards the emporium which contained mountains, piled high, of nylon-furred wallabies, kangaroos, lemurs, crocodiles, lions, wombats, duck-billed platypuses – and a sweet counter which Mrs Chambers had already reached. As she cleared the premises of Opportunity One pupils, this sensible woman told the assistant that the sweets should never have been allowed in such a shop. Did they care NOTHING for the dental health of future generations?

—Besides, you're asking for shoplifters if you put all that stuff at their level, she said, pointing an accusing finger at the liquorice snakes, candied mice and sea-horse-shaped humbugs.

—Where did we agree we wouldn't go? asked Mrs Chambers.

Even Mr Pollard joined in the rhythmic chanting of *In-the-shop-Miss-Iz-Chaym-Buzz*. In answer to a girl called Amy's relentless questioning, this highly competent person replied,

—How urgent is it, Amy? You went just before we left the school.

Later, Ella asked Mrs Chambers,

—They're right, aren't they, Miss?

Mrs Chambers answered,

—Maybe, Ella. Maybe.

The group pointed out by the child were standing in silent witness beside the tiger enclosure, holding a banner which read, 'TIGERS BELONG IN THE WILD, NOT IN THE ZOO'.

Eleanor stood beside her office window drinking coffee. She had seen Charles Nicolson approaching, and retreated to the depths of the room where she was invisible to the outside world. He had become a figure of nightmare to her. What had begun as a rather flattering flirtation was now a thing of total embarrassment. She had encouraged him. That was the undeniable, infuriating fact of the matter; but only because it had never occurred to her that he was, as far as she was concerned, a lunatic. Love – or whatever it was – had sent him round the bend. She felt threatened. If she had not been crazy enough to encourage him, just a little, in the initial stages . . . If she had not gone with him that time to the Botanic Gardens . . . If she had not yielded to his kiss, rather than pulling away, perhaps even smacking his cheek . . . Then, what?

The strong baritone of Penny Whistle had begun in the morning sunshine, which was already blazingly hot. Eleanor reflected upon the fact that she had been there for over three years, and he had sung every day, even on Christmas Morning. Apart from his occasional sallies into the hymnal – when he would, for example, sing Christmas carols – and Good Friday, during the hours he was not in the Cathedral, was devoted to 'There is a Green Hill', 'When I Survey', and so forth – he hardly ever repeated himself. His repertoire was prodigious. Not for the first time, she indulged the fancy that he had always been there – had stepped ashore in the 1700s with the famous sea-captain and the eminent botanist, and remained ever since, a man of the eighteenth century still chanting his old lays in the twenty-first.

> *Farewell an' adieu to you fair Spanish ladies,*
> *Farewell an' adieu to you ladies of Spain,*
> *For we've received orders for to sail for old England,*
> *An' hope very shortly to see you again.*
> *We'll rant an' we'll roar, like true British sailors,*
> *We'll rant an' we'll rave across the salt seas,*
> *'Till we strike soundings in the Channel of Old England,*
> *From Ushant to Scilly is thirty-four leagues.*

Penny Whistle wore capacious, frayed, blue cotton shorts, a red tee-shirt, already much-stained round the armpits, and – in readiness for another hot summer day in February – a wide-brimmed straw hat. This object, possibly the gift of a tourist, had begun its life as a sombrero. It now recalled the roof of a ruined cottage through which the sun's rays, the wind or the rain could make their incursions. Through the many gaps, the sun dappled Penny Whistle's weather-brown cheeks with flecks of light.

Her mind was in a state most conducive, in an almost literal sense, to reflection. That is, she was not forming coherent thoughts, but she was absorbing impressions, a hangover from her half-hour of liturgical observance in the Cathedral, when the repetition of familiar words, like the singing of an old song, or the hearing of a piece of music, moves the sensibilities into a receptive frame of mind without knowing what it receives. Is this what old song, old liturgy and serious music all make possible for us as human beings? And is it what amplified music, or new and unfamiliar liturgy, and all the artificial noise which we create around ourselves in a modern city drowns out? The possibility of being a reflective person? Penny Whistle sang so defiantly, his jerky blind head and his muscular shoulders moving in their marionette rhythms, and seeming to say – this is enough, this song, these words, the strange worlds which the words, which are not mine, evoke. To this extent, he was bardic, even hieratic. This was what the Church ought to be, but so seldom was. Because it wanted to interpret words, stories, rhythms and music which did not need to be interpreted? She put down her coffee cup. Time for a different sort of work. *Woman goeth forth unto her work, and to her labour, until evening.*

*

Aftershocks

Some of us heard the bang, and then saw the effects. Others of us saw the effects – the trees swaying, the cars rising in the air and descending upside down on top of other cars, the liquefaction of the earth, the unroofing of houses – and then heard the bang, louder than any explosion anyone had heard, even the army veterans among us, even our oldest inhabitant, Mr Tooth, a hundred and four years old, who had fought in Crete and Italy during the war, and taken part in battles where the pounding of high explosives went on for several days at a time. Mr Tooth was in a retirement home now, where the twenty residents and their carers were gathered round the television in a downstairs room overlooking the garden. It was a bungalow structure, built to modern specifications and quake-proofed, so that they were lucky. The building did not collapse around them. But the favourite soap opera which some of them enjoyed watching disappeared from the enormous plasma-screen as all the power went down. The two Chinese care workers, who were wheeling in a trolley of tea and biscuits, were thrown across the floor, the tea-urn upset, scalding one of them badly, and the biscuits suddenly flew up like a crowd of malignant insects.

The zoo, as all visitors to Aberdeen will remember, is on the edge of Gladstone Park.

Deborah Roskill, sixty-eight, a retired nurse, tall, bespectacled, summer-skirted, neat-bloused, was walking in Gladstone Park, near her flat in the suburbs. She strode briskly, in spite of the heat, occasionally whistling and calling to Finn, her energetic black Labrador, who bounded ahead of her in search of other dogs to play with. She saw the dog stand stock still, about eighty yards ahead of her. As she approached, he turned and ran back to her.

—What have you done? she asked. He was staring at her with wild, scared eyes, and he leapt at her with muddy paws.

—How did you get yourself so muddy? Her first thought was that he had been rolling in excrement, because the summer heat had seared the park, and there had been no mud when they set out on their walk. Now she looked, however, and saw human figures running. Some of them were screaming, but those who passed her had faces frozen with shock. All around, the parched lawns of Gladstone Park had split into fissures, and were oozing. This was not ordinary mud. It was liquefaction, and the park was turning into a swamp. We'd all seen this, six months before. She and Finn turned back from the lawn and made for the concrete path and the huge ornamental cast-iron gates, erected to commemorate the Silver Jubilee of King George V in 1935, which were now swaying like flimsy reeds. King George himself, who stood on a Lutyensesque plinth in the middle of the park beside the bandstand, was doing what, in life, he seldom did: he was wobbling.

The road which passed Gladstone Park, leading from the suburb of Kensington into the centre of the city, was already log-jammed with traffic. One woman was standing beside her immobile car shouting,

—My kid's in school in Benson Square! My kid's in school in Benson Square! Opportunity One!

No one could deny this, but nor could anyone do anything to help her. The traffic had come to a standstill. Hundreds of people, at the same moment, had formed the idea of racing into town by car to rescue their children, their wives, their friends. The concrete verges were cracking like cookies, and dusty grass had turned to a grey, smelly ooze as the liquefaction slopped onto the road. It was soon lapping the doors of the stationary cars. The woman yelling about her kid was now standing ankle deep in slime and the lique-faction was rising fast towards her waist.

The solid bronze statue of George V's grandmother, Queen Victoria, which had stood on its white stone plinth in the centre of Argyle Square opposite the Cathedral since 1903, swayed from side to side, as if that empress, as she sometimes did in life, had been over-indulging in good Highland malt. It tottered and fell on a camper van in which a young family had taken refuge. As it ripped through the roof of the van, it crushed a seven-year-old boy to death. At the same moment, the movement of the road beneath the van was hurling it about. The mother of the surviving two children, a gentle-faced hippy with black hair woven into plaits, was open-mouthed and screaming.

She was not the only person screaming. Many in the square had lost all control of themselves. Some yelled. Some shat them-selves. Bodies were being tossed as high as ten feet in the air before crashing back to what had been the ground, but was now a surging muddle of broken tarmac and liquefaction. Somewhere a gas main must have burst because the smell of gas was overpowering.

A policeman, who had risen to his feet again and was trying to stand upright, endeavoured to answer a woman in shorts and tee-shirt, who was yelling,

—Oh, where . . . where's MY . . . Where?

Was she searching for lost children? A dog? Her mind?

The bright summer day had turned into a scorcher. The shirt-sleeved policeman, Garry Hughes, touched her shoulder, and she flung herself into his arms. He stroked her mouse-coloured hair and squeezed her quivering body. Over her heaving shoulders, he could see Argyle Square, and the length of what had been King Edward Parade. The eucalyptus trees on either side of the ex-street were writhing as if in a hurricane. The branches were lashing out as if some vindictive maniac was using them as a carpet-beater. Many of them were uprooted, and were falling across what had been the surface of the road, but was now a great expanse of bubbling mud. In the time he had stood, trying to comfort the quivering woman, the young police officer could watch the city crumbling before his eyes and then vanishing in the clouds of dust which so much destruction caused. Some of the brand-new buildings which had been erected since the consciousness of seismology kicked in, a decade or so ago, were withstanding the Quake. Some, very few, older buildings had been quake-proofed. In Clarence Terrace, a parade of Edwardian shops and offices, some of them had been quake-proofed, others not, so that you saw about four out of twenty properties withstand the blast, while the rest quivered, rumbled, fell. Through billowing dust, you could dimly make out the old Adelphi, the most luxurious hotel on the Island, wobbling and turning to powder. Those police who were near could hear, through the din of collapsing masonry, the anguished, unchecked human screams.

All the Government offices at the end of King Edward Parade had already fallen.

When the woman had wept a little longer, she disentangled herself from Garry's arms and walked away, dazed, without a word.

—You must go to . . .

He wanted to tell her that there was some assembly point where people might find support, news of loved ones, hot sweet tea, which was supposed to be of comfort in times of disaster, though he had never been able to see why. He knew of no such place, however, and his mobile phone received no signals. Turning his body, he could see that the wreckage visible down King Edward Parade was repeated in all quarters of the city. Jubilee Park was filled with crowds. Most of them were standing still, some were looking upwards – as if expecting the Second Coming. Waikuku Road, Howley Street, Longden Road were no longer there – there was just a broad waste-land of rising dust and smouldering ruins. Further to the east, he could see the spire of the Cathedral snapping like an ice cream cone. Then the tower itself seemed to wobble.

Charlie woke up on a bench which was floating from side to side like the seats in a roller-coaster at the fair.

—If the Cathedral goes, we've all gone, said a voice at his side, but by the time he had taken in the fact of being addressed, the speaker, a red-faced man, so hot that he might just have been half-boiled, had vanished in the dust plumes which now filled the air.

Behind and within the dust and smoke were half a million instances of human despair. All that they took for granted, in the course of their daily lives, as solid – their houses, their offices, the shops, the pavements, the ground beneath their feet – was now in violent motion. Their limbs, their legs, their feet no longer properly functioned. If you stood up, you fell over again. Many were unable to stop shaking, from sheer fear. The fear was so powerful that, when they looked back on it afterwards, they realized the inade-quacy of the word. The occasions when they had used the word in their past – as children, fear of the dark, or, as adults, fear of attack by criminals in a darkened street, or the fear induced by nightmares or horror films – these, however strong, were mere twinges before the sensations brought to the surface by the Quake.

Others felt something different from this abject fear – it was immediate heartbreak, immediate consciousness that the person or persons they most loved were elsewhere, or threatened. Almost no mobile phones had signals in the first moments after the Quake, so that hundreds of thousands of people were stabbed with an instantaneous feeling of anguish – wanting to reach out for their wives, husbands, children, parents, and not being able to do so. Many had comparable feelings of anguish, bitterly regretting that their lives, which might be about to end, had taken some false turn or another – wishing that a broken friendship could be mended, or an act of cruelty undone.

Others in our city were stunned, literally stunned, and did not begin to feel the shock of the Quake until afterwards – in some cases, weeks afterwards. At the time of the Quake itself, they had been seized with numbness. They had felt nothing, literally nothing.

In the offices of Nicolson and Blake, Charlie Nicolson's PA, Harriet LeStrange, an intelligent woman aged twenty-two, was typing up a brief for him. It was not one of the big cases involving Rex Tone and Ricky Wong. It concerned an on-going dispute between two neighbours – a jam factory on the outskirts of town and St Frideswide's, one of the most prestigious private girls' schools in the country. The headmistress contended that Simpsons, the industrial jam makers, had built an extended workshop on property which belonged to the school. Simpsons-Jelly, represented by a big law firm in Derby, one of the larger, more industrial of the cities on the Island, contended that by the deeds last drawn up in 1928, this land had been part of the original factory site. It was the sort of case which Charlie enjoyed, gentle, expensive, and likely to be long lasting. A nice little earner.

Harriet was typing the words, 'the survey conducted in 1926, at the time of the building of the first Chemistry Laboratories, clearly show . . . ' As these words appeared on her computer screen, Harriet felt the whole room shake, and saw enormous cracks appear in the office ceiling. Cheryl, the receptionist, called out,

—This is bigger than a 5!

As she did so, both young women could see all the electric wiring behind the plasterwork of the ceiling. They could see lath and plaster, as dust began to come through the roof, and as the floor shook.

—Are you all right, Arlene? they called to Charlie's junior on the other side of the office.

None of them were all right, but the words came to Harriet's mouth anyway. The floor beneath her desk had begun to sway about like a boat in choppy water. She could hear Cheryl repeating that this was bigger than a 5, but she could no longer see her, or Arlene. An enormous slab of concrete had fallen, enclosing the young woman in a triangular cave. The movement threw her, and the bookcase beside her desk, containing directories and law books, collapsed as she grabbed it to steady herself. She was now lying face down in rubble. She heard Arlene and Cheryl shouting, screaming, for a while, but thereafter there was silence for what felt like forever.

In fact it was the inside of an hour. Through a gap in her concrete cave, Harriet could see light, and she could hear voices. She heard periodic applause, people clapping, presumably as other bodies were carried out of the wreckage by rescue workers. And then she heard a man's voice saying,

—I can see you, Harriet. I must be just above you.

—Below me, she said.

—Above you!

—Below me.

—Above you.

She tried to crawl towards him. For a while, her tortured spirit was liberated by sheer annoyance that he knew better than she did where she was. She realized that her hand was trapped by the fallen bookcase. She could not escape. She could, however, wiggle one of her legs towards the fissure at the top of her concrete cave, and by pushing her foot through the hole, she made her point.

—OK, Harriet, you're above me. I'm coming in.

The concrete slab was carefully drawn back.

—My hand! I can't move my hand!

—OK, Harriet, I'm going to get you out.

—I can't move my hand.

The fireman had a small saw, which he was using to cut around the fallen bookshelf.

—Look at me, Harriet. We are going to get you out.

—My hand is trapped.

—I know that, Harriet, we are cutting round your hand . . .

He managed to cut a semi-circle round the hand, and to pull her arm free. As he did so, they both saw that he had left all the fingers of her left hand trapped beneath the metal bookcase. She stared with shocked detachment at her hand, at the bleeding stumps, at the fingers, as if they belonged to someone else.

Outside the building, cars were being thrown about like small leaves blown by autumn wind. People were falling over, like joke drunkards. The hot tarmac surfaces of the road had become first cracks, then canyons, and the liquefaction, stinking black mud, was bubbling out like newly prospected crude oil.

Aftershocks

Two women who had agreed to meet in their favourite lunch spot, the Nosebag, a cheerful little café on the corner of Aberdeen Street and Hereford Square, had been thrown into the air about four feet and landed on their backs. One was in tears, the other lay for a moment, stunned, before getting up to help her friend.

—My God, Rosie – look!

As they staggered to their feet, they could see the wobbling structure of the Albert Hall, the fine Edwardian concert hall where they had sung together in the Aberdeen Choral Society – Mendelssohn's *Elijah*, Dvorak's *Stabat Mater, The Dream of Gerontius*. The roof was rippling like a silken bedspread before it lifted off, in seconds, and with a thunderous crash, the whole building, its millions of bricks, its white stone pilasters, its busts of the great composers, dotted in niches round the outside walls, had descended in a furious cloud.

The gibbons and the monkeys seemed to feel the shock more than the quadrupeds. They always sat and gibbered on their branches. Today, however, the gibbering was completely woeful. Those who heard and saw it felt it was quite as pitiable as the shock and suffering felt by the monkeys' cousins, the human beings. You could not 'explain' what was going on to anyone, but somehow, the fact of human consciousness, the knowledge that we had all (except Rex Tone apparently) been waiting for this quake to happen made some part of the experience intelligible. And we had all stored up our own experiences and memories of the more minor quake six months before. The animals were just nakedly suffering.

In our Tragedy class with Barnaby and Digby, we'd discussed what changed, or elevated, an extremely sad event into a tragedy; of course, it was all to do with how the sorrow is perceived, how it is received, how human beings are able to 'rise above' their sufferings, or endure, in defiance of the gods. I suppose, after the Quake, the difficulty for nearly all of us was our inability to do this. Some of us took refuge in legal battles with building inspectors or structural engineers. Some of us had long-running battles with our insurance companies. The public mood against Rex Tone, or the Federal Government, perfectly reasonable on one level, was really displaced anger against gods in whom we could not believe. Sophocles and friends, and Homer before them, gave tremendous dignity to the intolerable affliction which humanity felt. I wonder how many of us really felt that in Aberdeen. Was that what we were trying to do when we put on that production of *Trojan Women* in the months after the Quake – not make SENSE of the suffering, but to inject a note of dignity? Homer made the horses of Patroclus weep at his funeral. He made even the horses tragic. Our animals were not tragic. Their fear and vulnerability ripped open the nature of things, showed us the molten lava of screaming pain which lies beneath the apparently stable surface. The groaning of the rhinos, the howling – like alley-cats – of fearful tigers, the extra-wobbliness of the giraffes, who ran to and fro, unable to steady themselves on stick legs. No one who saw the zoo falling to bits, and the animals running free in panic among the crowds of screaming human beings, could ever forget, not just the pain of it, but the pointless pain. That was what was on display here – the absolute pointlessness.

CHAPTER EIGHT

DIGBY WAS IN HER TOWER ROOM. SHE HAD BEEN SOLIDLY AT work for half the morning, her meditations on the Greeks punctuated by the gurgling and grinding and clanking of the well-oiled Victorian works of the great Cathedral clock, and the striking of the quarters. Her long, cool white fingers moved rapidly across the keyboard of her laptop.

In the 1971 film version of *Trojan Women*, starring Katharine Hepburn, Michael Cacoyannis left out the gods. The film begins, not, as does Euripides' play, with a discussion between Poseidon and Athene, but with the women and children being escorted from the sacked, burning city. The Greeks had been waiting for the chance to make themselves rich with Trojan Gold. 'Fools,' says a voiceover, 'to lay a city waste and so soon to die themselves.'

You could say that Cacoyannis's film, though well acted by Hepburn (who plays Hecuba), is not really a tragedy at all. Just something that is very very sad – and, in a way, commonplace.

Hecuba, Cassandra, Andromache and Helen played their sad roles and told their sad stories, but there was not a tragic fault in any of them, there was no problem to resolve. The city of Troy had been devastated, reduced to ruins. The women, who were no more than chattels in the eyes of the conquering Greeks, had been brought back to Hellas.

In Euripides' play, the destruction of Troy is *not* accidental. The opening scene, which the film omits, makes it perfectly clear why all the devastation has happened, the whole fate of Troy is decided, neither by human beings, nor by blind accident, but by the gods. Poseidon, the protector of Troy, agrees with Athene that the city can be destroyed, on condition that he, God of the Sea, is allowed to cause havoc to the Greek fleet on their way home, with storms and shipwrecks.

She paused, and reached for a volume of the play. This was a moment to quote from Euripides. She loved this work so much that she knew much of it by heart, and was providing her own translations as she went along. She loved it because of its lyricism – it contained, she believed, some of the finest poetry Euripides ever wrote, which, for her money, meant some of the finest poetry ever written by anyone. She loved the raw, raw grief of the women, Hecuba's hopeless –

How can I ever stop crying? I have everything to weep for:
my homeland is gone, my children are gone and my husband.

Digby was overwhelmed by Andromache's undiluted grief for Hector. She also loved the frenzied, mad Cassandra, the virgin prophetess-priest who was now whooping with insane merriment at the prospect of being deflowered by Agamemnon. But the passage she wanted to quote must be from the beginning. It is Poseidon's sad acknowledgement:

O city, once so happy, I must leave
Your well-constructed towers and firm foundations . . .

Or should it be, as one translator had it:

Superb masonry farewell!
You would stand firm yet, were it not for Athene, daughter
    of Zeus.

Euripides was unconstrained by monotheism. He did not have to believe in a loving God, or a creator God. He put the gods on stage and demonstrated the extent to which their frivolous malice was the cause of human misfortunes. Ever since he did so, there had been debates about whether he was an atheist, whether he chose to satirize Greek religion, or whether – as perhaps the Bible does, with its depictions of Yahweh committing acts of genocide in Egypt and Canaan – it was simply a depiction of the way things were.

Mulling over possible epithets which were better than 'superb' for 'eutuchousa', the masonry of crumbling Troy, she leaned back in her chair, and looked up at the shelves of her tower library. How lucky she was to have this retreat! What cherished friends these books had been to her for the last thirty years. Here were her old school editions – the little blue *Aeneid* VI, which she had done for her first exams, and *Iphigenia in Tauris*. Here were her university books, to which had been added a substantial working library – now well over four thousand volumes lining the room.

Some of her simpler friends, such as Bob, the minor canon, had gazed at the shelves from floor to ceiling, and asked her if she had read them all. The simple answer was that she had, and that of the chief Greek texts – Homer, Euripides, Sophocles, Aeschylus, the major dialogues of Plato – her familiarity was total. She never lost her sense of what a privilege this knowledge was. True, friends in the English Faculty at Oxford were comparably familiar with Shakespeare and Milton (and she envied them that), but they had also been obliged to master many writers who were not worth the bother. And there were her many other colleagues on the Governing Body of her college – engineers, chemists, even the theologians (!) – who had only rudimentary reading, and who had, as it were, nothing to draw upon inside their heads.

There was smugness in this thought, certainly, but she was not a smug person, and she did not consider herself superior for knowing Greek – simply very very lucky. As she had the thought, she leaned right back in her chair, and rocked on its two back legs, a habit which had enraged her parents and teachers since she was a little girl. Her head was thrown back, and the rocking motion made her, at first, not notice that the room, and the whole tower, were in motion.

The ceiling itself was on the move, bouncing up and down as if the beams behind the plasterwork were made of rubber. Bringing her chair to an immediate upright position, she had no hesitation in knowing what was happening. Like every other human brain in the city, Digby's retained an indelible memory of the minor quake of six months before and there was no mistaking it. To say that 'she thought back' suggests some act of will. Rather, there was an instant replay in her mind of that day in the seminar room, when she had looked up at Barnaby and known there was a quake, and thought she was on the point of death, and wished she could touch him.

Ever methodical, she remembered to press 'Save', and closed her laptop. She stood up, making for the door of her room, and the winding stone staircase. But she could no longer move. The floor had become the deck of a ship in a hurricane. She decided that if she got down on her hands and knees, she would be able to crawl to the opposite side of the room. There was a long table there, standing against the bookshelves, on which various books and papers were piled high. They were slithering off the table on to the floor, but it was a substantial mahogany table, and she was sure that if she were only able to crawl underneath it, she would be safe if – when – the roof collapsed.

Even while she was having this practical thought, she was over-whelmed by a desire to live. *Le vent se lève – il faut tenter de vivre!* Specifically, she thought how sad it was that she had not had sex for nearly ten years.

It was strangely hard to kneel down. As she tried to do so, she was propelled forwards and fell. By now the floor was at a strange angle, pushing her backwards, away from the saving surface of that big old Victorian table. She clawed at the floor rugs, but this made her slither backwards further. And then she watched, as if it were all happening in slow motion, an enormous piece of masonry, a vast piece of carved stone fall on the mahogany table and crunch it to splinters. Had she decided half a minute earlier to try crawling under the table, she might have been successful, and that would have been her life, beneath the great ashlar lump of carved acan-thus. Superb masonry indeed.

She was now overwhelmed by a simple desire to be alive. More than that, to change her life. The past with its limitations, in which she had sometimes cynically rejoiced, was a plain beneath her. The future was the hill country above. It would be possible, it must be possible, to climb? Having previously felt that a human life could not realistically be filled with much emotional satisfaction, or much practical achievement, she now felt hungry for experience. Death was there, grasping at her with its long, cold rapist fingers, and she was pushing it away, with an unspoken, *not yet, oh, not yet.*

Yes, the gibbons, marmosets, chimpanzees and spider monkeys seemed to mind it all the most. Their screams rent the air. Near the picnic area, between the penguin ponds and the once tempting shop, the elephant, which had been offering rides to visitors, was thrown on to its side. The great howdah on its back, containing eight children, crashed to the tarmac. None of the children were killed, but three were trapped for a while beneath the great pachydermatous sides of the beast.

Flamingos, herons and parakeets swarmed, terrified, into the sky. The bars of the tiger cage, in defiance of the Green protesters' banner, remained in place, but the roof of the cages flew away like a flimsy umbrella. Animals and people were running around, none wiser than another about what to do. Two zebras, preceded by some baffled giraffes, lolloped through the clouds of dust. The windows of the aquarium and reptile house had been blasted out, and some of the zoo-keepers were saying through loud hailers,

—STAY AWAY FROM THE REPTILE HOUSE. STAY AWAY . . . THERE ARE DANGEROUS SNAKES AND OTHER REPTILES WHICH MIGHT BE AT LARGE. THAT'S REPEAT, STAY AWAY FROM THE . . .

An enormous water buffalo and a couple of hippopotami had accompanied two red river-hogs and a wildebeest on the march to freedom across Gladstone Park. Some of them joined the traffic jams on the highway going into town.

—THERE'S NO NEED TO PANIC, another zoo-keeper was shouting, in a voice which showed she was not following her own advice. DO NOT APPROACH ANY OF THE ANIMALS.

Ella looked this way and that and could see none of her school friends in the dust and heat. Mr Pollard had shouted at them, all the way on the bus, that whatever happened they were not to get separated, and now she had. Each child had been assigned a Buddy for the expedition, so that, even if they got separated from the bigger group, they would at least have one other person with them. Ella's Buddy was Stig. A few minutes before the Quake, he had said he was going off to look through the meshing at the crocs. Ella had told him they were seeing the crocodiles and alligators later that afternoon and that Mr Pollard had told them not to go off on their own. Mr Pollard, at the same moment, had been shouting,

—Ella! Stig! What did I TELL you? Keep up! We are going to see the monkeys now.

But even as he had said it the teacher had turned to another child and said,

—No, Gareth, you must wait till it's dinnertime, and in turning his head, he had lost sight of Stig.

Ella was keeping her eye on him, and was now torn between keeping up with the other children and holding on to her Buddy. She had opted for the latter course, and followed him towards the crocodiles just as the Quake hit.

There was an almighty roar, and the fencing around the crocodile enclosure was ripped away. Stig was hurled towards the water's edge at the moment that two crocodiles were thrown by the force of the Quake into the air. One of them belly-flopped back into the

water and surfaced to eye the little boy with drowsy malice. The
other crocodile, stunned, but very much alive, landed feet first on
the ground, about five feet away from the boy.

Ella shouted,

—Come back, Stig. Come here!, but he seemed frozen to the
spot.

She resolutely forced her little feet to stride towards her Buddy
and the croc.

There were two in the tower. But you had come to realize that,
reader? Two of them. Now and at the hour of our death. Five minutes before, the ceiling had been rising and falling, almost gently, its
four corners were those of a counterpane, shaken by invisible hands.
That is to say, it was probably five minutes. One of the things which
had happened, however, since the swaying of the room had changed
to angry shaking, up and down, was that any concept of time had
vanished. It might have been five minutes ago that the huge piece
of masonry had come through the ceiling and crashed on to the
mahogany table, crunching its thick sturdy Victorian certainty. It
might have just been a lifetime ago. Everything had changed now.

Now the ceiling had disappeared, and large hunks of masonry
lay across the room. Where the ceiling had been was a darkness,
strewn with electric cables, gunge, muck, lath and plaster, great
lumps of dust. Coldfingered Death was very close. Like a petulant
child, it shook the room up and down, trying to break it. It shook
the Two in the Tower together.

Digby thought – My book! My life! My book! The years and years
I have spent reading and rereading these texts, assembling these
notes, putting them into shape for a book, and . . . my head, so full

of Greek. Where is all that Greek going to go? Where are all the remembered lines of Homer, Sophocles, Euripides? Death is such a waste – a headful of knowledge, the lyrics of the greatest dramatist in Greek, the hundreds and hundreds of lines of wonderful poetry which she knew by heart, destroyed by one lump of masonry.

She did not even quite 'think' this. Rather, she sat in a slumped, hunched position on the floor and watched – rather than looked at – her twenty years of past endeavour, embodied in that laptop, those notebooks, those blue Oxford texts with their innumerable bits of paper stuck into them as bookmarks. She was floating away from it all. The disaster was lifting her away from the activity which had been central to her life since her late teens, the patient absorption in Greek. Other things had come and gone – feelings, for example: adolescent glooms, irritation with her parents, recognition, as Mum died, of how much she loved her mother, the constant, too close relationship with Dad . . .

Dad. What would Dad do? Now? Now and in the hour of our death. Dad's grief at her death. That was unbearable. This would break him. Break him up. How would they tell him? By telephone? No, NO! This could not be allowed to HAPPEN. Dad would pray for her. Would he? Or had they, all along, been kidding them-selves? Had Dad lived as a good priest AS IF HE BELIEVED not BECAUSE HE BELIEVED?

In such an hour, a priest would pray, no? Here was the Dean, Eleanor Bartlett, who knew that she should pray. Dean Bartlett. Praying did not even occur to her at that moment. All she could think of was the lack of sex in her life, the sheer, stupid lack of bloody sex. And lack of babies. And lack of involvement in the world . . . She was going to die, and she hadn't, since Doug, had a lover. The light petting with Barnaby did not count. She was forty bloody two and she wanted a lover, she wanted the fullness of life which having a lover brought.

She thought of the last time they had made love. Doug had been drunk. Oh, I don't want THIS to be my last memory! Get out of my head, Doug Bartlett, just get out . . . But the memory played itself relentlessly. It was after a college guest night. She knew he was seeing one of his graduates – an American called Sammie, who was doing a DPhil on Dickens and Small Women: the Marchioness, the Doll's Dressmaker, Little Nell. Sometimes, when he came to bed, Eleanor could smell Sammie. Sammie was small, like Dickens and his women. Small, conceited and smelly. When she made love with Eleanor's husband, she gave off a lot of post-coital pong. Doug had not even bothered to shower. But on that last night, he had not been with Sammie. Just been sitting up late with some cronies getting plastered. And when he had returned, he had had one last nightcap, some brandy which Dad had given them for Christmas. And after he had blundered into their bedroom, while she was lying there, reading, a novel – it was *To the North*, she remembered – she had known that he would want to make love.

She had asked him about the guest night. Their relationship, she sometimes thought, had been smothered by the habits of politeness which she could never shake off from childhood. His brandy-breath and the *boeuf-en-daube*, already slightly rotting between his teeth, or simply joining the plaque and rotten food already accumulated in his gums, had wafted towards her as he told of characters familiar to them both, rumours that the Master was in the running for a Nobel Prize (Organic Chemistry), thoughts about the Master's likely successor if she went back to Harvard. And that was how they spoke to one another, she and Doug, most of their married lives.

Bloody hell, I'm bloody DYING! And couldn't I think of the cliffs at St David's and the pounding of the Welsh sea, or remember some uplifting lines of Plato? It's my LAST THOUGHTS ON EARTH here, and I'm stuck with Doug. Bloody Doug.

When they had both switched out the light, he had reached over. They did not refuse one another when this happened, even though she was not in the mood, not in the least. So there they lay in the dark, she and Doug, and is there anything sadder in the world than two people who do not love one another, rutting out of routine? When it was over, she had the thought which had never, strangely enough, passed her mind – Well, that's the end of that. We'll never do that again. Even he, not the most sensitive of lovers, must have realized an ending had been reached, for there had been a rare energy in the restless last few minutes as he had pumped up and down, and she had felt nothing, except disgust.

And now the Dean, all these years later, and on the other side of the world, squatted in the corner of a Victorian tower that seemed to be on the point of collapse. And she thought, not of God or the afterlife, but of all the years she had spent not having sex, when she could have done so. That was what passed through the mind of the Very Reverend Eleanor, who was about to pass out of her partial existence.

The floor, in so far as there was one, was the deck of a boat in a storm. Her feet did not work. She tried to move, and it was like being paralysed. She did not think that she was injured – yet. She thought it very likely that at some point, very very soon, she was going to die.

Two in the Tower, Digby and the Dean; the two of them.

And that other pairing – the body and soul – the slumped, seemingly immobile body, and the thoughts and feelings which were swirling around like a swarm of bees.

She was not having an 'out of body experience'. She was, however, strangely detached.

Me, Ingrid, I'm really sorry, you'll probably think I'm just constructing a silly, tricksy narrative for the hell of it. This particular joke, however, I've been playing on you, people – writing about Digby and the Dean as if they were two separate people – was something which was inevitable. Because, until that moment in the tower, they really WERE two separate people. Probably had been since they/she were little. Being two people was what had kept her cool and balanced, what some people would call sane. For as long as she could remember, she had been the intensely emotional, inner, rather sad person longing to be loved; and the cerebral scholar who derived almost physical pleasure from the mere reading and writing of Greek characters. One of them was Nell, Dad's little pet, who wanted to be with Mum and Dad all the time, and who never, really, recovered from the ending of that Perfect Trinity of Love, and growing up, and going away to university. And the other – Digby – was never happier than when alone, thinking her often quite destructive thoughts. One was in love with God. The other did not believe in Him. One was happily at home in the 'grey Aristotelian city', and loved whatever home Mum had made for them in the bleak rectories of fogbound towns, or in the holiday cottage, 'Quam Dilecta', which they rented once a year in St David's. The other was almost a disembodied spirit, at one with Plato, happy when constructing dialogues – either Plato's or dialogues of her own making – in her disembodied, detached brain.

She says, that I, Ingrid Ashe, was the only one who had seen they were two separate people, and she had never seen it herself, not in that way. Everything I've written about them is true – about Digby being a non-believing classicist, and Eleanor being a

T.S. Eliot-reading, Chosen Frozen, Early Service believer; Digby fancying Barnaby in his cowboy boots, Eleanor wanting to go to concerts with Charlie Nicolson. They'd never allowed one another to admit, quite, that the other was . . . well, them. The real them, the whole them. They'd lived together all their lives, like twins who had never been properly introduced.

Longing to please Dad. Not realizing that Dad, with his gentle manners and quiet, shiny face, was actually making all kinds of demands on her, the only daughter, from an early age. With Mum, things had always been more straightforward. Good old Mum. But with Dad, if you wanted to be loved you had to join the Club. O Lord open thou our lips. Nothing opened his. He never spelt things out. But . . .

My God, am I CRAZY? I wanted to be a PRIEST, for God's sake!!!! When I'm like Euripides, I don't believe in the gods . . .

Digby and the Very Reverend Eleanor had gone by now. Together for the first time, in that tower, the New Woman came into being. Nellie. My Nellie? Oh, I so hope.

No, Nellie, it wasn't crazy, your wanting to be a priest like your dad, you weren't mad. You were responding to a real experience . . . There WAS something happening during those early Masses in fogbound Smethwick and Dudley, here we offer and present unto thee, O Lord, ourselves, our souls and bodies, to be a reasonable, holy and lively sacrifice unto thee . . . The sacrifice was a reasonable one. The 'something', the still small voice, had been heard by J.S. Bach, seen by Jan van Eyck, articulated by George Herbert and T.S. Eliot. Eliot the greatest poet of modern times – no? By miles and miles? These were more impressive witnesses than nice, genial but silly old David Hume and Freddie Hot Ayer. In the tower, their positions had been reversed. It was DIGBY telling the Dean that, whatever her doubts NOW, here, at the tower of her death, she would still rather belong to the blessed company of all faithful people; if she had to be in a gang, she would rather be in the Eliot-Herbert-Rose-Macaulay-John-Keble gang than in with the easy vacuities of materialism.

It was Nellie who said to Digby, though, (and they really liked one another! Why hadn't they dared to speak before now?)

—But it was all so bloody SILLY, so unreal, so out of kilter with the way everyone else was thinking. Was it surprising that only six people max ever came to those early Masses of Dad's?

—Come, now, Nellie – remember Bishop Gore, one of Dad's heroes – 'The majority are always wrong.' I love that about Dad and Uncle Lesley. Two Against the World.

She thought, Here I am in this tower, which is swaying about and about to fall down, and I'm remembering Dad's favourite quotations. 'Proud, pompous and prelatical' . . . 'The majority are always wrong' . . . 'I know I shall die a penitent Catholic but an impenitent Liberal' . . . 'My medieval knees lack health until they bend'. He repeated them so often that she had forgotten that most of them *were* quotations. They were 'Dad's sayings'. *Le vent se lève, il faut tenter de vivre.* That was another of them. And just for once, one of Dad's sayings, rather than provoking the light laugh, had an overwhelming effect. Too bloody right, *il faut tenter de vivre.* That's what you thought, Nellie, you told me.

I am going to get out of here alive, I am going to get out of here . . . ALIVE . . . Oh, my dear.

Deirdre Hadley, with brown breadsticks for arms, jutting from a sleeveless pale green jumpsuit, her brown, bird feet enclosed in ancient espadrilles, her blonde-grey hair tied back with a bandana, specs on her little nose, blue eyes bright and concentrated on her laptop, was in a train bound for Carmichael. It was a five hour journey, which she made once a week, when Parliament was sitting. She refused to fly, which took the inside of an hour. She invariably used the journey for work. Our national Parliament was about to close for its summer recess, and this would have been one of her last visits to the capital for a couple of months.

As well as many letters and emails relating to constituency business, Deidre was preparing for a summer conference, to be held here in Aberdeen, about the Man Drought. Her own paper to the conference was entitled *Does It Matter?*

In Deirdre's lifetime, the imbalance between the sexes had become more marked. Although overall, it was only something approaching forty-seven per cent versus fifty-three per cent, this was to take the divide between all male human beings and all females. In the employable educated classes, that is, among graduates between the ages of twenty-five and sixty, the difference was much greater, with only forty per cent males to sixty per cent females.

There were a number of implications which would be explored, she hoped, by the conference. One was employment. The numbers of those studying traditionally 'male' areas of expertise, such as engineering, architecture, experimental science, remained overwhelmingly male. There was already a shortage of Huia engineers, and research scientists necessitating the import of experts from overseas. Such figures usually, though not always, came with their partners or wives in tow, to ready-made jobs in Carmichael, Aberdeen or Derby, our three main cities. This increased the numbers of middle-class females who could be described as surplus to requirements.

Deirdre did not herself feel surplus to requirements in any respect other than the emotional one. Her work upset her, because for so much of the time, she was unearthing scandals or abuses which politicians, businesspeople, speculators, builders and investors were doing their best to suppress. She had made many enemies, and for much of the time, she was frightened. Nevertheless, she had no doubt that her work was worthwhile. And her professional success could not but satisfy her. She had moved from being a teacher who dreaded going to school every day, to being a public servant with a mission: to open the eyes of her fellow Huias to the environmental and other catastrophes which awaited them if they did not heed the warnings of conservationists such as herself.

This did not stop her feeling an emotional emptiness which was all but unendurable. She still saw Barnaby from time to time. They were meant to have become 'friends' in a very 'civilized' way, and he sometimes, for example – despite Bar's attempts to make him ban Deirdre from his life altogether – brought Stig for tea. Stig enjoyed Deirdre's company. He liked George Eliot, who was surprisingly tolerant (by her own exacting standards) of Stig. Quite often, the three of them bathed naked in the Windrush, from the jetty at the end of her very long thin garden. She still could not tell whether it was better to continue to see Barnaby on some terms or other, or whether she would actually find it easier not seeing him at all.

When he was leaving, he was sometimes clumsy enough to hold her spindly arm, and even to stroke it, as he used to in the old days, and to ask,

—All right, hun?

How was she meant to reply? Sometimes, she wanted to say,

—I am NOT all right. I think about you with yearning every hour of every day.

Aftershocks

This would only have made him run away from her. It would also have been so much an understatement as to be untrue. She yearned for him, not every day, but every second, all the time. His moving out of her house, shortly after Stig was born, had caused her pain of which she did not believe herself capable. It was far more upsetting than when her father, or various much-loved pets, had died. And infinitely more upsetting than the ending of any previous affair.

Until Bar had begun to prove so unreasonable, Deirdre had mapped out a strategy. She was prepared to share Barnaby. She was prepared to give him infinite licence to love other women, to sleep with them, even to bring them to live in her house in Harrow if this was what he needed to do. She was completely willing to help bring up Stig. She simply could not bear to lose him. He was the air she breathed, the life she lived.

When he had first come to be her lodger, she had noticed within herself a change which was something quite unlike any previous 'falling in love'. Not only was the sexual desire enormously stronger, but she felt herself surrendering emotionally, very very rapidly. Within days of his having moved in. She kept these feelings hidden for well over a year, and only slipped into his bedroom occasionally, and shared his bed, when he had made it clear that he was between girlfriends and was feeling lonely. The rapture they had enjoyed for two or three years had been something completely extraordinary. Perhaps such feelings cannot be expected to last, though she saw no reason why, in their case, they should not have lasted until one of them died. When he walked away from this rapture (and she knew that he had felt it too) she had felt baffled as well as hurt.

In some ways, she recognized this, it had helped her in her campaigning work, for she no longer had a private life or a home life worthy of the name (though she tried to make a home for George Eliot and to keep her company as well as she could, given her peripatetic existence).

For the forthcoming conference on the Man Drought, Deirdre knew that she could not address the central question of her life – whether, if the trend continued, and became more extreme, Huia women should consider polygamy as an option. She would love to have found a woman, preferably a young woman, to write a paper advocating this measure. She did not dare to write such a thesis herself. She knew it would be taken up and mocked by her political opponents, and she also knew that it was not a matter about which she could be balanced or rational.

So, she sat there in the train. Our lovely Island landscape slipped by. The train snaked northwards, out of our bay, and up through the mountain passes north of Aberdeen. It was a great Victorian engineering feat, building the Campbell-Bannerman Tunnel, which penetrates the entire range of the Hai-ruhri. When they burst through the eight-mile tunnel of darkness, the train whooshed out again into the vivid emerald of Chatsworth County. To the west of the train, on the gentle slopes of the Chilterns, the vineyards may be seen, acre upon acre of grapes. A knowing eye – for though an extremely moderate drinker, Deirdre had a discerning palate and knew a lot about wine – made out the ripening Pinot Noir. A little later, the landscape flattened a little. Huge sheep farms could be seen. Despite the high temperatures, everything was a vivid green.

And then, just as for a few illusory moments the beauty of the scene had soothed her everlasting sorrow, one of the young men in the carriage, who was looking at his phone screamed out,

—Jesus Christ, it's another one – it's a 6 this time.

Aftershocks

Everyone instantly knew what he meant. The train was pretty full – of Carmichael people going back, of Aberdeen people with business in the capital. A significant number felt, instantaneously, as Deirdre did, that they must return to Aberdeen at once.

She was already dialling Barnaby's number. She prayed the prayer so many of us were praying at that moment into phones which wouldn't fucking work – though we were making the prayers to hundreds of thousands of different people – Oh, be alive, beloved, be alive. Nearly half a million of us granted that prayer for one another, but about two hundred and fifty couldn't.

Cavan Cliffe always wound down after *Island Breakfast* with a paper cup of strong black coffee, taken whenever possible in the car park outside the Island Broadcasting Corporation building. This was to allow her to smoke a much-needed cig. Thus refreshed, she would go back upstairs, two storeys, so she took the lift when possible. At eleven, there was a meeting with her producer. They would discuss how the morning's programme had gone; pick up on any 'matters arising'; decide a rough outline of the programme for the following morning. This was always provisional because, as Gill Frang (the producer) liked to end every such discussion, in her bright, much-inflected voice – *You nee-ver know!*

Well, that morning, she never spoke a truer word.

Cavan occasionally glanced at her watch during that particular meeting, because it was going on longer than usual. Rex Tone's office had sent a complaint almost before they came off air, saying that *Island Breakfast*, and the IBC generally, were filled with Green propagandists, that Deirdre had been given more air-time than him, that she was always on the radio, people were sick to death of being told negative, doom-laden predictions, when Rex and his team had our future and our safety sorted.

Obviously, this was all bullshit, but the Director of the IBC had come down to the office to talk to Cavan and Gill about this. Clearly, they needed to decide on a strategy. There were elections coming up. Deirdre was an extremely popular and conscientious MP, but there were other parties, and Rex was the Mayor of Aberdeen. He had his point of view, and, amazingly, he had his supporters. Our other MP, Tam Dawkins, was Labour and in many respects she was much closer to Rex than she was to Deirdre. Everyone agreed that Deirdre was an 'extremist' who went too far. And of course, in spite of the fact that there had been a severe quake only six months before, everyone hoped that this would be a one-off, never to be repeated.

So all these things were discussed, and for that reason, Cavan was delayed. Normally, she would have been out of the IBC building by noon and rowing back home down the Windrush. On this occasion, though, she was there, two storeys up, when the Quake struck.

The third or fourth time she looked at her watch, Gill Frang had said,

—Cavan, we'll be through this soon, I promise – would you like to go outside for a puff?

And Cavan had laughed and said she'd be OK. Then, she'd changed her mind, and said,

—Actually, I would like a break.

They were in an upstairs meeting room – simply furnished, it had a long Scandinavian-style table, round which were ten office chairs. There was a jug of water with some glasses on the table. On the walls were huge blown-up photographs of Island scenery – the Southern Alps, the Bay of Promise, Holy Trinity Cathedral in glorious sunshine with summer sun blazing down upon its spire.

Just as she was saying, 'Actually', the plate glass of the window, which overlooked the car park and, beyond, Banks University's Faculty of Law, shattered with what seemed like a bomb explosion. The block-mounted photographs of beauty spots were hurled off the wall. The picture of the Cathedral came at the Director's head as an offensive weapon. The surgeon who treated him afterwards said it was as if a vindictive maniac had tried to beat him to death with a plank of wood. If they'd been able to look out of the window at that moment, they'd have seen the whole of that part of town coming down – the Law Faculty buildings crumbling like sandcastles before the waves, the car park breaking up into liquefaction, the houses and shops in Howley Street and Temple Street disappearing in clouds of their own rubble.

But they did not see this. That was because the floor beneath them and the ceiling above them both seemed to collapse at the same time.

I was in the garden when it happened, lying in a hammock, reading *King Lear*. I was really looking forward to the next seminar, which was to be on Shakespeare, and hearing Digby and Barnaby debate whether *Lear* was a tragedy in the sense we had been discussing, when we were talking about the Greeks, say. Now I'd grasped the concept, which Digby and Barnaby seemed agreed upon – that the essence of tragedy is the contingency of value – I felt I could understand *Lear* in a new way. Gloucester, for all his moments of insight ('I stumbled when I saw'), remains trapped in the idea that the gods are moral, and that humanity is sinfully paying for its sins when bad things happen. Edgar clings to this, at the end, with his –

A. N. Wilson

The gods are just, and of our pleasant vices
Make instruments to plague us.

But we know, the audience knows, this is bullshit, crap. *Howl, howl, howl* – that is the last word, really, corresponding to the *Io, moi, moi* and the *ee ee* of the chorus in *Trojan Women*. Hecuba's *aiai* . . . Undiluted human pain . . . It was what you saw every night on the news in some horrible scene: a bombed-out city in the Middle East, where the population had been gassed, arbitrarily shot, their houses destroyed, their children eviscerated . . . An African plain, where starving families dragged their stick bodies through the dust in search of water . . . A screaming crowd, anywhere in the world, where terrorists had, with the tug of one cord in a grenade, destroyed the happiness of hundreds of human beings, taken away daughters, lovers, parents . . . This was reality. *Nature's above art in that respect . . . Thou art the thing itself.* Why did we try to kid ourselves? *Every consolation is fake* – an Iris Murdoch saying that Digby liked quoting. I suppose I can stop saying 'Digby' and 'Eleanor' now, and settle for 'Nellie'. (How much I'd have liked to listen to Nellie's talk with Iris Murdoch! We so love reading her books together.) Our moments of pleasure, in food, in sex, in art, were merely distractions from the reality we all knew to be there – the raw suffering, which was not simply to be seen every day in the TV news, it was waiting for us. We all knew that. The cancer diagnosis. The telephone call from the police, to say that they were afraid to say that . . . The arbitrary removal of our capacity to be happy, or at peace.

I was yet to know the slightly different way in which you read it, Nellie – but that lies in the future. You may not believe it, reader, but, as I lay in that hammock, I had got to *Rumble thy bellyful! Spit, fire! Spout, rain!* . . . And in that precise moment, the hammock gave an almighty jerk, and I was swung to and fro between the apple trees. I watched our solitary chimney come down, and the house shook, and immediately became a Leaning Tower of Harrow, all wonky and on one side. The neighbours' house, the Whitworths', wobbled even more, their windows smashed, and the extension they had built on the side, which included a conservatory, collapsed instantly. Over garden walls, I could hear screams, invective being shouted – FUCKING HELL! and the like.

King Lear had flown out of my hand, and its contents had flown out of my head. Having written that sentence, I want to rewrite it as '*King Lear* had flown out of my hand, and I had flown into its waves and storms, its world of absolute pain'. I immediately reached into the pocket of my shorts and rang Mum. No signal. It's a sign of how immature I was/am, perhaps, but at twenty-seven, I was ringing to tell Mum the Quake had happened, ringing to tell her the chimney had fallen down, ringing for her to *come home*. I did not explicitly want her to come home and look after me, but that was what instinct clawed for, on the front of that mobile phone. I needed Mum, and it was only a few seconds later that I began to realize – if she's not answering the phone, and if she's not home yet, that means she's in the middle of town . . .

I acted impulsively. As I stood on the lawn, I fell over, because it was shaking, but I got up again and went to the garden shed. Its door had been ripped off, but the bike, together with the garden tools and the lawn-mower, was still inside. Some of you, if you'd seen the inside of that shed, would think the Quake had made a real mess of things in there, but that wasn't the Quake, that was me and Mum, who aren't the sort of people who arrange all the garden forks and rakes and hoes in neat little rows and all the flower pots in stacks as though we were the Flopsy Bunnies or someone. We tend to make a chaos of pots, deckchairs, old oil cans, trugs, boxes of lawnseed, plastic bottles of fertiliser which we would keep hidden when Deirdre comes round for a cup of mint tea, etc. That's the way we are. Were.

I hauled the bike out of the shed. Don't know if I picked up its front wheel and gave it two hefty bumps up and down – or why I did this – or whether it was the Quake just shaking us up, me and the bike. But on I got and pedalled off towards town. Not ideal cycling conditions, but I was not thinking.

I'll never forget that ride, and nor will I ever know how I managed to do it without being killed. The road into town which would normally, at lunchtime, be busy but full of motion was solid with cars, both ways. Adding to the surreality of it all, I wobbled past two bewildered zebras. *What were THEY doing in a traffic jam?* As many people were trying to get out of town as in. So many that they'd caused a jam, and real anger and panic were on display, with people standing beside their swelteringly hot cars, yelling abuse at the vehicles in front of them, shouting with real hatred at people they did not know, and who – they could see – were simply stuck in the traffic, like themselves.

Why can't you get a move on, you stupid fucking CUNTS?

Some of the time, I was in the cycle-paths which, thanks to Deirdre, had now been installed on all our major highways. Some of the time, however, these paths no longer existed, and great bogs of bubbling liquefaction had taken the place of the road surface.

DON'T TRY RIDING INTO THE CITY, LADY was among the more polite bits of advice which got shouted at me. YOU FUCKING MAD? CAN'T YOU SEE WHAT'S FUCKING HAPPENING IN THERE? was the more usual sort of question, but I was not really hearing, or only hearing with half an ear and Mum, Mum, MUM was all I was thinking. Normally, cycling into town from Harrow takes ten minutes, quarter of an hour if you get into a real snarl-up of buses and the like. It's an old bike – an ancient Pashley which Mum bought me second-hand when I went to drama school in Carmichael. Although they're upright bikes which look like what George Orwell must have had in mind when he talked about old maids biking to Holy Communion through the mists of the autumn whatsitsname, or whatever it was he said, they can get up quite a speed, those Pashleys; they are all hand-made, in England, and the few gears can easily match the multi-geared mountain bike if you know how to handle them. This was behaving like a bucking bronco, thanks to the Quake, but like a well-trained rodeo rider I stayed in the saddle.

It was boilingly hot, but I did not think about that. I'd taken off my bandana, my hair and brow were sweaty, and I'd tied the spotted handkerchief round my nose and mouth, because the heat and dust were now overwhelming. By the time I'd reached what would have been Gladstone Park, it did not really exist. It was like you imagine a battlefield, like Stendhal's description of Waterloo, when Fabrice just staggers about in the fog, unable to see a thing. In the midst of the cloud, there was just pure, raw, naked suffering – screams, heat, more screams, people calling out names, and making the equivalent of the *moi moi, ee ee* or *aiai* of tragic utterance. Through these sounds, there was also a roar – or so I remember – whether the roar of machinery (diggers, already trying to clear rubble and rescue survivors) or aftershocks, which were frequent and loud, I couldn't say. I wasn't carefully taking down every impression and putting it in a notebook. I was just trying very very hard to concentrate on where the fuck I was. By now, if I was cycling round the planted roundabout on the edge of Gladstone Park, with its floral clock and the name ABERDEEN picked out in lobelias and aubretia and zinnias, I'd look left and see old George V on his plinth, turn right into Prince of Wales Parade, whiz down until I hit Davidson Street, do a right at Gloucester, cross Oriel Street, with Borough Market on my right, and then be in shouting distance of the IBC building.

—YOU CAN'T GO DOWN THERE, LADY, IT'S NOT SAFE.

Some policeman was bellowing this through a megaphone at me, and he continued to bellow,

—THIS IS AN OFFICIAL ANNOUNCEMENT. YOU ARE ALL ADVISED TO LEAVE THE CITY. YOU ARE ALL ADVISED TO LEAVE THE CITY. THE EXITS ARE VERY CONGESTED AT THE MOMENT BUT IF YOU LEAVE SOUTH BY LEICES-TER SQUARE THERE ARE FREE LANES OPEN ON THE HIGHWAY. REPEAT YOU ARE ALL ADVISED TO LEAVE THE . . .

The clouds of dust were so thick that they could not see you if you crossed the makeshift barriers which had been erected. For a moment, I got off the bike and tried to work out where I was. You literally couldn't tell any more. All the familiar buildings had come down – the concert hall, the Dyce Gallery – where I began this story – Rex Tone's Convention Centre – they had all gone. At one point, I found myself near the Cathedral, so I knew I was now more or less in the centre of the city, and only a third of a mile from the IBC building and Mum.

The dust cleared enough for me to stare in momentary wonder at what had been the Cathedral. The spire was down. The tower was a stump. Obviously, I did not know then that you'd been in the tower, Nellie. But although my stomach was wrenched by the sight of the ravaged Cathedral, and I thought of you – course I did, when at this point of my life, did I NOT think of you? – I was confused. Confused but focused on my chief consideration, which was to find Mum.

I don't know how I blundered on through dust, noise and heat. I made many mistakes, but eventually, something about the line of trees which I had now approached, and the proximity of the river, made me realize that I was opposite the IBC building. I paused. My bandana was once again tied round my mouth and nose. I could see the river water, which was choppy like an ocean. Never normally like that. And then I saw it, tied to its mooring with the skill of the sea-guide who had won her special guides' badge for knotting: the wooden skiff with my name painted round the prow; *Little Ingrid*.

That was when tears and panic took over, and my own versions of *aiai, ee ee* came forth from my lips. I don't know what I was shouting, but it was mainly MUM, MUM MUM!

I must've left the river behind me then, because someone had got me quite tightly by the arm and was saying,

—You can't go in there You can't go any further.

It was a man in uniform, and I was, like, screaming, I guess, and he was calming me down, trying to.

Eventually, I got my voice, and I said the three fateful syllables,

—IBC?

—Yeah, that's the IBC building. I'm sorry, lady, but you aren't helping, you can't go—

—My Mum, my MUM, my MUM!

I stood and watched. There was this heap of smouldering rubble. On the other side of what had been the square, there were fire engines hosing the half of the Law Faculty building which was still standing, and which had burst into flames. In the ruins of what I now realized was the IBC building where Mum worked, trucks and diggers were already moving huge slabs of concrete and wood, and already a few bodies were being carried out.

—Your mum's in there?

I must have indicated to the man in uniform – policeman or paramedic I did not know by then – that this was the case.

—It doesn't look good, he said. I'm sorry, lady.

She was in her bedroom, her childish bedroom, in one of those fog-bound West Midland towns. Had Dad just finished reading George MacDonald, as he so often did, one of those strange sequences where you can't tell whether someone is dreaming, or whether the world is being changed, and you've stepped into a new place, which both is, and is not, your bedroom? Curdie blinks . . . Is that a beautiful lady or just a pile of straw and sacking? Is it a green carpet, or a meadow, running with streams of living water?

No, it was Smethwick, or Dudley. That was where it seemed to be, but, rather as in that confused state of mind, when we wake in a strange bed, perhaps in a hotel, and are not sure where we are, or as in those ever-vivid George MacDonald moments. Curtains flapped out of existence. The sad West Midland fogs were swallowed in dust and heat. She could see the large yellow helmet at the window, and something resembling an axe smashing the coat of arms of Bishop Gladstone. Her English ears heard a Huia voice calling *Ilinor! Ilinor!* Only it wasn't Mum's voice, it was a man-Huia. *Don't speak to strangers, Nillie. Promise me that, you must NIVER speak with strangers.* And she could hear the voice, a man's voice – *Ilinor? Nillie? . . . Are you all right, Nillie* – on holiday in Wales when she was nine. She had wandered from Mum and Dad, slithered down some tufts of thick, springy grass and found a spot, just beneath the clifftop, where golden rod and field scabious grew, and she had sat and sat there, with her apple and *Oliver Twist*, with the great ocean blue beneath her – Nellie! Nellie! Mum's anxious Huia voice which made her name sound like Nillie – and then Dad – and she had heard the fear in their voices, before she had replied – *I'm here* . . . But now it was a man calling – *Eleanor, Eleanor!* She recognized his invisible, sinister, alluring face. Oh, I know you – you're a Stranger. You are Death. I can't speak to you. I can't speak to strangers. Break into a run. Just run for it. Try screaming, even though no sound comes to your mouth. – *You just stay nice and calm, Eleanor, we're going to get you out of there*, and she had wanted to say, *you can't come in, it's not safe*, and it was as if she was watching it all happening to somebody else – she could not speak, and when she tried to move she did not know if it was the room moving, her moving, the whole tower moving – *I think she's alive, just dazed*, the voice was saying and she was thinking, I'm safe here on my clifftop, don't take me back to the world, I'm ready to go, I am floating. O, I am so tired, my lover. Take me, Death, take me. Come away, come away, Death, and in sad cypress let me be laid, Fly away, fly away, *I've got you, now Eleanor, just relax*, is that the Angel in a yellow helmet or the firefighter not a friend not a friend greet my poor corpse, oh Nilly, you little silly, as Mum hugged her, coming through the gorse and the bracken at the top of the cliff and finding Mum there – We thought we'd lost you! Oh, Nilly, we thought we'd lost you – but it's all right now, Mum, I'm here, I'm here – Mum is there now, and she is coming, Eleanor is leaving behind the body in the fireman-angel's arms, and moving towards Mum. Oh, it will be so easy, so gentle, to die . . . In the bright yellow light beyond her eyes, she can see her mother's smooth, smiling face. What about Dad? I can't leave him – He'll be OK, we'll soon see him, Our Nill, we'll see him . . . He'll follow us, Nilly, he'll soon be on his way . . . Part of his host hath crossed the flood and part is crossing now . . . Oh, Mum, I've missed you so, so much, here all is love, the fire and the rose are one, *ma già volgeva il mio disiro e il velle, sì come rota ch'egualmente è mossa* . . . *Ialemoi tous thanatos apueis* . . . she had just been reading that line before the first thud of the Quake, how did she render it? It is the Dead you cry to in your lament! . . . that our sinful bodies may be made clean by his body . . . Barnaby? Is that you making love to me? Barnaby Farrell is the last person on earth I have kissed as a lover, and I do not love . . . no, Doug, I don't want that, no – I want to make LOVE, not be slobbered over by you, Doug, I want to MAKE LOVE, not just HAVE SEX, what a phrase, and our souls washed through his most precious . . . O mistress mine, where are you roaming . . . In the yellow dusty light, through the choking dust and heat, Mum's arm is stretched out, not Mum's arm – *That's right, Eleanor, just hold on, hold on, darling.* No! It is not Mum's arm, tugging her towards Death, it is another arm, a young, smooth arm, drawing her towards life and love. Her cheek is held against the hot, dusty, shiny yellow of the fireman's protective gilet, but it is not his arm that holds her, O stay and hear your true love's coming, who is this that holds her? Who? Who? The long, bare girl's arm which reaches out to her, follow it with your eye, Nellie, follow the long white fingers which stroke you, up to the bare elbow, the round white shoulder on which her thick springy mouse-blonde hair cascades, look up into her brown eyes, lover, look at her, look at Ingrid, live for her, my darling.

Rats ran. I'd never been aware of lots of rats in our neighbourhood, but evidently they were everywhere, all over the city. Our Harrow neighbours told me they were scurrying in crowds, across what remained of their floors. You'd go out on the lawn, and feel their fur and their cold tails slithering past your ankles.

George Eliot watched them from her cage. She was beside herself with terror, at all the movement and shaking. The cage had fallen over on its side, and she alternated. Sometimes, in impotent anger, she flapped her wings to be let out, and sometimes, she was just lying on her side.

She heard voices.

—Jeez, Norm, there's a fucking bird.

—Take it.

As darkness fell, the city was still reverberating, quivering. There were several aftershocks that day. They continued for months. Not every day. But you would suddenly feel the ground beneath you shudder. You'd be in a room and the picture would fall off the wall. You'd be trying to get on your bike, and you'd think – hey, I'm not drunk, but I feel, dizzy, sort of, and you'd fall over. And that was because the ground beneath you, and the bike, had given a little jump. Since the first big Quake to date, there have been over *seven thousand* aftershocks. So that first day, you wondered, will the earth ever stop moving?

Ever been seasick? When the heaving of the waves just won't stop, and you've thrown up everything inside you and still your body heaves and retches, and the cruel movement of the sea just won't STOP and you think you are going MAD? Maybe you haven't. People don't have that sort of seasickness nowadays unless they are sportswomen/men yachting. Read Darwin's *Voyage of the Beagle*. He's good on the subject. He was sick on a regular basis for three years. In his case, puking became the habit of a lifetime.

It was a bit like that with the Quake. Every time there was a tremor, and aftershock, you thought – Christ, this is another of the fuckers. If you were in a building, you wanted to get out pdq, if you were outside you looked about anxiously thinking – will that car over there fly into the air and land on my head? Will that tree suddenly uproot itself and land on me? It's just so, SO weird. All the expressions you used to use – safe as houses, firm as a rock, with your feet on the ground . . . They all become jokes. Houses are the least safe things you ever saw. Rocks are like fireworks. The last place you'd put your feet is on the ground, you'd rather put your feet on the fire.

But that first night, we had not got into the aftershocks routine, so . . . Every little aftershock was a torture. I can't write about all the destruction and loss of that day. Not at the moment. I just can't go on with describing myself, standing there, looking at the rubble of the wrecked IBC building, and knowing that Mum was underneath the rubble. I just can't write it. Course, I'll tell you what's happened to everyone in our story, but not at the moment. Just for now, it is so upsetting, just thinking about it, that I'm going to have to take a break, as I remember the shadows falling on our city. In fact, I do not even remember anything about the few hours after that man in uniform (police? paramedic?) took my arm and told me there was nothing I could do, while I watched through the clouds of dust, as they took bodies out of what had been the IBC building. One of which was Mum.

Later, later that day, afternoon, evening, whatever, I was in shock. And I was somewhere in a hospital corridor, shivering, and drinking sweet tea. But I do remember, before They – who were they? Some very kind people – took me to the hospital, I remember one of the truly weirdest things about that day. We were somehow all being led away from the desolation which was the IBC building, back through Howley Street and across what remained of Argyle Square. The police had cleared the whole square. Our ruined Cathedral loomed over the scene, a vast, holed ship about to go under cruel waters.

And as we crossed the square, in the gloaming, with the light falling, and the dust still filling our lungs, and the ground shaking every few minutes, we heard this deep baritone voice, singing through the shadows.

> *Through many dangers, toils and snares*
> *We have already come.*

> *'Twas grace that brought us safe thus far*
> *And grace will lead us home.*

As night fell, the town became completely dark. Some electric appliances, funnily enough, seemed to work, even after the Quake, but the street lamps went out. I think I spent that night in the hospital, so I'll finish this dreadful day with what I've pieced together from the accounts of others.

—What would we want with a fucking bird?

—Take it. Yer never know. The cage'd fetch something.

The two men, one of whom was evidently Norm, were standing with electric pocket flashlights in what remained of Deirdre Hadley's kitchen. 'Evidently Norm' because George Eliot was able to tell Deirdre, and later the police, that his friend had kept saying, *Jeez, Norm.*

George Eliot felt them picking up her cage and setting it upright.

For this she was grateful. She stared at the unfamiliar faces which had pressed themselves against the wire meshing.

—It's a parrot, I'd reckon.

—Course it's a fucking parrot.

—Could be a budgie.

—Christ, you're stupid. Don't open the fucking cage or we'd never get the fucking bird . . .

But there was no need to finish this sentence, because the advice went unheeded, and George Eliot was not one to hang about. She gave a fierce peck to the tobacco-sticky thumb which was resting on the latch of the cage, heard the cry of pain with some satisfaction, and broke free.

—Jeez, Norm, don't blame me.

—Course I bleeding blame you, I told you not to open the fucking cage.

—Let's take the cage.

—Put it on the cart.

They piled the parrot cage on top of next door's lawn-mower, and the small heap of laptops and televisions which were assembled on the large barrow, and moved off into the dark. The random collections continued until the sad dawning of the next day. All through the dark hours, as people were gathered into temporary rescue centres, huddled in church halls and gyms and garages, comforting one another as best they could through each aftershock, their shaken, wrecked homes were being plundered. Scarcely a shop went unrobbed. The scavengers were picking them over even as the earth rumbled and masonry fell. Into vans which could scarcely negotiate the potholes and fissures and swamps of liquefaction which had once been roads, wobbled and lurched from shop to shop, weighed down with loot – washing machines, televisions, computers, clothes, three-piece suites, toys were indiscriminately seized. Most of them were by now broken, or so filthy as to be unsaleable, but it did not stop the greedy hands which reached out for them.

Deirdre knew it was her duty, as one of our MPs, to be in one of the rescue centres. She had got the first train back as far as the small town of Weston, twenty miles north of Aberdeen. From there, it had been quite a journey, not least because the police were urging everyone to leave our city, and there were barriers closing the highway. She'd paid a Tangata cabbie called Elizabeth to defy the police, and somehow or other they'd got through.

The actual drive, until they came to the outskirts of Aberdeen, was relatively easy, except where the road had been torn open by the Quake, and there were large squelchy patches, hundreds of yards across, of liquefaction. The Exodus was crawling the other way, cars crowded with people, with belongings dangling from their roofs – bikes, baby-buggies, one had a harpsichord strapped to the roof, and reminded Deirdre of the moment in Pepys, during the Great Fire of London, when he watched his neighbours carrying spinets out of their houses.

Elizabeth, who was a fearless driver, negotiated the darkness, the potholes, the liquefaction and the fear and they somehow were led, by the wings of the angels, to Harrow, and the cavernous church hall of St Thomas of Canterbury. It was late when they got there. Some of the families were already hunkered down in sleeping bags. Elizabeth ate a well-deserved lamb burger washed down with tea. How many gallons of tea we Aberdonians all drank that night! Deirdre set to work at once, helping to sort out the blankets, clothes, shopping bags full of tinned food, which had spontaneously been assembled. By some wonderful chance, while she was handing out trays of tea in one such meeting place, her phone rang, and it was Barnaby.

—You OK? was his voice.

—Much better now you've rung. Stig?

—I thought I'd lost him. He went on an outing to the zoo.

Barnaby's voice was trembling. Now he was openly weeping.

—Oh, Deirdre, the cages were blown sky high, the animals got loose. They found Stig face to face with a crocodile . . .

—But he's all right?

—The crocodile took one look at Stig's Buddy and ran.

There was a moment of laughter.

—Who was the Buddy?

—He says, Dad, Ella's really scary. Even the croc was scared, Dad . . . Oh, Deirdre, if he'd stayed at school. You heard . . .

—What?

—The new block of classrooms in Opportunity One collapsed. About ten kids were killed.

—Oh, Barnaby, oh my dear.

Down their phones they wept together. We were all having conversations like this with one another over the next few days. They got Mum out of the rubble in the IBC building after she'd been under there ten hours. It was dark, and they did it under arc-lights. Gill Frang, her producer, was dead. Gill was alive when they got her out of the rubble, but she died in hospital. When Mum came to, she told me she'd gone out into the corridor, because she needed to smoke, and was making her way down the passage when the Quake struck. She happened to be standing in a doorway and although she was buried in rubble, the lintel stopped the heaviest masonry from falling on her head.

Of the other figures in our story, not all were so lucky. Charlie Nicolson and his wife survived. Ella, who had saved Stig from the crocodile, and become the heroine of the Zoo Outing, was alive.

Aftershocks

Her brother Josh had been in the cricket pavilion at St Augustine's when it collapsed on top of him. He was dead. Many of the two hundred and fifty-three dead in Aberdeen were children.

The Dean of our Cathedral was carried from the tower by a fire-man and got away with just a broken arm. From now on, Digby, the sceptical classical scholar, and the Very Reverend Eleanor Bartlett were at one. Their strange divided life was at an end. As a united being, they felt strong to face life's paradoxes. This became apparent to the people of Aberdeen ten days after the Quake. Services in the wrecked Cathedral were impossible, but ten days after the Quake struck, it was announced that the choir and congregation would assemble to sing Merbecke's setting of the Mass in Argyle Square. With her arm in a plastic casing, and held up by a sling around her amiced neck, a new Nellie spoke to us.

Realizing that the service would be televised, and that it would attract a huge crowd, Bishop Dionne had telephoned Nellie imme-diately to tell her that she would preach at the service herself. The Dean had been most uncharacteristically emphatic. It was very kind of Dionne to suggest it, but she, the Dean, had been scheduled to preach that Sunday. She was the Dean of the wrecked Cathedral. She would speak as scheduled.

—What did the Pontiff make of that? asked the Skyped dis-torted face of her dad.

Christianity came into being because a city was reduced to rubble. In AD 70, the Roman armies of the Emperor Titus reduced Jerusalem to ruins. The immense temple, built by Herod, was levelled to the ground. The population was massacred or driven into the hills, and hardly a stone of the place was left standing on another. Josephus tells us the story in horrifying, graphic detail – the absolute devastation and loss visited on families, the loss of life for which there could be no consolations.

We tend to think that the stories concerning Jesus, which were written down in the Gospels, must have grown up during his lifetime, or immediately afterwards. This is not necessarily the case. All the four Gospels mention the destruction of Jerusalem, the utter ruin of the city. So we know they were written after the Romans wrecked the place. And not just the place – they destroyed the Temple, which was the centre of the Jewish religion. So in some senses, the Christians, who had all started out as Jews who worshipped in the Temple, were encouraged to believe that in Jesus, a new religion had begun. A complete break with the past had occurred. Perhaps that's why, when Jesus died, there was an earthquake. Or so it says in Matthew's Gospel. 'Jesus, when he had cried again with a loud voice, yielded up the ghost. And behold, the veil of the temple was rent in twain from the top to the bottom; and the earth did quake, and the rocks rent; And the graves were opened; and many bodies of the saints which slept arose, And came out of the graves after his resurrection, and went into the holy city, and appeared unto many.'

The other Gospels do not tell us anything about this story. So, why does Matthew tell us it happened? One reason could be that some of the Jews, filled with Messianic hopes, believed that when the Redeemer of Israel came, the graves would open and there would be a general resurrection. Jesus is not the only one in Matthew to be raised up. Many other good Jews are raised too, to show the readers of the Gospel that the Messianic Age has truly begun.

Well, Matthew's account was written fifty years or so after the events it is describing, so what are we to make of this scene painted by Stanley Spencer, of people climbing out of their graves? To tell you the truth, I do not know. And were they supposed to live forever, or did they have to die all over again one day? Matthew hasn't, apparently, really thought about that.

Here, however, are a few thoughts. Jesus on the Cross, in his moment of total desolation, cries out from the Psalms – 'Eli, Eli, lama sabachthani? My God, my God, why hast thou forsaken me?' It is the cry of religious humanity, time out of mind, when calamity strikes. It is the cry of the women of Troy in Euripides' great tragedy. It is our cry now, as we assemble in our ruined city. Why did my child, my lover, my father, have to die in this pointless way? Where is God when you need Him?

I don't know what Matthew meant by his Gospel, I'll be honest with you. But this is what I extract from this passage now, as we stand in the ruins of Aberdeen, as we remember our dead, as we look at our Cathedral, our art gallery, so many of the familiar city landmarks in ruins.

Wounded humanity, innocent humanity, has always looked to Heaven for justice, for explanations, for consolations – for consolations which are not there. They have hoped that a religious explanation of the world will somehow make the pain and unfairness of things easier to bear. And this illusion actually makes the pain worse. A complete atheist could not EXPECT blind Nature to be fair or kind or loving. We know from a purely material point of view how and why earthquakes happen, and we do not think they happen because God has forgotten to be kind, or because God is a secret sadist. Things just happen. For geological, scientific reasons. Our city was not destroyed by God or the gods, it was destroyed by geology, blind Nature.

Jesus cries out to a God who has forsaken him, and you could say that the human being closest to God in the world at this point in history here takes leave of God. The holiest prophet takes leave of *religion. The veil of the Temple is torn down. 'That vast moth-eaten musical brocade' – religion – is demolished in the earthquake at the end of Matthew's Gospel, just as, in real life, the Temple and all the rituals of Jewish worship had been expunged by the Roman Army which levelled the city to the ground in* AD *70, a decade or so before Matthew wrote.*

So where does it leave us, who call ourselves Christian, and who meet today in God's name? It leaves us without the old God, that is for sure. The God that William Blake called Nobodaddy. Nobodaddy forsook Jesus, and Jesus, on the Cross, forsook him. He asks us to forsake him because he is an illusion. A tortured human soul, crying out from the Cross, is the emblem of all suffering humanity, the figurehead of all abused, innocent victims. He is our symbol as we try to come to terms with the Quake, just as he is the unrepresented millions who have died in famines and wars and plagues throughout history.

Our Godhead is not to be found in the forces of Nature, or in some supposed male Creator figure. Rather, we try to enter into what the first Christians discovered. That is, that the Glory of God can only shine out of a human face; and the face on the Cross is in the greatest possible pain. We are not going to try, at this point in the cycle of our grief and rage, to be like Job's comforters and say that Nature, still less Jehovah, punishes humanity for its sin. On the contrary, we are going to say goodbye to the Temple, and the priestly veil, and the legends about Jehovah or the immortal gods of Olympus. We embrace instead the divinity within each human being. What is divine is to do good. What is divine is to love. What is divine is to make a good vision out of these terrible events.

Some of us will want to go on, struggling to reconcile the vanished theologies of the past with the perceptions which have been granted to us since the Earthquake here in Aberdeen. That is their privilege.

Aftershocks

It is not my way. I find in the Four Gospels an everlastingly rich set of stories, liberating me to become more human. It does not worry me in the least whether they are what you would call true – if by that you mean whether they actually happened in history.

Jesus died. And the Fourth Gospel says that this was his Glory. The moment of Glory was not the moment when he burst from the tomb. It was the moment when he gave himself up to death. That is not to glory in death. It is to say, in death, or in life, our glory is our humanity. It is by belief in one another, belief in the power of love to overcome greed and hate, that this city will pick itself out of the ruins and rubble and build itself up, turn itself into an abode of love.

CHAPTER NINE

FOR THE FIRST TIME IN OVER FIVE YEARS, CHARLIE AND Pamela Nicolson had felt togetherness, in a great wave of joy when their daughter returned from the trip to the zoo. Somehow, in spite of the chaos and disruption of that day, both Charles and Pamela had found their way home to their large house in Kensington, and, as we all did that afternoon and evening, they had been exchanging experiences. Charlie did not know at that point that Harriet, his PA, had lost her fingers, but he did know that his offices had been destroyed, and that all the staff had escaped. Pamela's building, quake-proofed, had survived intact, without injuries to the occupants or damage to the structure. She knew how lucky she was. Stories had circulated Aberdeen for hours about the effects of the Quake on the zoo, and they had, obviously enough, been thinking of nothing but Ella and the school trip. They did not know, at that time, that, had she stayed at school, she might well have been among the children who were killed by the collapse of the new concrete classroom block in Opportunity One.

Their only anxiety had been for Ella. So, when she appeared, looking as she nearly always did, so cool and collected and on top of things, they had both wept with relief. Pamela surprised herself by throwing herself at Charlie, hugging him with a greedy ecstasy before enfolding Ella in her arms. Charlie had bustled round the kitchen trying to prepare the little girl's favourite high tea – fish fingers and frozen peas – and her mother had quizzed her for questions, and a happy half hour in which Ella mercilessly and exactly recited the events of the day, the incompetence of Mr Pollard, the common sense of Mrs Chambers, the erratic behaviour of Stig, the timorousness (in comparison with herself) of the crocodile, the elephants being thrown to one side, the screams of the monkeys, the animals running amok. Much of this was becoming the common parlance of our city, but Charlie and Pamela knew nothing of it, because there was no television, radio signals flickered and most people's phones were still down, and there was only sporadic contact on social media. It was strange to think that, as the little six-year-old narrator told her parents about what had happened, the lions and tigers, the giraffes and orangutans were making their bewildered way through the ruins of our streets and squares, peering at cinemas and department stores which had burst into flames, wondering, as they surveyed half-demolished churches and theatres, where the next food would come from, and, in some cases, feeling homesick for the security of cage or compound.

—Anyway, said Ella, nobody can say that zoos are for babies NOW.

Her parents had not forgotten their son, of course they had not. But they had no reason to suppose that he was in danger. Some neighbours, whose sons also attended St Augustine's, had come round only an hour before to share the good news that his school had remained, robust Victorian building, upright. It would have been surprising that Josh had not yet come home, had they not picked up on the general panic, which was being passed around the neighbourhood, about the zoo – the collapse of the flimsily built cages, the escape of the animals, the deaths of a number of children beneath the wreckage of buildings. Josh's entry into the most highly regarded boys' school, not only in Aberdeen, but on the Island, had caused them joy and his membership of that exclusive and envied band made them doubly glad when the Johnsons had been round to reassure them that all was well. The school had lost a few panes of glass, but no buildings had collapsed – they heard – everything was fine.

—I wonder why he's so long, said Pamela.

—He'll be fine, Mrs Johnson – Sue – had said.

There had been no reason, especially, to doubt this.

Nevertheless, when Ella's relentlessly self-congratulatory account of her day at the zoo had progressed for the better part of half an hour, both parents had begun to think more about Josh. Public transport (he normally came home by the school bus, which dropped him off only a few streets away from the house) was, like everything else, in abeyance. But he would, surely, soon be home.

The normal telly news was down. The IBC building had fallen, after all. But it was possible to get some reception online, and they managed to hear some of the news which was being broadcast from Carmichael, while Ella, with callous hunger, devoured four fish fingers and a small mountain of frozen peas.

It is quite hard for anyone to know what happened, precisely, after that. Time passed, but whether it was five minutes or two hours after the little girl had satisfied her hunger (and neither parent had any appetite), the two grown-ups began to be gnawed by anxiety. The lateness of Josh was to be explained by the Quake, the appalling travelling conditions . . .

—We should have gone to the school?

Charlie's question.

—But David Johnson made it home on the bus.

Pamela began this as a simple reply, but it turned into a gulp, almost a yelp. And from that moment anxiety gripped them.

—I'm going to the school, Pamela said suddenly, after half an hour of pacing about the kitchen, vainly tapping at her phone, going to the Johnsons to ask David whether he had any idea why Josh had not come home.

—Let's all go to the school, said Charlie.

And Ella said,

—Can I come?

Then the doorbell rang.

—He's forgotten his key, said Charlie, as relief flooded through them all.

He stood back in the kitchen and allowed Pamela the pleasure of greeting their son. There would be another recitation of a child's day – this time, Joshie's – the maths test, the cricketing practice, the man's talk about the school's prospects for the coming season, the preparation of a favourite meal. Charlie was hoping there was a steak for the boy in the fridge.

These thoughts, if they were thoughts exactly, flitted through his brain in a matter of seconds and were instantly dispelled by the voices he heard from the hall.

—What is it? What have you come to say? – Pamela.

And a man's voice saying,

—Am I speaking to Joshua's mum?

—Yes – yes, I'm his mum, what is it, what's happened?

They looked up, Charlie and Ella, as Pamela followed a uniformed policeman into the room.

Nellie was sobbing. Waves of incoherent, howling grief.

—Oh, DAD!

—Well, Nellie. The distorted face on the screen smiled, but she could not see it.

—There's nothing more awful than a child's death, he said, nothing.

—They were both so, so HOSTILE . . . Oh God! It doesn't matter how I feel, but I was just standing there on their doorstep and I . . . of course I had to go round there . . . of course I did . . . Bob drove me.

—How is the arm, by the way?

She sniffed away some of the tears.

—It's fine, Dad. It'll be fine. I was in hospital a few days, that was all. You know that. I've got a small fracture in my left arm. Think of what other people are going through. Think of Ingrid and Cavan – oh my God! And Charlie and . . .

More tears.

—And Bob was so discreet, so kind, he stayed in the car. I went up to the front door. It's strange, for some reason almost none of the houses in Kensington have been much affected by the Quake. The house next door had broken windows, but . . . well, maybe the Nicolsons' place did too, I wasn't looking.

—Of course not.

—And she opened. Pamela. Dad, he was in the choir . . .

Another outpouring of tears.

—I know, I know.

—I just didn't know what to say, when I saw her standing there. I did not recognize her at first. Her face was not twisted or anything, but it was like a kind of mask. I honestly wondered if she was some distant relation of Pamela's, or perhaps a sister who had come to be with them at this . . . to be with them . . . but it was her. And she looked at me as if I was an encyclopaedia salesman or a Jehovah's Witness or something, the sort of annoying person who turns up on a doorstep, and just repeated, 'Yes?' And I asked if I could come in, and she said, 'No'.

—What did she actually say?

—She said they wanted to be alone together.

—That's understandable.

There was a very long pause.

—Dad, I've handled things so badly.

She had never told him about 'her and Charlie' – whatever there was to tell. She had told him about accompanying the man to concerts; she'd told him about Josh in the choir, and the amazing Top Cs his lark-treble hit during Stanford's *Te Deum*; and she'd told him about Pamela's unfriendliness, and . . . well, perhaps she had, on occasion, 'gone on' about the Nicolsons.

—Lesley always says that it's the unforeseen hazard of parochial life. People projecting on to the clergy. I mean, even Lesley! Can you imagine being in love with Lesley?

Here the light laugh was almost turning into a hoot.

—It would be like falling in love with a chair, her father announced in a still voice. But people can fall in love with chairs, just as a duckling thinks a shoebox on a string is its mother.

The implied snub shook her out of her tears.

—Charles is not one of those pathetic people who fall in love with the vicar, Dad. We got together . . . He developed this sort of crush on me . . . quite independently of church.

Ignoring the pardonable vanity of this, her father said,

—Lesley thought Charles Nicolson was getting in too deep. Do you remember Mrs Ballard?

—Well, I remember you telling me about her, said Nellie, quite literally sniffily. She could remember, at the time when her crush on Miss Firebrace was raging at the grammar school, that Mum and Dad had gossiped, not maliciously exactly, but with a heartless humour, about one of Uncle Lesley's parishioners, who could not be dissuaded from knitting him socks and mufflers.

—Dad, I don't think you or Uncle Lesley . . .

She was not angry, exactly, but she was taken aback that the whole Charles and her 'thing', which she did not completely understand herself, should have been discussed by the two old gossips. She went on,

—I mean, I think it all had more to do with Charles and Pamela having difficulties, rather than . . . He honestly wasn't knitting me mufflers.

—He was doing the masculine, sophisticated equivalent.

—I suppose we – the clergy – we are prone to . . . I know what you mean about projection, but he hadn't been to the Cathedral much when . . . I mean, it began very early, very soon after I arrived here.

—Poor Nellie. I'm sure you did not encourage it.

—The awful thing is, Dad—

—Or not really, he added quickly, to signal the unnecessity of going into detail. And now they are lost in grief, poor souls, lost in that unbearable pain together; and it is a pain which binds together and rips apart at the same time, and neither of them want to be reminded of something which was so . . . well, so unimportant, so . . . silly! as his infatuation. So they froze you out.

There was a long silence.

She was aghast at his words, and yet, at the same time, she was grateful for them, and as the weeks passed after he had said them, she came to realize how much they had learnt, he and Uncle Lesley, in those fogbound places, about the secrets of the human heart.

—You know, we're both cool under fire, you and I. Probably too cool. And maybe you're not admitting to what a shock it has all been. Not just poor little Josh, but all of it. You've been through an earthquake, Nellie! You're bound to be horribly upset.

—I'm fine.

—No one could be fine in such a situation. I don't suppose, um . . . I don't imagine you've been in touch with . . .

Doug had, as it happened, sent an email. All it said was 'You OK?' with two xx. She had read Auden's poem about the Old Masters being 'never wrong' about suffering, and everything turning away quite leisurely from the disaster, but she felt, even by Doug's standards, that this was taking things a little far. So she chose to ignore her father's inability, even at this moment, to say her husband's name.

—But, Dad.

—Yes, angel?

—What am I to do? Josh was in the choir. If the Cathedral had not been . . . oh Lord . . . if we had a Cathedral, of course we'd have the funeral in the Cathedral, and I'd have taken the service . . .

—I think you should write to them. Say that you are always there for them. Say how utterly devastated the whole choir is to have lost him, and how they want to honour him. Have the service in their parish church, and ask the incumbent if the choir can come and sing for the child. Offer to take the service, but say that you quite understand that this is their choice. And don't just say you'll pray for them. Do it.

There was another long pause.

—I haven't found prayer very easy since they took me out of the tower.

—It would be most peculiar if you had.

The next pause was even longer.

—I miss you so much, Dad.

—Yes, well. Darling girl.

She wrote the letter, Abel delivered it by hand, bless his heart. Some hours later came an email from Charles to say that they would like her to visit them after all. She would dearly have loved someone to go with her. Going alone, by taxi, was the bravest thing she ever did. She wore her clerical collar, a black linen trouser-suit and black espadrilles. It was still very hot.

Ella was watching television with a grandmother – Pamela's mother – so it was with the two parents that she was engaged. Charles made mugs of tea for each of them, the default comfort drink despite the heat. There was a terrible stillness about the pair, and for much of the time, none of the three said anything, so that the noise of *Finding Nemo* blared from the neighbouring room and swallowed their unsayable words.

—I wondered if you'd . . . whether my idea of the choir coming . . .

—That would be so wonderful, said Pamela. We should both like that so very much.

Aftershocks

—Derek Marsh could come down and talk to you about music, Pamela. I don't know what you think of this, but you could choose . . . music that he . . . that Joshie . . . had especially sung . . . Oh, dear, I'm so sorry. I am meant to be here to bring comfort to you.

Her voice had cracked, and her eyes welled.

—We have thought, said Charles.

—We thought of hymns, said Pamela, but not so much of the music. Fauré's *Pie Jesu*? You both know so much about music than I do.

The silence seemed to acknowledge, and if not to condone, to place behind them, the follies of the previous months. Nellie so respected Pamela for this.

—I think you should choose the music together, she said. But Derek is very experienced, and he is a wonderful musician, and he adored Josh.

When she rose to go, she had recovered her composure, and became a chip off the old block. She thought of the professionalism of her dad and of Uncle Lesley. She held both their hands and said the *Anima Christi*. Then the Lord's Prayer, in which they joined.

A week later, she accompanied the choir, Abel, the sacristan, and a couple of the retired clergy who helped out at the Cathedral to the Nicolsons' large parish church in Kensington. They all drove there in a Macnaughton's bus. Bob, who was being 'marvellous', had been down to see the Nicolsons most days, prayed with them, been with them the previous evening, when they received the boy's body into the church. (He'd asked if they wanted a requiem after the coffin was laid on the altar steps but they had not wanted this.)

The Nicolsons were not in church when the Macnaughton's bus pulled up, but most of the seats, half an hour before the service began, had filled up. It was one of the first post-Quake funerals, and maybe people attended, partly in awestruck horror at the loss of a life so young, partly to touch base, to recognize that the Quake had meant death on an enormous scale. (Altogether, Nellie attended over twenty funerals in the following weeks, on one day alone going to four, two of which she conducted.)

There's no doubt they helped all of us, in one way, to recognize the terrible realities which we had lived through. In other ways, they were simply unbearable, a repetition of the inevitable rites, the inevitable clichés and untruisms. Nellie found herself longing for the simple Prayer Book service – perhaps with appropriate adaptations. Instead, most of the funerals she attended were a mishmash of bad poems, read out in choking voices, or of badly constructed 'memories' of the dead person. She grew especially tired of a poem by an Edwardian clergyman called Henry Scott Holland:

> *Death is nothing at all.*
> *It does not count*
> *I have only slipped away into the next room,*
> *Nothing has happened.*
> *Everything remains exactly as it was . . .*

It was so palpably and obviously untrue. At all the funerals where it was read out, it was clear that everything did NOT remain exactly as it was. Without the presence of the one they loved, people were desolated. True, time heals the wound of bereavement, but to say that it does not count or that it is nothing at all was simply stupid. Nellie still missed her mum, though it was eight years since she had died; and she knew of her father's patient loneliness, and the wretchedness of life in that little modern flat where he now lived eating his ready-prepared meals for one, purchased at a super-market. None of the day to day companionship which the presence of another brought. None of the affection, none of the irritation, none of the sheer physical comfort. Even supposing there was life after death (and Dad surely DID suppose that he and Mum would meet again?) . . . it could not be like slipping away into the next room. For one thing, there is nothing to stop us going into the next room any time we like, and the thing which really enraged Nellie about Canon Scott Holland's poem was its callousness – it ignored the heartbreak of knowing you couldn't see the person you loved, couldn't reach out to them, or hold their hand, or see their smile. Hoping that you would meet in Heaven was not, and could not, be the same thing as believing they had slipped out into the next room. And in her present frame of mind she found it rather hard to hope for anything.

The formality of Joshie's funeral, and the music, enabled her to get through the next hour. The choir, in their scarlet cassocks, ruffs and surplices, followed the crucifer into the church. Nellie, wearing her choir robes, sat in the sanctuary with the Cathedral clergy. Bob and the incumbent of the church, a nice clergyman called Timmy Mills, stood beside the shockingly small coffin.

Charlie and Pamela came in at the very last moment, with Ella and some older people, presumably one set of grandparents. Ella, paper-pale, stared at her brother's coffin. Pamela was wearing dark glasses. Both Pamela and Charles looked as if they might be on some kind of tranquillizer, they were zonked, stunned. The choir were in wonderful voice. 'I will lift up mine eyes unto the hills'; 'Jerusalem the Golden'; the *Pie Jesu*; and one verse of a beautiful motet by Johann Christian Bach which Derek had suggested to them. No one, however, had been prepared for the ending. Six of the senior choristers came forward and lifted the coffin on to their shoulders. They turned with such poise and slowness and delicacy that they must have been rehearsing it for days – there was none of that wobble which even professional undertakers usually make, before they get the coffin straight. It appeared that they were going to walk out in silence, because at first, there was no organ music. Pamela, who had now crumpled, and was leaning against Charles's shoulder, led the way, and they followed immediately behind the coffin. Charles had one hand round her waist, and with the other he held Ella's hand. The little girl, behind her pallor and her specs, was still impossible to read. And then, when the procession had begun, one of the boy choristers, Jason McCann, suddenly burst forth with Geoffrey Burgon's solo *Nunc Dimittis*. Most of us only know it, if we have heard it at all, as the title music for the BBC TV version of Le Carré's *Tinker Tailor Soldier Spy*. Hearing it in church, so surprising, so familiar, so pure in its sound, was both thrilling and almost eerie, for it did seem, as this one child's un-broken voice filled the church with unaccompanied sound followed by the almost sobbing of organ music, as if the voice had come from Josh himself.

To be a light – to lighten the Gentiles – and to be the GLORY of thy people Israel.

—I think that's JUST RIGHT, Cavan. Just right. We don't need histrionics at this point. Everything has gone wrong that could go wrong. Troy is destroyed. The city is in ruins. It's an ex-city. You remember that devastating phrase at the very end of the play spoken by the Chorus – *Megalopolis, Apolis* – Great City, Non-city – you, the great women of Troy, are all about to be taken into slavery, to be the enforced concubines of your conquerors, and in case that isn't enough, the Greeks have just taken Andromache's little son, Astyanax, and killed him, thrown him from the city walls, and here he is, lying dead on his father's shield. The situation is what speaks here, louder than the words. So – right – go ahead again, please.

Cavan, who was playing Hecuba, said the unbearably pitiable lines:

> *Poor boy, how horribly your own home's walls,*
> *the ramparts of Apollo, crushed your head*
> *and ripped the curls your mother doted on:*
> *she often used to kiss you, there where blood*
> *laughs out between the broken bits of skull . . .*

There was no connection between the gratuitous murder of Astyanax in the old play and the almost capricious accidental nature of Josh Nicolson's death. But we were all thinking about him, and about the other kids who'd been killed.

> *But I'll set out an answer to the charges*
> *That I anticipate you'll make against me.*

When the first rumble of the Quake had occurred, the other St Augustine's boys, out practising in the nets, had stayed out of doors. He had gone into the pavilion – perhaps to use the lavatory, perhaps in search of some more gloves or another cricket ball. No one seemed clear. He was the only person killed when the pavilion came down.

Two hundred and fifty-three people died in the Quake – remarkably few, given the extent of the devastation, the more or less obliteration of the centre of our city. Thousands of our houses became uninhabitable. Rex Tone's City Hall came down within seconds of the Quake and the majority of deaths were in this building, though Rex himself was not there. He was in a meeting on the other side of town, but many of his staff – the local planning officers, about twenty-five secretaries and other office workers, cleaners and odd-job people – were killed. The other major area of casualty was in Opportunity One. The name now seemed so grotesquely inappropriate that there were strong moves to give the school its old name, St Michael's Primary. Twenty children died when a concrete ceiling collapsed and the whole of the first floor fell through to the ground. Had the Year Ones not been on the zoo expedition, the death toll would have been much, much higher.

Inevitably, though, those of us who were even casually acquainted with the Nicolsons responded to Hecuba as if it was the Nicolsons' tragedy. Perhaps what gives the piece its wrenching power to move us two thousand four hundred years after it was written is precisely the fact that it individualizes the general devastation. And, as Nellie had said to us before the first read-through, this play is so unlike most Greek tragedies. It is not about weird people, such as Phaedra or Medea or Oedipus or Ajax or Philoctetes. It is about essentially normal people. And it isn't about heroes. It is about women. And most of the main characters, except the Greek herald, who comes and goes to tell them what hideous punishment has been assigned to each, and Menelaus, are female.

It had been Nellie's idea to approach Cavan and ask her to consider playing Hecuba, the most demanding role in the play, who is on stage throughout.

Aftershocks

One of the good things to come out of the Quake – and there have not been many good things to date – is that all sorts of initiatives were formed to bring us together. In the vast warehouse spaces on the Carmichael Highway, two and a half miles out of town, the Aberdeen Choral Society, accompanied by the Philharmonic, put on a concert just a week after the major Quake. They did a rerun of Haydn's *Creation* which they had performed in happier days, only two months before at the Albert Hall. There was a big aftershock which trembled through the entire warehouse while they sang *The Heavens are telling* . . . It was remarkable that, although some people called out swear words – Holy shit and the like – everyone stayed in place. No one ran. It was as if we were all determined to sit it out, to defy the fates and whatever calamity they decided to throw at us.

Since that first brave concert, there have been performances of one sort or another almost every week in Aberdeen since the disaster. Brass bands and silver bands have played at the many spots in town where food banks and temporary shelters have been set up. Schools have staged revivals of old standbys such as *Joseph and the Amazing Technicolour Dreamcoat* and *The Wizard of Oz*. The Aberdeen G and S society had a two-week run of *Ruddigore*, which was wildly successful, attracting far bigger audiences than they ever did in the opera house.

Nellie suggested the idea of doing *Trojan Women* to me in the hospital, in the week that Mum turned the corner and we all knew there was, after all, going to be a future. I'd been in the hospital day and night, sitting by Mum's bed. Because Cavan Cliffe is not just my mum but an Aberdeen Institution, there had been a lot of media attention. Of all the two hundred and fifty-three deaths, the TV news and *The Press* had concentrated, in too much detail, on the deaths of the kids, and on Mum's ten hours trapped under the rubble of the Island Radio building. Her remark to the fireman who eventually, with immense skill, lifted the iron girder and concrete slab beneath which she lay passed into Aberdeen legend – 'Mine's no milk, but make it strong'. People even had it printed on tee-shirts. That's how legends are made. Actually, the very first thing she said to the firemen was, 'I'd kill for a ciggy', but such is the mania against smoking nowadays that you'd probably be prosecuted for printing that on a tee-shirt. She had eventually said the thing about coffee, but it was smoking that was the first thing on her mind – and the fireman had, in fact, got a pack of fags in his pocket and shared one with Cavan.

As they lifted her on to a stretcher, she had winced, but not cried out. It was Mum all over, of course, to give an example of simple, unshowy heroism. It made it harder for me, having to cope with all the publicity. Journalists and photographers were banned from the wards, but they were waiting for me every time I stepped out into the car park. And because I am, not well known, but an actress who has appeared on the stage of the Garrick, they felt justified in accosting me all the time, asking for pictures and so on. It was hard. I did not want to share with them all the distressing details of her injuries, especially when it really looked as if we were going to lose her.

Nellie, who had been in hospital for so much shorter a time with the broken arm, was soon up and running, as Mum put it. She returned often to the hospital to visit the wounded, and to offer comfort to the bereaved.

Cavan was hoping to learn to walk with the prosthetic leg, but it was going to take a long time. While we were rehearsing, we all agreed it was totally appropriate for Hecuba, the mother of Troy, to be in a wheelchair. Nellie said there were some lines in which Hecuba threw herself on the ground, but we could rewrite or omit these. No one was surprised that Cavan, almost from the time she came out of hospital, had learnt to manipulate the chariot with particular vim. Her rower's arms and shoulders saw to that. There was an electronic device which put her on automatic, but more often than not, she resorted to manual, turning her chair this way and that with conversational jolts and confrontational energy. A jolly Boudicca, usually with smoke coming out of her nostrils. She was so full of life, and so happy to be alive, that I think these weeks were ones of happiness for her, even though none of us could be completely happy; felt, indeed, that with some parts of ourselves, we would never be completely happy again. Happiness seemed a cheap need, one which, for the time being, it was more tasteful to be without.

It's difficult, knowing how to frame this narrative. I'm not tricksing you, people, really! It is just hard to know how to tell the story I want to tell, without too many extraneous details. As I said at the beginning, we are all post-Quake and post-just-about-everything-else here in Aberdeen. The things which I think are important – in the story of the city, in my own personal story – are much clearer to me now, eight years – my God, eight years, it is unbelievable! – after the Quake, than they were at the time.

Anyhow, back to the rehearsal. We were rehearsing in St Luke's Church Hall, near us in Harrow. Mum was home now, after a couple of months in the Rutherford Orthopaedic, learning to use the prosthetic leg, and so on. She was even going in once a week to compere *Island Breakfast* and life was – not going back to normal, it felt like it was never going to do that – but developing its own level, its own routines and momentum. And, obviously, although she said she was fine, did not need help, bla bla bla, she definitely needed me. Those weeks, when I helped her into bed at night, and made hot milk, were truly beautiful. Her bedtimes felt like my bedtimes as a kid, and we, who had always been close, drew closer. The hot chocolate now had whisky poured into it, but otherwise the routines were remarkably similar, ending always with a lovely hug. We were all just so inexpressibly grateful for being alive, all the more because it was Love among the Ruins.

The rehearsals lasted a bit over an hour. Nellie was fantastic, a natural as a theatre director. But each rehearsal also felt like the most instructive seminar. We were all really coming to grips with the play. When we'd done the scene with dead Astyanax on the shield, we all broke up for the evening. It was during the next rehearsal, with just me, Mum and a professional actor called Lewis Compton, that the Moment occurred.

Lewis was playing Menelaus, the wronged husband of Helen – that was me. As everybody in the world knows, the Trojan War started because I left my husband, Menelaus, and ran off to Troy with Paris – known by his other name as Alexander in this play. After many a long year, Troy has been defeated by the Greeks. Menelaus comes to claim his bride back. He is so angry that he intends to have me put to death. Ritually, of course. My big scene is the one where I plead for my life. It was not my fault I ran off with Alexander. It woz the gods wot done it. Love could not be resisted, because Aphrodite the Goddess of Love put it into Alexander's mind to carry me off, and into my mind to yield to him. But the minute he had been killed and Troy was destroyed, I'd tried to go back to the Greeks and to my lawful husband, honest. And Hecuba, meanwhile, is going, like, Menelaus, don't believe this hussy, she's no better than she oughta be.

Anyhow, it's a great scene and a fantastic part. Hecuba warns Menelaus not to take me back to Greece on the same ship as himself. Why not? he asks. Because she'll seduce you on the way home, and then you won't have the heart to sacrifice her, is Hecuba's callous reply. 'Once a lover, always a lover.' It's one of the passages which make people think Euripides was a complete atheist, 'cause Hecuba says all that stuff about me being in the grip of Aphrodite is a load of total horseshit and there's no such person as Aphrodite, I'm just a slag – but Euripides puts it much better than that, you won't be surprised to hear.

The way Nellie was staging the scene was this. Hecuba, in her wheelchair, with her prosthetic leg sticking out like a walking stick (she was always forgetting to bend its artificial knee!), was dead centre stage. Menelaus was front-stage left, not with his back to the audience, but with one shoulder turned in that direction, so you had this sense of him really staring at the furious Hecuba. And then I'm a bit back-stage right, cowering, terrified by both of them, but I come forward as I make the very long speech in my defence. I'm the only woman who is decently dressed, by the way. Hecuba, the former Queen of Troy, is in rags, preparing to be a maid to Odysseus, and I'm in this, like, really swanky Greek dress.

—Start speaking, and then move, Ingrid. Don't move then speak.

—So, when do I come forward?

—Hang on!

It was lovely, she was getting her little harrumph back, the little Madcap of the Remove hoot in her voice, which, ever since coming out of hospital, had been low and unlike herself.

—Yes . . .

And having fiddled about with her script, she came behind me and began to say my lines.

—*I'll set* – Yes, that's the moment to go – *I'll set out an answer to the charges* – AND MOVE. –*that I anticipate you'll make against me.*

She had come behind me and placed two hands on my shoulders. We must have touched one another before, I'm sure we had. We air-kissed when she'd been to our house for drinks once, before the Quake, but when she came to see Mum in hospital once or twice, we had not. That was a sign, of course, that we could not kiss one another, not just in a social way, any more. That something had already happened.

And now I felt her long white hands on my shoulder blades. Don't laugh at me, reader, when I say that I practically swooned. I looked back over my right shoulder with a nervous smile and I could feel myself blushing so deeply. And our eyes met. And that was when we both knew, because there was a silence – it was probably only about five seconds, but it felt like forever. Life changed.

And, I was thinking, this is incredible, in front of Mum, and Lewis Compton. All she was doing was marching me forward a few paces, and saying the lines of the play while I walked, and she kept her hands on my shoulder blades. But it felt as if we were making love. That was because we were making love.

—And then when you get to *But Greek delight cost me my ruin*, stand still, she said. Her hands were removed.

It was like that deep heat treatment you get sometimes for aching joints. Her long white hands had the power to scald. I wanted those hands to grab me by my thick mousey hair, and turn me round to face her, and I wanted her open, smiling mouth to kiss mine, and I wanted her to start tearing at my clothes.

Instead, she let go of me and said,

—Right, let's try it. Menelaus, if you give her her cue – *If you want to, speak.*

Instead of shouting, *Nellie, I love you! Nellie, I give myself to you, body and soul*, I went through the lines like a good professional.

This is what I mean about it being difficult, knowing how to frame this narrative. Because I now know so much more than I did that evening, eight years ago, about what was passing through people's heads. And I know what would happen in the end. So I'm just going to try to write it all, like a narrative in a novel, with an all-knowing or almost-all-knowing narrator; only forgive me, reader, if I sometimes butt in, because, as you'll have realized by now, that's what I'm like.

The rehearsal broke up. Lewis offered to give Nellie a lift back to the centre of town. Her flat in the Deanery had been put back into some kind of shape by then – the windows replaced, and so on. Nearly all her books had been destroyed when the Cathedral tower came down, but the fireman saved a few hundred of them, crumpled and dusty as they might have been. She was a punctilious backer-up of her material, so though the laptop, and that morning's work, had been destroyed, much of *Euripides and the Masks of God* survived on memory sticks, even though she had not looked at her book since the Quake.

You, reader, are going to have to get used to the new Nellie – the one who is both Digby and Eleanor Bartlett. She was much more confident. She got on better with Dionne now, because there was less to hide. She did not attempt, when talking to Mum and me, to disguise Dionne's follies, but nor was she blind – as Digby had always been – to the woman's virtues – a warm(ish) heart, and (on the whole) good intentions. Troubles lay ahead – most notably, in the many rows Dionne would have with the people of Aberdeen about the future of their Cathedral. Dionne was one of the many Bishops of our Church who hated architecture. She did not know this. She just thought that buildings, and beautiful objects, and tradition got in the way of the urgent mission to which she and her generation were called. But, like I say, all this lay ahead.

Nellie, her Dean, no longer shied away from telling Dionne when she disagreed with her. She recognized much good that Dionne did – for example, in forging links with the social services and making churches and parish halls available throughout the diocese to help people post-Quake.

Nellie was definitely Nellie now, to more and more people. Her students still referred to her as Digby, and even the Cathedral Folk had been asked to call her Nellie Digby – the 'Bartlett' was a thing of the past.

She went back to her flat that evening with her heart pounding. On the one hand, the rehearsal had gone well. *Trojan Women* was going to be a success, she could feel it, and she also felt a new empowerment, with the two sides to her nature – the scholar and the priest, the public and the private self, come together. For Digby would never have been public-spirited enough to direct a play for semi-professionals and amateurs; she would have been too diffident. And Dean Eleanor would have been too frozen to let Euripides, and his dangerous notions, speak through her. Nellie knew that the masks of God slipped sometimes, and that Euripides was good at snatching the masks away. But Nellie was also relaxed enough about her Anglicanism, now, to let these ideas – God versus no-God, even – dance about in her adorable head, and on her cherry lips. There was no need for Keeping Up Appearances any more. The Quake had torn off our Appearances. We had only what was left beneath, and with any luck, if you have been living a wise life, when

Aftershocks

Appearance is torn away, you will be left with Reality. And – I'm
obsessed by those poems now, thanks to her! –

> *In order to arrive at what you are not*
> *You must go through the way in which you are not.*

What happened to her that night of the Helen/Hecuba/Menelaus
rehearsal was a pivotal moment on the journey. Before she had even
got in to the flat, she found herself mentally packing up her bags,
and ready to go back to England.

In no particular order, she had these thoughts: I am not cut out
to be in the professional clergy. To be a priest, and to say Mass, yes,
but my main task, with what years I have left to run, is to finish my
book, and continue my life as a scholar. And then, there is Dad.
He is the most important person in my life, and I can't leave him
for another few years alone in England. The Quake had made her
realize how dependent she was on her father. Something similar
had happened between me and Mum – I was quite as dependent
on her as she was on me. And if the course of my relationship with
Nellie had been a bit confused, and zigzaggy, this was very much
down to the Quake, and the way the big shake-up made us both so
preoccupied with our parents.

Nellie was thinking – first, I'll get all my things packed up, and
start sending belongings ahead of me to England. There was not
that much, not now the library had been obliterated. Then I'll go
and tell Dionne that I'm resigning as Dean. I'll save up telling Dad
until it is all a *fait accompli*, a lovely present for him. She had begun
to compose a letter, in her head, to the Master at Oxford, exploring
the possibility of becoming a research fellow at the college, while
she looked round for an academic post. She was far from being

fixated on Oxford, and would in many ways welcome a change of scene if she could find an appointment somewhere else.

These were the thoughts, doggedly specific, which had been provoked in her practical brain by the shoulder-blades moment, by the moment when our eyes met and we both knew that we were . . . I do not want to use those two words yet . . . in . . . Yes, we were, deep in it. That thing which moves the sun and other stars.

Nellie found it deeply worrying and upsetting. She had not yet fully admitted to herself what it was that was so disturbing her. She felt that maybe those were right, her father included, who had warned her she had not yet made sufficient allowance for the effect of the Quake. She was all bright and breezy and saying she was fine, and all that was wrong with her was a slightly wonky arm. She was temperamentally equipped, after an upbringing in a series of draughty houses which her parents could not afford to heat, to say, when she was cold and miserable, that she was fine. And for generation before generation, on her father's side, there had been English people saying the opposite of what they meant, that unpalatable food was lovely, that cold picnics on wet beaches were the greatest possible summer treat. Moreover, those English forebears had all mastered the trick of hiding, from themselves, the secrets of the heart. No one wanted to be thought soppy. As for being soppy in a manner of which the Church had traditionally disapproved – soppy about your own sex – well, it was a phase which adolescents passed through, wasn't it? The other thing was for Americans and exhibitionists or people in London. She remembered the rueful way in which her father and Uncle Lesley meditated on the fates of their fellow clergy who 'came a cropper'. And she thought of Mum, good old Mum, laughing quietly at her husband, when he had said, about two parishioners, Miss Kelly and Miss Summers,

—The things people will say! They are perfectly respectable women. It's a poor lookout if two people can't share a house without other people drawing conclusions.

—I agree with you, it's mean to gossip, Mum had said with a laugh.

—Yes, but you don't think . . .

Nellie could still remember the astonished expression on her father's face when Mum had failed to reply. When recounting this exchange to one of her friends, Mum had added,

—He said they were sharing a house, but it's a one-bedroomed cottage.

Love between women, of that sort, was something which was not discussed, probably not understood. She was so close to her father, even closer to him since the Earthquake. The strange feelings, quite new to her, which now possessed her were creating their own earthquakes and aftershocks. She saw utter disruption, the embarrassment of public avowal yawning before her. She saw the awful challenge of complete abandonment. She had never let go, never in her life, never given in to emotion, and never felt emotion so strong. It was not possible to yield to such feelings. Chaos would come. And the thought of it shook her with holy joy, making her realize she must burn her boats fast, resign and leave the Island now, before the Thing Got Out of Control. She surely was in Control still? Though she must make sure never, ever, to be with the Girl alone. Never.

—No, it is lovely to break the routine.

Normally they Skyped at fixed hours, at the beginning or end of one day or the other. But she had had to speak to her father, and it was the first thing she did, that evening, on returning to the flat. Half past ten at night our time, so 11.30 in the morning in Winchester.

—Lesley was on the blower this morning. Says your Pontiff was on the television news.

It was Nellie's turn for the light laugh.

—She was saying the Cathedral will have to come down.

—It's far too early to say, Dad. We'll need structural engineers to look at it. The tower came down.

—With you in it.

—With me in it. The spire collapsed. But the basic structure of the nave remains. I do not see why it should not be repaired and rebuilt. Oswald Fish never wanted the tower in the first place. It was only the then Pontiff who required it.

—'Proud pompous and prelatical'.

They jointly laughed at one of their shared church anecdotes.

—There'll be a hullabaloo if Dionne is serious.

—Well, you're the Dean. You have the ultimate say-so.

—That's where you're wrong, Dad. Our canon law on the Island is different from the English. The Bishops have far more executive power over all the fabric of the churches, even the Cathedrals. Deans and Chapters aren't really autonomous.

—But why would the donkey want to pull the Cathedral down, if it can be saved?

—You know what Bishops are like. Oh, Dad. Not for anyone, not even for Uncle Lesley, but there has been something so much on my mind.

—Go on.

—Dionne and Brian were very kind, offering me a bed when I came out of hospital, and I am really grateful to them. But while I was there . . .

—Go on.

—It was the second or third day. I came down from my bedroom in the middle of the morning. Dionne was letting a man out of her study. They were scurrying to the front door.

—The thought of your Pontiff scurrying is—

—Don't be mean, Dad.

—Lesley said she reminded him of William Temple. Physically. Not intellectually.

—She did not want me to see her, and the guest, who tried to be matey, was hustled out of the door. Dionne went back into her study, and I went into the kitchen to make myself some coffee. Brian was there. He was having a day off work, and getting ready to go to the Links. Out of the window, he watched the guest being shown into the back of an enormous limo. He said, 'You know who that was?' And I said, 'No', hadn't the foggiest. 'Only Ricky Wong,' said Brian. Don't tell, Dad, but I'm so afraid he was making Dionne some kind of offer.

It was not the canon's way to be ribald, so that his splutter of mirth signalled an understanding that the Bishop and the cele- brated Shanghai businessman were hatching some scheme, and that his daughter was naïve in the extreme if she placed any but the most lurid interpretation on the visit.

—Well, do keep me posted.

She paused, because she wanted, and did not want, to speak of the things which had passed through her head as she came home. She would not have said directly, I have fallen in love with a woman, nor, I can't face what this means so I am coming home, but she would have her own way of speaking about it. Rather, he said,

—How are all the others? How's the family of the poor little boy?

—Devastated. Angry. Vulnerable. Pitiable to behold.

A huge sigh came from England.

—And Cavan?

—Dad, she's so GOOD as Hecuba. She doesn't declaim. She does it as quiet, almost whispered grief, shame, anger. We're going to mike her up, so she won't need to project at all. At first I thought it wouldn't work, with her in a wheelchair, but it is really, really affecting.

—And Cassandra?

—I'm glad that Deirdre said she couldn't do it after all. There's something so undignified about poor Cassandra in her madness. Anne Roberts is superb.

—She's the young actress, the friend of your friend Ingrid.

—She's not especially my friend, Dad.

After a long silence, he said,

—Well, I wish I was going to see this production.

They spoke every day after that, Nellie and her dad. He had obviously broken his word, and been unable to hold back from discussing the Ricky Wong business with Lesley Mannock, and Nellie had broken her own inner resolution, 'cause she had told me and Mum about it, and we were wondering whether we ought to tell Deirdre.

Here might be the moment to keep you readers up to speed on what happened to our cast of characters in the future, 'cause after this chapter, it's going to be the question of whether I ever managed to persuade this maddening, beautiful person to admit she was in love for the first time in her life, in love with me.

Deirdre? Well, one effect of the Quake was that the Fuck Bar policy was now in full operation. Barnaby had not moved back in with Deirdre, but he had defied Bar, and allowed Stig to become

part of our lives down in Harrow. Mum lent *Little Ingrid* to Stig
and Barnaby, and we all three – he, me and the kid – went rowing
several times. Deirdre tried to take Stig rowing, but her stick arms
are thinner than the oars and she caught more crabs than there
are in Aberdeen Harbour. Nellie did eventually warn her about
Ricky Wong's ambitions. He'd persuaded Bishop Dionne that the
Cathedral was a prime site for development. If, like Dionne, you
believed that the old Anglican Communion was, in a very real sense,
a Community of Outreach, and so much more than a collection of
fusty old buildings and hymn books and such, Ricky Wong's advice
would have been music to your ears, as it was to hers. After all, he
was offering her millions and millions of Island Dollars. All she
would have to do is spend a fraction of this on some modest quake-
proof replacement (Ricky reminded her that when they had the big
quake in Christchurch, New Zealand, they had built a cardboard
cathedral). The rest could be spent on educational programmes,
galvanizing the young, oh, there were no end of things which could
be done with the money. We're talking about eight years ago and,
would you believe, the lawsuits are still going on. Deirdre led the
charge, of course, but there were many others. Our Island was
settled, very largely, by Anglicans. Anglicanism is in the blood.
Many, many of us who aren't Anglicans look to that Cathedral as a
symbol. The thought of selling it off to Ricky Wong was abhorrent
to thousands of people. But that's not part of our story. Not my story,
anyhow, except in so far as it impacted on Nellie and she on it.

Stig eventually did move in with Deirdre! There was nothing
that Bar and her husband could do about it, really. He hit it off with
George Eliot at first, squealing with delight as GE repeated 'Course
it's a fucking parrot' and 'Jeez, Norm, don't blame me' at inappropriate moments. I was there when GE did it once, and it quite took

me back to when I was sixteen and did not get the point of Deirdre, because she turned, in a flustered way, to the parrot and said, 'I really don't think . . . ' 'Course it's a fucking parrot' . . . 'I really don't think that you should say that, George Eliot' . . . 'Course it's a fucking parrot', and we were back at St Hilda's, and Rachael Newton and the gang were taking the piss as poor old Badley Dreary tried to get them to share Lily Briscoe's Vision.

Some people are not very good at being happy, and it is a knack, not just a matter of luck. And I don't think poor Deirdre would ever be happy. That's why she had so skilfully chosen to fall in love with Barnaby who, though a decent bloke, was quite thick emotionally, and thought, when she said that she loved him so much, she'd have him on any terms, even if it meant him loving other women as well, that she meant it. What she meant, as anyone who understood anything could have told that dunderhead Barnaby, was, she wanted him and him alone, come live with me and be my love. Whereas, he thought she meant, leave the kid in my house, while you go off and shag your way round Aberdeen. So she shed a lot of tears over the time between then and now, and she did a lot of tearful staring out of the train window looking at the giant sheep farms and lush vineyards, as she sped towards Carmichael and her parliamentary life, but she never stopped loving our Barn, and maybe some people are just like that, want to be miserable, because they are programmed to be so.

I only know about Pamela and Charles and Ella from Nellie, so I can't tell you much about what was going on in their inner lives. As soon as they possibly could, they left Aberdeen and he took up his role as a High Court Judge in Carmichael. A few years later, we read that His Honour Judge Nicolson and Pamela Dobson, the distinguished company lawyer whose firm had relocated from

Aberdeen to Carmichael, had, with the greatest regret, decided to separate. Like I say, I don't know them. A friend of mine who does says that Ella, who's in her early teens now, is anorexic and driving both parents up the wall with guilt and worry. But it's not the main story here.

Oh. And some of you will ask, what about old Penny Whistle? Something which makes us think he's something paranormal, or supernatural – that he is left over from the eighteenth century – is that he is STILL THERE! Every day, his brown face and arms and legs, beneath the shorts, are to be seen in Argyle Square, jerkily moving like a marionette. His day starts with Morning Prayer – the Davidson Hall, next to the Cathedral, which is used for social gatherings, fetes and the like, has been kitted out as a church, and Penny Whistle is to be found there, coming in with the responses several beats before everyone else. Then, it's a few swigs of coffee from his thermos flask, and out into the square. Only when Abel, the handsome sacristan who may or may not have been a mystic, died a few years after the Quake did we find out that they had been living together for years. It was Abel who had washed Penny Whistle's tee-shirts and shorts, Abel who had made him his thermos of coffee, Abel who cooked him his evening meal. Only at Abel's funeral did we learn Penny Whistle's name – he is called Desmond Grainger, but everyone calls him Penny Whistle. His heart is broken, but on he goes. Now he lives on pizzas, but he still comes out each day. I heard him only this morning.

Ae fond kiss and then we sever
Ae farewell, alas, for ever!
Deep in heart-wrung tears I'll pledge thee,
Warring sighs and groans I'll wage thee . . .

But – back to the time in the aftermath of the shoulder-blade moment, the epiphany. On one of her daily Skypes – Nellie's 7 p.m., Canon Digby's 8 a.m. – her dad was saying,

—I still can't get over the Pontiff wanting to sell the Cathedral to this dreadful-sounding spiv.

—Dionne and Brian have been very kind. They had me to stay – I could still be there if I'd wanted it. Their house was one of the few in Gloucester Street to be completely unaffected.

—The sure foundation, lightly laughed her father.

—Anyway, I'm fine. My flat was shaken up, but it's perfectly habitable now. I'm much happier on my own turf.

—You're one of the ruins that Cromwell knocked about a bit.

—Deirdre says Wong is buying up land all over the city, sometimes in his own name, usually in the name of dodgy or defunct companies. We can have no idea how much he has already bought. Good old Evans and Cosh . . .

—Oh, that shop is splendid! We so loved it, said her father, the real old-fashioned department store. Do you remember your mother buying that hat?

—Well, Evans and Cosh moved the bulldozers in the very next day, after the Quake. And through all the aftershocks, they have been rebuilding. They reckon they'll have finished in four months. They aim to make it *exactly* as it was before. It will be so reassuring when it's finished. But I can't tell you how desolate the middle of town is.

—Your mother loved it all so much. The river winding through. The little bridges over the Windrush, and the Victoriany lamp-posts. And that lovely parade of shops – is it the Promenade?

—It *was* the Promenade. You can't even see where the Promenade was. All the outlines of the streets have disappeared. And it is months now – what? Four months, and hardly any new building or any clearing. It is as if we are all just getting used to life among the ruins. We are trying our best to come to terms with it all, but it's as if we've had a sort of collective nervous breakdown. And there are so many complicated insurance problems – or so I gather.

—Well, Lesley says you should just ignore the Pontiff and Wong and get on with the Cathedral rebuild.

—Dad, that's what I am worried about. We've had the meeting. We've had all the reports from the structural surveyor. There's no way we'll ever be able to rebuild the tower and the spire, but they should never have been built in the first place. But we could repair the nave of the Cathedral, and the sanctuary.

—How much of all the lovely iron-work has survived?

—Surprisingly, quite a lot of the rood screen. Of course, all the glass has gone, and the regimental banners, and all but one of the beautiful reredoses. But Atalanta is safe. She's propped up in my hall . . .

—Dear Atalanta. Send her my love.

—I will. Course, we could repair, or at least the nave. We could.

—Is it money?

—It's delay. It's lack of will. Although I have executive respons-ibility for the fabric – in terms of the fittings and decorations – I'm not like an English dean. And the Chapter are not like an English chapter, which would be autonomous. If this were Winchester Cathedral, the Dean and Chapter would have sole responsibility for the rebuild. And obviously, there would be an appeal committee and all that – well, we've set that up here. But the ultimate decisions are to be made—

—By the Pontiff.

After a pause, the canon said,

—You aren't saying that the Pontiff would really be tempted to sell the Cathedral to Ricky Wong?

—Since you last came here, Dad, the whole of one side of Argyle Square, the side opposite the Law Courts, is dominated by this SOCKING great American-style hotel. It all but abuts on the Cathedral. He must have had it proofed, because it survived the Quake. Of course – he'd love to get his hands on the Cathedral.

—But why would she love to sell it to him?

To that, there was no answer, or none that Nellie could give.

She fell to giving an account of rehearsals for *Trojan Women*. In the middle of this description, I walked behind her chair, and the old canon exclaimed,

—Who's there?

—Hi, Nellie's Dad!

I waved into the screen.

Mum had told me she was perfectly capable of making supper for herself once in a while. She was making brilliant progress with the leg, but I had immediately raised a whole number of objections – what if she slipped on the kitchen floor and was left lying there?

—Then I'll lie there till you come back – a roar of laughter.

—Hi! said the old man back to me. You could tell that it would have been more natural for him to say 'Good evening' – only for him it would have been 'Good morning!'

—I'm Ingrid, Ingrid Ashe.

We all laughed – and while Nellie finished saying goodbye to her father – I could hear her saying,

—No, it's a chicken pilaf. It smells completely delicious. I don't know, I'll ask her.

She called,

—Do you use black cardamoms?

—I could only get green.

While I stirred, I could hear the canon's well-modulated tones saying,

—If one can get black, they are even more delicious. Do you remember Mr Chakrabati sold the most wonderful cardamoms in Smethwick? Oh, all the spicy smells of that shop!

When she'd said goodbye to her father, Nellie returned to the kitchen-end of her large living room. So much for her resolution never to be alone with 'the Girl'.

Over our pilaf, which was damn good, even with green cardamom, she talked about losing all the books and papers.

—You know, the funny thing is, it is a liberation. I backed up the *Masks* book, I have not really lost it. But I am not sure I want to write it any more. It's really weird, I can't quite . . . I can't really put it into words, but . . .

—Is it that you were putting two selves into two different compartments? That the Digby side was writing the book, but ignoring all the spiritual insights and gentleness of Eleanor? And Eleanor was clutching her copy of *Four Quartets* and safely rereading Jane Austen every year, rather afraid of what would happen to her prayer life if she allowed herself to think Digby's radical thoughts?

When I had blurted all this out, I felt embarrassed, because it implied I had been thinking about her so obsessively, and we did not, at that stage, in spite of the shoulder-blade moment, really know one another very well.

—What a strange way of putting it, was all she had said.

But when I'd said it we'd crossed over a border.

We had spent quite a number of evenings together now. Sometimes, Nellie came round to see me and Mum, and Mum would usually leave us chatting in the kitchen or in the garden while she went to an early bed. (Mum had soon persuaded me that she would call me when needed, but that she did not need help putting on a nightie or getting herself to the loo. And she had resumed *Island Breakfast*, though getting herself to work in a taxi, rather than in *Little Ingrid*.) So, sometimes Nellie came to us, and sometimes I went to spend the evening with her, and usually, wherever we were having supper, I did the cooking. We'd usually drink a carafe of red wine between us, usually one of the delicious Island Pinot Noirs which Nellie says knock spots off nearly all the Burgundy she has ever tasted.

During these evenings, which were quiet, and gentle, and loving, I used to be reminded of a Carol Ann Duffy poem which I really liked, 'The Laughter of Stafford Girls' High', in which two of the schoolmistresses, Miss Batt and Miss Fife, had supper together regularly twice a week, and Miss Fife played Bach on the piano while Miss Batt marked history essays. They loved one another but

nights like this
twice a week, after school, for them both, seemed enough.

In the poem, Miss Batt and Miss Fife eventually go much further – become lovers – but Nellie and I had not reached that stage, perhaps never would. I loved her now more than I had ever thought it was possible to love another human being, and I think she loved me, but I did not want to broach the subject for fear that, in talking it over, it would be over. If necessary, I'd have been happy to go on seeing Nellie every week, several times a week, for the rest of my life, rather than having some sort of scene which she found embarrassing.

There was no one with whom I could discuss it, not really. Mum would have been sympathetic, but I am not sure I wanted, or needed, sympathy. The only person I wanted to talk to about it was YOU, Nellie. And I couldn't. One evening, which had been especially nice, I felt I was coming close to being able to say the three simple words, 'I love you' – and Nellie had begun to talk about Dionne. Somehow, the words 'I love you' did not come easily into a paragraph devoted to Dionne.

We all need to let off steam about work colleagues, and Nellie was saying some of the things she did not like about 'the Pontiff': that she did not trust her; that she was self-important; that she was actually rather an intolerant person but masked it by blathering modern clichés, such as liking to begin all her sermons with the declaration that her diocese was 'open and inclusive, to different ethnicities, and to different sexualities . . . we are open in my diocese – open to the gay community, open to the transsexual community, open to LGBTs and . . . '

—It's all humbug, Nellie had said with one of her laughs. And if Christianity were even half true, you would not need to SAY these things, since obviously, it is inclusive. That is its *raison d'être*.

Nevertheless, I felt that deep down – and I'm like this, too, to this day – we both are – she did not want to have a label beginning with a capital L hung round her neck. I reckoned she was beginning to love me, but that she would have found it difficult to explain by Skype to the old man, because he was old-fashioned; difficult to explain to Dionne, because she would be so 'understanding' about it; and difficult to admit to Doug.

That evening – the evening I cooked the pilaf with the green cardamoms – we talked a bit about Doug. She told me about the unfaithfulnesses, and finding the porn on the computer. She did not exactly spell out when the sexual side of her marriage fizzled out – I learnt that later.

—Why don't you divorce him? I asked.

—That was truly, very delicious, she said, forking in the last bit of her second helping.

I topped up her glass.

—Oh, I don't know, Ingrid.

She looked across her little table at me. We stared and stared. She must have seen all the love in my eager, pathetically young eyes. And I did genuinely wonder whether she would reach across the table and take my hand, or whether we would even kiss passionately. But we just stared.

It was about a month after that that she dropped her bombshell, on a perfect, unseasonably warm winter's day, as we were rowing on the Windrush. Nellie was a very good oarswoman. That's Oxford for you, I suppose. The original idea was that we would take Mum out for a treat in *Little Ingrid*, and Nellie, suddenly rather Christopher Robin, had turned up at our house for an early lunch, wearing white shorts, an aertex shirt and a sunhat and eau-de-nil Converse. Mum had been getting on fine with the leg and the wheelchair, and the physio and all. But when we'd had a nice lunch, of olives and cheese and salami and home-made lemonade, Mum suddenly said,

—You know what? The old woman wants a siesta. You two go out on your own.

There was no dissuading her. Afterwards, I wondered whether Nellie had tipped her the wink, and they'd decided a boat trip would be a good way of breaking the bad news to me.

We'd all been on a high for the ten days since *Trojan Women*, which had been such a success. Although it was a semi-amateur thing, performed in a warehouse, we had got really excellent audiences. It had been reviewed in *The Press*. Nellie had written an article for the paper, explaining why it had been such an appropriate piece to perform in Aberdeen at this juncture. Hale Jackson – director of the Redgrave Theatre in Carmichael – came to the performance on our final night, and was really, *really* encouraging. She said there was every chance of developing the production professionally, and she asked me – Hale Jackson asked me!! – if I would consider taking the role either of Helen or Andromache, and if I'd also like to be involved on the production side. So we were all in a kind of dream of happiness. The city was still in ruins. The future of Aberdeen did not look especially bright. Deirdre seemed to think that all sorts of skulduggery were afoot – with Rex Tone and Ricky Wong – to quote Deirdre – 'in it up to their elbows'. And we were a broken city, we were bereaved, we were wounded birds. Mum's leg wasn't going to come back, and the very fact that she was being so brave actually made it more poignant, not less. Nevertheless, we were all on a high – I was especially – which actually made that afternoon a particularly painful one on which to drop the bomb. But dropped it had to be, I could see that, as soon as it fell.

She pushed out, with an expert shove of the oar, gave her little giggle – 'Oh Lor!' as the right oar wobbled a little in its rowlock, and then set out, with confident, clean strokes. I sat in the back of the boat, with my hair loose over my shoulders. I was wearing a stripy summer frock, and bare legs and sandals. Although it was June by now, it was warm as a summer day. Her blue-black met my pleading brown eyes and she smiled – pityingly, I now see.

We left Harrow behind us, and were rowing out of town. It was too sad to visit the ruined city unless you had to. The banks were overhung with willows. Once past the industrial estates, which now doubled in the evenings as the city brothels – for the hookers' quarter between the junctions of Davidson and Harcourt streets was now a pile of unreconstituted rubble – we came to allotments, little gardens, and then open meadowland.

We talked of Mum's leg – was she just being brave, or was real progress being made? We relived some of our old triumphs, dwelling on an exceptionally nice article about the play which had appeared in the monthly magazine *Island Culture*. And then we were silent, and my happiness, which had been as bubblingly irrepressible as it had ever been in its life, suddenly *evaporated*. I could see in her face that she was about to say something. And then she did.

—Ingrid . . .

One of the things which made me realize I was falling for Nellie in the first place was her impassive expression, which I (rightly) conjectured was a mask for a whole lot of intense emotions, interesting thoughts and . . . well, vulnerability. *The Masks of God* might have been destroyed when the tower came down. The Masks of Nellie were still in full operation. And I could not tell whether she was completely in control of herself and was actually suffering a lot, or whether she was cold as Christmas and was just worried about upsetting me. That's how flipping mysterious she was. My first thought was, *she is about to tell me she has got cancer.*

—Ingrid . . . it's Dad.

She stopped rowing, and allowed the boat to drift. Little drops of water fell into the brownish-green surface of the Windrush. Waterfowl scudded this way and that, blue duck and paradise shelduck. On the muddy banks, black stilts pecked for worms. Through the reeds, a creature swam with a sudden dart, too quick to be spotted, though I guessed it was a water rat.

—What about him? I asked, suddenly sounding like a sulky adolescent.

—Lesley Mannock rang me yesterday. Dad's had a stroke.

I wanted to punish her by pretending that I did not know who Lesley Mannock was; but of course I knew he was her dad's best friend – *Les Silences de Lesley Mannock* and all that. Of course, of course, because I could remember every flipping word she had ever said to me, I could remember every glance, every accidental (or was it accidental?) touch . . . I was in it up to my neck.

—Oh, that's terrible.

—The thing is . . . oh LOR. There's no easy way of saying this. Ever since . . . ever since the Quake . . .

And I was, like, suddenly realizing she was about to say goodbye to me, like, goodbye FOREVER. And inside, I was wanting to say, Yes, ever since the Quake, when you must have realized I was IN LOVE WITH YOU . . .

— . . . ever since the second Earthquake, something has happened to me.

—Something's happened to all of us, I said, hardly able to say the words.

—I've wondered . . . I've felt . . . I've been homesick, without really knowing where home is. And Skyping Dad has been a real lifeline, actually.

And I'm like, haven't I been a lifeline? But I just sat there, hoping I wasn't going to cry and then finding it was a bit late for that thought, as the tears splodged on to my stripy cotton dress.

—Oh my dear. It's awful. There's no easy way of telling you.

—But, I gasped . . . You'll come back. Of course you have to go and see your dad, but you'll come back?

—It's rather hopeless timing, isn't it?

She could not say much more after that. She seemed to be saying that she was going back to see her sick father, but that she had decided, whether he got better or not, to return to England permanently. The next day, she came out to Harrow (how? Bus or bike?) and slipped a note through the door. It ended – *Saying goodbye to you will be the hardest thing I do this week. N*

Part Three

CHAPTER TEN

I AM THE RESURRECTION AND THE LIFE . . .

There were fewer people at Canon Digby's funeral in the Cathedral than she would have expected. She had developed the clerical habit of counting heads, and including two vergers, and the cafeteria-women who were going to supply tea and sandwiches afterwards, there were twenty-nine in the congregation and rather more in the choir stalls, lay vicars, canons, as well as choristers. No Bishops. And the Dean had written a note to Nellie explaining the reason for his absence (the General Synod in York), a note so perfunctory that she considered it would have been kinder not to write at all. About ten clergy were gathered 'robed and in the sanctuary', as it used to say on invitations to inductions and similar ceremonies. The choir were there. The Master of Music has been solicitous, asked Nellie if there was any particular music she thought her father would have liked. Her equivocal reply had been 'Duruflé', because this was the Requiem setting which she herself liked the best; and as far as church music was concerned, there was no one on earth left to please but herself.

The music, which is at the same time poignant and sharp – it has an almost citrous quality – brought comfort. They had asked her to robe and sit in the sanctuary, to take some part in the rites, but this was not where she wished to be. She sat in the front row, staring at the wicker coffin, unable to register the fact of his death. She had most definitely not wanted to attend this rite dressed as a priest. She wanted to go as his daughter. And, though he would not have recognized a designer label if it had been pasted on to his *English Missal*, and though he could not tell the difference between Gucci and a jumble sale, she wanted to do herself proud? No, not quite. She wanted, in clothes she could not quite afford, to register a protest at the expected Church dinginess. A good second-hand dealer – Vestiaire Collective – enabled her to buy a Chanel black suit with a skirt which verged on the outrageously short, and shoes from the same house. Beneath it, she wore an extremely good white silk shirt. Her father had loved Augustus Hare. One of the oft-repeated quotations had been the remark made, as far as she recalled, by one of Hare's aunts, that the consciousness of being perfectly dressed brought an inner peace which religion was powerless to bestow.

She was conscious of being well dressed. The shoes were especially good. The skirt, only an inch or so above the knee, reminded her of something she had forgotten – how very good her legs were. She had watched other people in this condition at funerals. To a certain extent, although Charles's shoulders had heaved with grief at Josh's funeral (by far the most harrowing she had ever attended), the Nicolsons had all been in this condition: not taking it in. With the dispassionate knowledge of a professional – like a medic self-diagnosing some particular condition such as malaria or the early stages of meningitis – she knew that grief would probably 'catch up with' or 'hit' her some time in the near or distant future, but it had not done so yet. Here she was back in England, and it was the impression of this, quite as much as the loss of her father, which made most impact.

It was over three years since she had left. She had not forgotten any aspect of England, but she had very much ceased to be accustomed to it. The light itself was totally different. It was more subdued. Morning and evening skies had far less yellow in them. She was struck anew by the antiquity of the buildings. In Aberdeen, she had grown so used to nothing being older than a century. For all its cast-iron lamp-posts made in Birmingham, its students in straw boaters punting tourists on the Windrush, there was something patently and clearly non-European about Aberdeen, and, obviously, about the Island as a whole – its vegetation, its birdlife, the whole feel of the place. She had found that refreshing. Here, however, once again, the old stones of the Cathedral, the tombs of Bishops and barons who antedated the arrival of the Katanga in our Island, drew her back into that sense which never leaves you in England, of an older world; and these sensations had begun long before she saw the Cathedral itself. They had swept over her with the first glimpse of green turf, seen beyond the wing of the plane before it landed, and been prompted every few miles, if not yards, of the railway journey – the stock-brick backs of London houses as the train pulled out of Waterloo, the elms soughing on the border of bowls clubs and football pitches, unthreatened by earthquake, the cows munching inconsequentially in immemorial meadowland, the Georgian Corn Exchanges in small market towns, the far cooling towers, the sprawling housing estates, all still, still, safe and still. Here was land which could be relied upon not to erupt.

Dad had died while she was in the air. She had reached the hospital merely to stare at the pale waxwork which both was and was not him, so unlike him, because so white, and so uncharacteristic without the spectacles. She had decided to stay in his flat, whatever the pain this caused. Apart from any other consideration, she deplored the idea of paying hotel bills, and, despite invitations to stay with some cousins who lived quite nearby, she wished to be alone. In the days before the funeral, she had time to sort the 'things'. The task was completely simple, the 'things' falling into two easy categories – what she did and did not wish to keep. After Mum died, the canon had lived a life of the utmost simplicity. Three dark suits were taken to a charity shop. The smalls and the socks were recycled. There was not much clerical garb. He had not been one of those clergymen who had a personal collection of vestments. When asked to officiate in a church or cathedral, he wore what they gave him to wear. Two frayed soutanes on coat hangers she decided to keep. And it was touching to find his biretta in the wardrobe, alongside a broad-brimmed black fedora, which she could remember him wearing for parish visiting in the fogbound Midland towns. She could not quite bear to think of these obsolete and now almost comic items of attire appearing in a local charity shop, and it was obvious that no stranger would wish to finger them other than as some form of fancy dress. For the time being she retained them in the flat, torn between feeling she should destroy them, and wanting to take them to whatever the next destination would be. Otherwise, the black priest's shirts, and the clerical collars, she offered to Lesley Mannock, who had driven over from Worcester, where he lived, and would preside at the funeral Eucharist, and who was staying for a while at the largest hotel in the town. Dear old Lesley, with his bald crown, tufts of white hair, his bushy eyebrows, his silences. This left the papers and the books, and – a surprise, this – an extensive collection of diaries. Something told her not to read the diaries, not yet.

All the letters she had ever written to her parents were arranged in order of date and tied up with rubber bands or pieces of string. She put these into a box, realizing that the time was not yet right for her to read these either. The I. Compton-Burnett novels, a complete set, were always worth reading again, so those were put into the pile to be retained. Some of the devotional volumes, especially *The English Missal* and a volume called *The Monastic Diurnal* – a rendering of the old Roman Breviary into 'Prayer Booky' English – came into the same category, as far as she could see, as the dusty biretta. They were survivors of a vanished world of piety. She could not quite bear to think of hands other than her own poring over them as 'curiosities' in a charity shop. She found a man who took away the television set and the trashier detective stories. The small Roberts radio she retained. With what she recognized as absurdity, she half felt that the programmes which it was transmitting, quiz games with roars of studio laughter, *The Archers*, even the News, had been preserved for her in the years she had been away.

So, the work of clearing out the flat took little more than a day, and for much of the remaining time, she would sit quietly, utterly unable to think beyond this week, but realizing that, when the funeral was over, there would be decisions to make.

She had not, it turned out, told anyone but me and Mum about her idea that she would probably not be returning to the Island. In idle moments in the flat, however, she wrote letters to Dionne, explaining the choice; letters which she did not post. She toyed with a return to Oxford – it seemed the obvious destination – and yet, could she be confident of recovering her fellowship? Getting another job? For some reason, she could not much concentrate upon reading for long, though when she returned to *A House and Its*

Head, it was with quiet and deeply absorbed admiration. The simple formula which that wonderful novelist had evolved was to write plots which the Greeks would have used for tragedies and make them into comic melodramas. Sophocles rewritten in the manner of Mrs Henry Wood. No one could quite match the special atmosphere of those books.

Her father had asked very specifically that there should be no panegyric. Nellie and he had always savoured the egoism of the clergy, and she wondered, as the funeral took its stately pace, whether this typically self-effacing request had been interpreted by some of the clergy as a comment on their inability to match the occasion; perhaps, even, whether it was the reason the Dean had stayed away.

As the music spoke more eloquently than any clergy, she thought with deep affection of her father, and was back in the fogbound Midland towns, where, with such complete dedication and professionalism, he had cycled to sickbeds, attended school assemblies wearing his frayed cassocks, made by Wippell and Co. of Exeter, conducted weddings and christenings for people who never came to his church for any other purpose ('It doesn't MATTER. We are here for THEM, not the other way'), conducted funerals, nearly always more than one a week, either in church or at the crematorium, said Mass in the old people's homes, visited the lonely and the housebound, prepared an ever-diminishing number of people for baptism and confirmation, helped the illiterate with their benefits forms, made a weekly round of the local hospital wards – in the days when there was a mental hospital as well as one for the physically sick, not to poach on the chaplains' work but to see parishioners about to undergo surgery – visited the prisons, and, in latter days, given evidence on behalf of asylum-seekers and so-called illegals, and tried to teach some of the Asian neighbours English. These relentless parochial routines would be punctuated by the recitation of Morning and Evening Prayer (BCP) which he did, not privately in his study, but aloud in the church, even though it was unusual for anyone to join him – still he would say the words – '*I pray and beseech you as many as are here present* . . . ' And after the Morning Prayer, and Mass on Thursdays, he would return to the study in the Vicarage, fuggy with tobacco smoke, for everyone smoked in those days, for an hour or so of Greek – the New Testament, and the Fathers, above all the two brothers Basil and Gregory of Nyssa. It was in those rooms, her father's studies in the three parishes of her childhood, that Nellie had learnt Greek . . . There was something wholly satisfactory about her father's life. Her mother never complained about poverty or loneliness or boredom, though these three things were what she embraced when she left our Island and chose to be his wife. Not for the first time, Nellie found herself wondering why she was an only child.

She had not been concentrating on the funeral Mass; perhaps it was impossible in such circumstances to concentrate. And what would one concentrate *upon*? On the thought of Dad, in that wicker basket, pale and alone, the thin lips no longer capable of the light laugh? Already – good heavens, she must have been daydreaming – most of the congregation were shuffling forward for Communion, distributed by old Lesley Mannock and a minor canon of the Cathedral. A sacristan came and led Eleanor so that she would be the first at the rail. When she turned to go back to her seat, she took in the congregation. There were some old faces from the sad Midland towns – that was nice. And then, to her horror, she saw Doug. Sitting there. Looking up at her, most inappropriately grinning and giving a little wave.

*

—Will you be coming back?

She hoped, and then realized the vanity of the hope, that he did not mean what she feared he meant.

—To Oxford, that is, he said, leaving once more open the chance that he spoke only of her travel arrangements, in England, over the next few days, not her plans for the future, with or without him.

At last, they were alone together. There had been the service in the Cathedral – whose idea had it been to add two hymns on top of Duruflé? Not hers. There had been her journey to the cemetery on the border of the town, with Lesley Mannock, the few cousins, whom she seldom saw, and a gaggle of the former parishioners from the sad Midland towns. Lesley, dressed in a soutane and cotta, had pronounced a blessing over the coffin before it was consigned to the ground. Whenever possible, Lesley and her father had spent their days off together – Lesley's parish, of a similar high-church West Midland dimness, being only ten miles or so away. Her dad had always said that Lesley was the most faithful priest he had known. Unmarried. ('Very' unmarried? One could not be sure.) Austere. Quietly humorous. Like Ronald, clever, bookish. He had read his entire way through Barth, Balthasar, Rahner. Always appeared to have read the latest Papal Encyclical.

—So useful, Dad would say. Obviates the need for one to read them oneself.

Lesley asked Nellie to stand beside the grave and throw in a handful of earth. She wondered if she would return to this spot to commune with her father? He and Lesley had been long agreed on the dignity of being buried in unmarked graves, so, if she wanted to come back, she would have to take careful note of where they were burying Dad.

Aftershocks

Perfect weather. Near the grave, an old copper beech soughing in sunshine and light breeze. The familiar words of the burial
service. What would remain of her faith now he was dead? Tribal
Anglican she would still be. But would anyone, anyone at all, in
future, be Anglo-Catholics in the Lesley and Ronald mould, the
faithful recitation of offices and Masses in almost empty churches,
the maintenance of the Catholic faith in defiance of all the changes
within the Church itself, the fasting communions, the monthly
confessions, the almost Tractarian correctness of demeanour and
belief?

Tribal Anglican she might remain, but what was happening to
the Church of England? She felt, as they stood by the red earth
inadequately covered by the vivid Astroturf beside the gaping hole,
that they were burying all that was good and decent about the
Church of England by law established. Ever since she had landed
in England, the papers had been full of an especially nauseating
sexual scandal. Bishops and Archbishops had contrived to hush
up the misdemeanours of one of their number. The guilty man
had been sent to prison, but only after a string of his victims had
been constrained, by the brutal silence of the authorities, to fight
for justice. There had been at least one suicide among the victims,
and the offences had been of a peculiarly creepy kind, involving
nudity in church, buggery, canings. The pervert himself – he was
evidently a pathetic creep, perhaps in denial about the psychological
damage he was causing the boys. Such figures would appear anywhere, especially – she could see that plainly – especially in church,
which released so many strange demons and visited so many weird
areas of the psyche. No, what worried her was the attitude of the
Establishment – the Archbishop himself, sitting in Lambeth Palace
taking advice from lawyers rather than asking every single one of

the young men to accept his abject apology, his promise that all would be done in future to avoid such a thing being repeated. No – their attitude was not merely that the matter should be hushed up, that the Church should be spared 'scandal'. It was worse than that. It was almost as if they were living on a different moral planet where such practices – now known to cause a lifetime's harm – were somehow unserious, all part and parcel of the Church's life. Any barrel has its rotten apple. This should not turn us away from the essence of the Church's mission, which was, obviously enough, the appointments of 'suitable' – i.e. neo-liberal but not too liberal – men and women to deaneries and bishoprics; the smooth running of the Synods, local and General; the management of the Church's finances; the pompous holding on to their seats in the House of Lords, even though fewer than seven per cent of the population were now even nominal Anglicans . . .

She felt sick at the thought of her Church. As the earth was thrown in, and they buried it, she hated the Church of England, hated its cant, hated its buried sexual perversions, its delusional belief in its own virtue, its mindless wishy-washy political liberalism, its sheer lack of effectualness. She had said nothing of this to Lesley, as they had returned together to the much-dreaded (by her) funeral baked meats. The cafeteria of the Cathedral had been set aside for this rather gruesome part of the afternoon, and in order to reach it, she and Lesley had passed back through the Cathedral where her father had worshipped daily ever since she had been Down Under. Neither of them had planned to do so, but they had both by instinct paused by the grave of Jane Austen.

When Digby was claiming the Upper Hand over her mind, Eleanor Bartlett would try to hold on to the thought of her father's, and Lesley's, faithful ministries in the fogbound Midland towns.

If she thought – well, that is all right for THEM, but we can't live like that NOW, and the world has moved on . . . then she would think of George Herbert. Samuel Johnson. T.S. Eliot. Surely one would rather be at one with them, than apart from them? Surely, whatever some sordid bishop had done to adolescent boys in the 1990s, one could remain at one with George Herbert – at one in a way that non-communicants never quite could be. (*You must sit downe, sayes Love, and taste my meat;/So I did sit, and eat.*) If the appalling cliché-ridden nonsense of the latest pronouncement of the General Synod made one wish to give up any association with religion in general, and with the Church of England in particular, could not two pages of Boswell's *Life of Johnson* draw one back into the robust, moral universe of the greatest English conversationalist? If the vulgarity of the Happy Clappers, or sheer vacuity of a broadcast by this or that Archbishop, the cringe-making infelicity of phrase, made one wish to join the Society of Friends, did not a rereading of *Four Quartets* make one wish to remain 'where prayer has been valid'? And if none of these measures could prevent Eleanor from thinking, with Digby, that the whole of Christianity was an unbelievable and unsustainable nonsense, she would think of Jane Austen. Even if there is no one on the planet alive with whom I feel a spiritual affinity, I am, when I go to church, at one with Herbert, Johnson, Eliot and Jane Austen. And this is far more than simple sentimentality about the past. For without the past, we cannot be sane; and if the first few lines of *Burnt Norton* are true (and, for Nellie, nothing was more true than those lines) then a novelist who died in 1817 had just as much to say to us as one who was still alive. For the first time that day, she prayed – and now they were together, and fused, the prayers of Dean Eleanor and Digby, of Nellie, were more robust, more mystical, looser, less troubled by 'realism'.

Jane, who in your dying, expressed the thought that you were not sure we all should not be evangelicals . . . Jane, who grew up as I did in a Parsonage House and saw all that was best of our Church of England tradition, its subdued pieties, its respect for the intellect, its unshowy holiness of living . . . Jane, who was always funny, and could not restrain your malicious pen from satire . . . Jane, who has helped me to live alongside Bishop Dionne, and Bob, and the Island Synod . . . Jane, who was wise as well as clever, give me wisdom, give me patience . . . Jane, if Doug has been clumsy enough to stay for the tea and sandwiches in the cafeteria, please keep me calm, please keep me from saying the wrong thing.

He was still there, of course, one of the very few guests who had somehow managed to winkle a glass of red wine out of the waitresses.

It had been a difficult hour and a half in the cafeteria, the whiff of fish paste, or was it smoked salmon, in the air. She never ate fishy snacks at parties for the same reason that she never drank fizzy wine. Those who did so seemed unaware of the fact that it invariably produces appalling halitosis. With her mouth frozen in a party smile, she peered into the faces of those approaching her, hoping that they would not read in her own eyes an absolute ignorance of who they were. Sometimes she could place them – old parishioners of Dad's, a couple of former curates, wives of ditto, Cathedral ladies who had evidently been 'kind' to the canon in his latter days and offered Sunday luncheons and weekday sup-pers . . . Everyone repeated the same little phrases to her, some venturing on the tactless path of suggesting that she must feel relief that his sufferings were over . . . some blundering around the subject that she had been down on the Island when he died and how strange it must have been to be on the opposite side of the world, others, gentler in their intrusiveness, unrealistically wondering if she would continue to live in the canon's rented flat. The cousins, one a dentist in Bognor Regis, and a couple called Kath and Simon, relations of Dad's mother, who lived in a suburb of Bournemouth called Ferndown, spoke more warmly of Ronald, and one of them, Kath, had brought her a photograph of Dad when young, riding a bicycle, which Nellie had been glad to have. Doug had come up to stand beside her during this exchange with Kath, and, because the cousins in her family met so seldom, it was obvious that Kath did not know their circumstances, because she had asked Doug – 'Well, Nellie is obviously loving the Island, but how do you like it?' Somehow she had shaken him off, while she finished doing the rounds of the room. She knew from her father's example that she should speak a few words to every person in the cafeteria. It was a curiously exhausting challenge. When she found herself talking to a woman who turned out to be the Dean's wife, she realized with a stab of almost humorous disappointment that there would be no one to share this experience with. Ronald would have so enjoyed the fact, as would Jane Austen, that the Dean's excuse for not being there, conveyed by the curt letter, would just about have been passable, had he not instructed his wife to go as his proxy, and to say afterwards to Nellie that her husband was truly 'desolated' not to have been present.

No one afterwards, either, with whom she could talk about the party. The bereavement had not kicked in, but she did, most intensely, miss Dad (which is something rather different) as her companion for a post-mortem. When the last of the clergy-wives and the mysterious old people in their pale grey cagoules and white cardigans shuffled away, she would so loved to have had his commentary on them all. She had always liked Lesley – they were having lunch together on the morrow, at his hotel, before he went home – but she suspected him of being too high-minded to enjoy life's absurdities or to notice the foibles of others. By the time he had leaned over her and kissed her cheek as, in an avuncular way, he had done for as long as she could remember, she had realized, with some alarm, that the party was breaking up.

It suddenly ended. She had thanked the minor canon for helping with the service and for arranging the party. (It was he, it transpired, who had added the two hymns, including one which Nellie had never liked – 'Thine Be the Glory', set to 'See the Conquering Hero Comes'). And there she was, alone with Doug, to whom the minor canon, as a blundering parting shot, had said, 'Well, you two will probably want to be going.'

That was when Doug said, 'Will you be coming back?'

She did not want him in her father's flat, so they walked around the Cathedral precincts a number of times, and then started drifting through the town. It was very Oxford, but also very Doug, that he had not bothered with a suit for the funeral. Just the normal grey tweed jacket, an open necked shirt, flannel trousers, the sort of brown shoes she and her father used to call Cornish Pasties, casual lace-ups with a kind of rim.

—Tell me how things have been, Doug? You are happy at Duke?

Then it had all come out. Or rather, Doug had allowed as much of it to come out as made him seem vulnerable, even pitiable. Only afterwards did she guess that what lay behind the story must have been a failed relationship. Some graduate student or the wife of a colleague had either demanded too much of him, or given him the heave-ho. Doug had retained his college fellowship while he did a stint at North Carolina, now coming to an end. So, he could return to England in the autumn. There was a readership at Oxford for which he felt he would be eligible. He had not been idle in the United States. A new book – to Nellie it sounded a rather tired repeat of the old one, but of course she did not say so – was complete and had been accepted by Oxford University Press. It was about Dickens's narrative techniques. Ye Gods, does anyone want to read another such book? Just when everyone else had quietly confined them to the dustbin of history, Doug had begun to apply the techniques of 'Theory' – Derrida, Barthes and friends – to his rather laborious readings of *Bleak House* and *Our Mutual Friend*.

She allowed Doug to prose for some time about it. Being an academic herself, Nellie knew the need, from time to time, to bore about one's subject, regardless of whether one's audience was remotely interested.

—It came upon me when I was working on *Barnaby Rudge*.

Whereas the rest of the world read and reread the novels of Dickens for pleasure, Doug 'worked on' them.

—There's that passage where he says – Dickens, that is – *Chroniclers are privileged to enter where they list, to come and go through keyholes, to ride upon the wind, to overcome, in their soarings up and down, all obstacles of distance, time and place . . .*

—Where's that? She was struck by it, but listening with half an ear.

—*Barnaby Rudge* – some 'edge' in his voice, as he had turned into a tutor, impatient with an inattentive undergraduate . . .

—Sorry. Yes. You said.

—And I was really struck by the narrative sophistication of that. It's so *modern*, for God's sake. If Nabokov had written it, or Beckett, we'd not be surprised, but Dickens is aware of how the novel takes on these different narrative voices and vantage-points . . . It's something the novel, as a form, is uniquely placed to do, actually.

—What about the Chorus in a tragedy?

—You couldn't get that ambiguity in a drama – he brushed the remark aside with some testiness; her job, surely she remembered, *was to listen to him*, not to pick holes – because the Chorus is on the stage, there, in front of you, so to that extent, the Choric voice HAS TO BE TRUSTED, whereas the . . .

She allowed the lecture to go on. It was better than an analysis of their marriage. But, then, he repeated,

—So, Nell, are you going to come back? Are we going to try to make a go of it together?

Staring very hard at the ground, she paced silently.

They had taken a turning down a street behind the Cathedral, followed a crumbling sandstone wall, and come to the playing fields where about five games of cricket were still, at that late afternoon hour, in progress. She walked out, a little ahead of him.

—Nell! Are we? You have no future in the Dominions.

He had adopted this whimsical way of describing our Island ever since she had received the offer of the Deanery at Aberdeen. She looked at him, the beads of sweat on a bald forehead, the specs and the clever eyes, the imperfectly shaven round chin, the teeth which an American dentist had not straightened but had, miraculously, cleaned. The paunch, incipient when he had set out to the USA, had become a four or five month baby in the womb. There were splodges of red wine on the very slightly pongy shirt. Doug at Sixty.

She asked, or perhaps the prayers of Jane Austen allowed her to ask, whether, for more than five minutes, she would have considered him a desirable match if she had met him that afternoon for the first time in her life.

—I thought marriage meant something, he had begun to say, earnestly.

Meant something to whom, she wanted to retort. Now was not the time to recall Sammie, or Lanka that Indian graduate who was doing an MPhil on *The Moonstone*, or some of the others which might have been mere flirtations, but which still had possessed, at the time, the power to make her feel stabs of humiliation and pain. Nor was it the time to tell him what, of course, pride had always forbidden, that she had seen the porn on the laptop – seen its extent.

—It can't be easy for you, being . . . well, separated, or whatever we have been, the last few years.

Again, this did not seem worthy of a rational response. Jane was continuing to pray.

—I have not kept up with what the clergy think of conventional morality any more, I suppose, he said, with a pompous harrumph. It was a college noise.

At this point, she did turn, and say,

—I beg your pardon?

—Sorry, it was a thoughtless . . . I just thought of this Bishop . . . I mean, some of us thought it was just the Papists who weren't to be trusted with the nippers.

—I don't get your drift, Doug, she said coldly.

He did what he often did if he realized he had strayed into tactlessness. He supplied a quotation.

—*You should not take a fellow eight years old/And make him swear to never kiss the girls* . . .

—Shall I walk you to the station, Douglas?

He said he would rather walk alone. Oxford was only an hour away by train. He had begun to rehearse gastronomic options. If he caught the five something, he had told her, as if it were a matter of concern to her, there would be time for a college dinner. Otherwise, a new Thai had opened near the station which he was keen to try out. One of Doug's many rules of life with which she profoundly disagreed was that 'you can't go wrong with a curry'.

It had been blessedly easy to shake him off, but later that evening, when, presumably, drink had been taken, he had sent an email, saying what he had not been able to put into spoken words that afternoon. He really hoped she would consider returning to England to be his wife. He missed her. He felt they had not given their marriage a chance, and she had just seemed to, well, to walk away from it. He was sorry that he had made what sounded like cheap gibes against the Church, but he had actually meant what he said rather sincerely: he had assumed that as a priest she would take her marriage vows seriously.

This from Doug who had admitted to her on a number of occasions that he was an unbeliever, had never been a believer, and only attended college Evensongs and the like in the same spirit that he would attend a garden party, as a traditional olde tyme English 'thing', a ritual.

Nellie's mum, in allusion to the title of an amusing Maurois novel she and Ronald both used to enjoy, would talk about *Les Silences de Lesley Mannock*. Certainly, as a child, Nellie remembered them, when he would come over for Sunday supper. Even quite trivial inquiries – 'Did you have a decent day, Lesley?' – could be greeted with long pauses as he meditated the question. Sometimes three minutes would pass before he would reply, 'Yes. Yes, I think I HAVE', and then smile broadly. Ronald considered his friend holy. Gwen had not disputed this, but she had considered the holiness was scarcely an excuse for the maddening uselessness of the man. When his sister Jean, a doctor in Malvern, had been widowed, he had caught the train at once and sat with her in silence all afternoon. When he had asked her if there was anything she would like him to do, she had replied that there were two lightbulbs which needed changing (Jean is a short woman); and she was so tired, she would be really grateful if he could make them some scrambled eggs. He had smiled helplessly, and spread out his hands in that gesture of wonder and openness to spiritual adventure with which he often accompanied his conversation – when the talk began.

—He could not change a lightbulb. He could not scramble an IGG, Gwen had said with great Huia emphasis on the monosyllable as she recounted this moment in Lesley's life, which she often did, always with much affectionate laughter.

People nowadays, and especially male people, could not get away with personal incompetence on this scale – could they? Or were teenagers all like this, and was it only Nellie's generation, rising in age as far as the baby-boomers, who were actually capable of holding down jobs, mastering basic DIY and domestic skills? Being childless, she did not know.

Anyway, lunch at Lesley's hotel, before he caught his train, promised to be a stiff affair, if he was in one of his silent phases. This turned out to be wrong. Without asking what she wanted, he had ordered two large schooners of Amontillado sherry, which were on the table in front of him in the bar when she arrived and found him there.

Lesley Mannock is a tall man, always well dressed in the manner of the old-fashioned clergyman, a charcoal grey suit with a hint of pinstripe, and a soft linen clerical collar. (The Principal of Cuddesdon, when Ronald and Lesley trained for the priesthood, had said that only a true gentleman could get away with wearing black. To be on the safe side, charcoal grey: think how common Roman Catholic priests always looked.) He beamed at her as she entered the bar, and for the first time during that visit to England she wondered if she was going to burst into tears. Lesley was the last real contact with her parents, the last link with childhood. He had always been there, every few weeks of her life, between the time of her birth and her going up to the University. Many of the harmless shared jokes which she had enjoyed with Ronald had been ones which, she realized slowly, had also been shared with the old man who now sat opposite.

But after the first two or three sips of the sherry, she realized that this was a conversation which she would never ever be able to have with anyone else, ever again in her life. Here was a Christian priest of deep experience, total integrity, who had known her all her life. She did not want to go to confession, though she could imagine, if she did, no wiser confessor than Lesley. But she did want to be totally honest.

Over the lunch – a salmon mousse sort of thing, tasteless as it sat in its little salad nest, the inevitable 'pan-fried sea-bass' (how do you fry, other than in a pan?) and (for only optimists expect much from a 'Desserts Menu') the cheese board, washed down with a Muscadet which was too cold, the ice bucket killed the taste of the wine – her tongue was loosened. She told the truth.

Aftershocks

It was me who made up the two figures – E.L. Digby and Eleanor Bartlett, who only came together when the tower collapsed. That was just my way of trying to say something true about you, Nellie.

What she told Lesley Mannock, though, was basically that she had always been two people – on the one hand, the ardent Greek scholar, who was a religious sceptic, and on the other, the pious little girl who had been in love with Ronald; and not only with Ronald, but with the Church, its language and liturgy, its spiritual tradition, its mystics, its theology, its hymns, its architecture.

And now that she was beginning to recover from the Earthquake, and was also facing up to the death of her father, something had happened. The two sides of her nature had coalesced. She no longer needed to shield the priest Eleanor from what Digby was thinking about the gods, or about God. She could let Digby read the New Testament, and still inhabit the body and soul of Nellie the priest. The priest could admit that she was lonely, and desperate for some sex. The Greek scholar could stop being so priggish about her secretly held, almost Victorian scepticism, and allow that she loved hymns. The lover of the Gospels – both their varied Greek – Mark's so plain, so stark, John's so elaborately Semitic, while employing Hellenic tropes, Luke's so much as you imagine the conversation in the Koine Greek (i.e. the common Greek lingua franca of the Eastern Mediterranean) of some civil servant or merchant – and of their crazy, ragamuffin anarchism. This lover of the Gospels, however, could not believe – did it horrify Lesley to hear this? She could not believe in God.

When she came out with this, the sea-bass and what had been described as seasonal vegetables (the snap-peas and miniature corn on the cob imported from Kenya and Peru, so presumably seasonal somewhere) had all been consumed. The dining room was very quiet at that point, and her bell-like St Trinian's voice had carried audibly as far as the cheese board.

—You see, Uncle Lesley, I don't believe in God. I believe in Jesus, and I believe in the Holy Spirit.

He was still beaming, but her admission had provoked one of the famous *silences de Lesley Mannock*.

At first, she thought he was going to respond in the most maddeningly annoying way possible. She thought that he was going to ignore her confession, or, even worse, to laugh it away as that of the grief-stricken female.

The cheese board came. He dithered between Stilton and Roquefort. Asked her if she wanted port. Her head was swimming and she said no. She chose some Brie.

Then he said with great emphasis and a huge smile,

—It doesn't matter. It doesn't MATTER. Nellie. In your priesthood, in your SELF, all you have to do is to be true. Your father and I used to laugh at the motto at Cuddesdon.

—*Ten kalen paratheken phulaxon dia Pneumatos Hagiou tou enoikountos en hemin*, she repeated, with her mouth still full of cream cracker and Brie.

—Guard the deposit! Guard the deposit, he repeated, beaming with laughter. We thought it was so funny.

When she had swallowed, Nellie said,

—Dad used to say it had made you all laugh, but that after five years as a priest it was what kept him going. *That good thing which was committed unto thee, keep by the Holy Ghost which dwelleth in us.*

—It's the only thing we can do, Nellie. The only thing. We guard what has been deposited with us, and we try to pass it on. And, my golly gumdrops, Ronald was a good priest! And we'll so miss him.

Aftershocks

—I know.

She said it quite simply, and, whether because of the alcohol, or because she was talking to Lesley so intimately and intently, on so much deeper a level than she had ever imagined she would, she felt no choking emotion. She simply acknowledged the fact that her father had been a wonderfully good man, whom she would continue to miss, achingly, forever. The gulping moment of shock, of bereavement 'kicking in', never happened with her, and years later, she concluded that there was a reason for this. Her love for him had been uncomplicated by any unfinished business. It was true that she feared upsetting him, and that some of the actions she took, after he died, were ones about which she would have hesitated had he been alive. But there was nothing to grieve about – forty-two years of uncomplicated and uninterrupted love.

—When we guard the deposit, said Lesley, very carefully slicing a wedge of his Stilton and balancing it on a piece of celery, we are all different. It is the same deposit – perhaps, *perhaps*. Though Bultmann . . .

He laughed, for reasons which could only have been known to himself, and was silent for about two minutes.

—Well, never mind Bultmann! But we are all different. Our minds, in 2018, can't be the same minds as those in 1618 or 1918. And the sacred deposit which we pass on will mean different things to different people at different times and at different stages of your life. And for the present, in your life, it has all gone. It is blanked out. Nellie, you've just lived through an earthquake! You cannot expect that not to affect you. It would be far, far better not to believe in God than to believe He had sent the Earthquake, still worse, sent it to punish you all on the Island. Far better to get rid of that God altogether. Tell Him . . .

He smiled quietly, and then whispered,

—Tell Him to bugger off. You can tell God to bugger off some-times, you know.

She responded with an astonished stare.

—Live without Him for a while. But in so far as you can – guard the deposit. Who knows? Maybe we live in the end of days, as those late pastoral epistles said. Maybe Christianity itself – or certainly the sort of Christianity you and I were brought up to believe – is on its way out. Who knows what will happen? Go on worshipping Christ, Nellie. Go on worshipping Jesus in the Holy Sacrament. Go on reciting the liturgy – if you can, if you CAN.

She looked down at her Brie.

They took their coffee on a wooden bench in the garden. The gentle summer sunshine was wonderful. He wondered again, although she had already said no, whether she would not like a glass of port, but she was not to be tempted. They stirred their coffee-cans meditatively, and stared across the lawn to the slight mess the hotel people had made of the old garden – the climbing frame for nippers, the plastic tables with umbrellas. Nevertheless, it was a good scene, with an old brick wall against which a rambling rose rampaged . . .

She had no intention of becoming an old maid living in a small flat in a cathedral town. But Dad's flat was as good a place as any to spend a few weeks before the next stage was decided, and the law-yers had established, via the letting agency, that she could stay on for a few weeks. The rent was still being paid by the canon's estate.

She was quite sure, had been, really ever since being carried out of the tower as a wounded bird, that her life in Aberdeen was over.

A number of factors contributed to this realization. *Pace* Lesley Mannock's words, she was not sure, any longer, that she wanted to be a priest. If this feeling persisted, to be the Dean would quite quickly start to feel anomalous. She was sure she could revive *The Masks of God*, and if this certainty turned out to be an illusion, she still had a big enough body of published work to find an academic post. She did not want to go back to Oxford. Not really. Some other university would be just as good, better, for the present purpose which was . . . what? The old book still provided the right words, even if she had lost, perhaps forever, the knack of belief: *Grant that we may ever hereafter serve and please thee in newness of life . . .* That was what was needed. Newness.

That had been, of course, what had led her to go in the first place to the Island. The offer of the Deanery, held jointly with the research fellowship at Banks, had been newness of life in abundance. It had forced the two sides of her nature into hiding from one another. Clever Ingrid, she thought – while trying not even to think the word 'Ingrid' – to have spotted that about her. She had always been at least two people. No doubt most souls are divided, but in Nellie's case, the divisions were extreme. She really was a different person when she sat in the seminar room or stood at the podium in the Davin Lecture Theatre from the stately priest in her surplice, cassock, scarf and hood, seated in her decanal stall while the choir sang Wood in the Fridge. It had taken an earthquake to make her see it.

It had also taken an earthquake to confirm which she had previously only allowed herself to grasp in little grabbing gestures, which were subsequently suppressed or denied, that she had come to the Island in pursuit of Love. Here the sense of failure was more bitter than the consciousness that her life as a priest had unravelled. It had all seemed more or less clear when she had emigrated: she must get away from Doug. Her husband was, objectively speaking, awful. She could not function, while trapped in the marriage. She could not, quite, tell Dad that the marriage was over, and the new post in Aberdeen solved the problem admirably.

Only now did she admit to herself, only now, that Doug was only half the problem. Although a priest, Nellie had very little pastoral experience. As an ordained teaching fellow of her college, she had occasionally, quite literally, been a shoulder on which depressed graduates wept, but although these tears were usually occasioned by 'relationships', it was as often as not their lack as their complexity which made the young people unhappy. During her training, she had attended a few courses of a pastoral character, and been told about marital breakdown. She had very little practical experience of it.

This was one of the reasons she had been so troubled, shocked, by Charles Nicolson's outbursts about Pamela. Of all the mistakes she had made during her time at Aberdeen, the foolish flirtation, or whatever it was, with Charles weighed heaviest upon her. If she had never allowed it to happen, she just might have been of some small use to them when the blow fell and Josh was killed. As it was, she, the senior priest in the Cathedral where their son sang, merely added to their pain. It was apparent in the cold hatred with which Pamela regarded her. It was obvious from the studied way in which they asked Bob to take the funeral, and in the fact that, when they had packed and left for Carmichael, they did not even say goodbye to her.

Apart from cringing as she thought of the sheer silly vanity which had delighted in accompanying a handsome, distinguished lawyer on visits to concerts, and on afternoon walks, the sheer professional muddle was making her wince. Her certainty that Dionne and Ricky Wong were up to no good, that the very fabric of the Cathedral was probably threatened, would in normal circumstances have led her to consult the firm of Nicolson and Blake. It was precisely the sort of case in which Charles was an expert.

O, irony upon irony, reader! Allow a narrator to interrupt here and say that Nellie's fears about the Dionne/Wong axis did not paint the situation in nearly lurid enough colours! Even while she was away in England, Dionne, who had rather Rex-Tone-type feelings about Gothic architecture, was speaking about the damage done to the Cathedral's fabric as 'in a very real sense, a godsend'. She addressed the Chapter, in Nellie's absence, about the possibility of erecting a temporary structure. In Christchurch, New Zealand, after their quake, a Japanese architect had built them a cathedral out of cardboard. Dionne did not like the word 'Church'. She preferred to think of them all as a 'Community of Outreach'. What sort of signal did it give to the world if a Community of Outreach were to spend the money on offer from the insurance company – and we were talking hundreds of thousands of dollars here – shoring up some old-time building which quite frankly did not speak to today's younger people, let alone those on the margins of society? How much better to level the Cathedral to the ground, rebuild a light, airy contemporary structure which would reflect the values of a Community of Outreach. And there was a bonus. God was really and truly speaking to and through Dionne here, of that she was convinced. Ricky Wong, one of the most respected members of our Chinese community, could use the site of the Cathedral as an extension of his magnificent hotel, and the construction of a new multi-storey Convention Centre, which would bring to Aberdeen all the things we so desperately needed – business, foreign investment, especially from South-East Asia. A lot of people made remarks about the Chinese community which Dionne considered to be frankly racist. Wasn't Zacchaeus, the publican, the man who was the supposed wideboy and swindler of his day, wasn't he a friend of Jesus? Did not Jesus tell his followers to make friends with the Mammon of Unrighteousness?

Yes, all this was going on while Nellie sat in her father's little flat. And in the times to come, when Bishop Dionne's plans for the Cathedral were challenged by an alliance of conservationists, the Victorian Society in London, Deirdre Hadley and others, the case would eventually go all the way up to the High Court in Carmichael where it was heard by His Honour Mr Justice Nicolson.

That all lay in the future. Nellie knew none of it as she sat alone, meditating on the wreckage of her friendship with the Nicolsons. She thought, too, of the clumsiness, the ineptitude of the way she had handled the advances of Barnaby Farrell. She liked Barnaby, and the seminars had been the high point of her professional life after her arrival in the Island. She also fancied him, and it did not matter to her in the least that she was not in love with him.

Some readers might think – well, of course, she could not go to bed with him: she was a priest of the Church of England and they are supposed to be chaste!

Nellie had a different way of thinking about this, particularly when she had hurried home after their last evening together, wishing that she had, in fact, spent the night with him. She thought – one of the reasons I became a priest was because I am afraid of my own sexual nature. It was fear, not a love of chastity, which made me reject Barnaby. And yet she longed for sex, while fearing it, longed for gentle, sensual touching, and longed to be possessed, body and soul, by someone else's consuming passion.

Reading her dad's diaries made her contemplate, as she had so often done in the past, the mystery of her parents' life in that regard. She knew now the real loneliness of the only child. She had often observed, in families visited by death, that siblings squabbled about funeral arrangements, or about possessions – often quite trivial possessions – presumably because that set of not very valuable egg-cups, that chair, were symbolic of some all-but-lost part of childhood, a life-belt to be grasped as one bobbed about in the water. She did not envy her friends these squabbles, which could often turn nasty. What she did envy now, however, was the shared memory which even quarrelsome siblings could bring to the experience of loss. There was no one to talk to about Dad. She could hardly ask Cousin Kath whether she believed that Ronald and Gwen had any fun in the sack, and even if she had done so, there was no reason to suppose that she would have been in a position to know. The diaries, as she might have expected, shed no light upon Ronald's life with Gwen whatsoever.

Her dad had been an obsessive diary-reader, especially of clerical diaries. Parson Woodforde, Parson Kilvert and Bishop Hensley Henson were all great favourites. He also enjoyed political diaries, from Harold Nicolson to Barbara Castle, literary ones, especially Virginia Woolf, and of course the bizarre snobberies and unstoppable anecdotalism of Augustus Hare took first prize among all diaries. When it came to penning his own journals, however, Ronald was flat. The long years in the fogbound towns of the West Midlands contained almost no Kilvert-style evocations of the characters of his parishioners. He listed the names of old ladies visited, sick communions dispensed. Sometimes there would be a paragraph or two about some current piece of ecclesiastical politics. The crisis caused, during the 1970s, by the then Archbishop, Michael Ramsey, trying to force through reunion with the Methodists was the closest that particular volume rose to the heat of passion. 'Long conversation with L. about the Methodists. He says that there is no real provision for the ordination of their ministers, and that their superintendents are being talked up as Bishops, but with no apostolic succession. South India all over again. Or the Jerusalem Bishopric.' It went on for pages, Lesley and Ronald's agony over the question. She was astonished to discover that they had both gone so far as to visit a Roman Catholic monastery in Lesley's parish and made arrangements that they would 'go over' if the Ramsey measure was passed. The short entry – 'Methodist Reunion defeated in Synod. DG' – was eloquent in its way.

Apart from these Lilliputian concerns, whose pettiness and remoteness from anything that might be considered important were troubling, the diaries said little. When Gwen died, he simply wrote, 'G. died this morning. Woke and found her dead beside me. Kissed her forehead before getting up and ringing Haycraft.' The account of her mum's funeral merely listed the hymns – 'The Day Thou Gavest' and 'Soul of My Saviour'.

What made tears start to Nellie's eyes was the amount of space in the diaries devoted to her. From her girlhood onwards, he chronicled her sayings, her academic achievements, her school prizes, her Oxford prizes (the Gaisford, the Chancellor's Latin Prose Prize, the Ellerton Theological Essay Prize).

About Whatsisname her dad was characteristically reticent. 'Nellie married' was all that he wrote on her wedding day. And, during the first holiday with Doug at 'Quam Dilecta' – 'HC early at Cathedral. Nice cliff walk afterwards with N. Her husband does not join us at church. Nice to have some time with her, just the two of us.'

One thing which shocked her was that he must have been talking about the state of her marriage, both with Lesley Mannock and, more embarrassingly, with the chaplain of her college, Tony Gilmore, for, when she took the job in Aberdeen, her father wrote, 'L. was right – and T.G. – and my Nellie wanted to leave the man. Suppose this was the neat way of doing it.'

Oh, Dad! Why didn't you ask me? Why could we not talk about it?

Because we were the Chosen Frozen and that was the way we wanted to keep it. That was the sensible answer.

Only a few weeks before he died, Ronald had written, 'So now, it is this girl Ingrid. Hope it won't make N. unhappy. Bless her and keep her.' And about a week later – 'Glimpsed the famous Ingrid on N.'s Skype-machine. Rather fleshy face, which surprised me, but nice smile. Fringe cut very straight. Long hair, schoolgirlish. Betjeman girl?'

Nellie put down the notebook on her father's writing table.

This was the reason she had decided to leave the Island. The other things – the sense of disillusion with the Church, the sense she had made a mess of things with Barnaby and Charles – these could be lived with. What was happening between her and Ingrid could not. They had once – laughing, jokily, as though it could have nothing whatsoever to do with them – agreed that they disliked the use of a word beginning with an L.

She had meant, of course, reference to a Greek island and burning Sappho. (The closest Lesley and Ronald ever came to the ribald, in their shared quotations and jokes, was the notice placed in a newspaper – in the days when the upper classes announced their summer travels – *Lord Berners has left Lesbos and is making his way to the Isle of Man.*)

The phrase 'coming out' implied that one had ever been 'in'.

Nellie looked back on her schooldays and her crush on Miss Fire-brace. That had been a love which was deep, painful, intense, and it had lasted two years. After this, however, there had been no recurrence of a word beginning with an L – until Doug. And the word which she dreaded, as she knew now, was not Lesbian, but Love. Maybe if Doug had not been such a Pill, the feeling of being 'in love' with him would have lasted? And she would have 'made a go of it' if he and she had made babies . . . It was too late to ask questions such as that. Whatever it was she had felt for her husband had evaporated, and changed to contempt.

Perhaps, though, and this was what she only confronted after her final encounter with him at the funeral (and it was a final encounter – she never set eyes on him again in her life), perhaps she had not been equipped to love anyone at that point. And that was because she had been a divided nature who did not love herself?

Ingrid wasn't little, she was almost as tall as Nellie, but Nellie found herself patronizingly saying, inside her head, that 'clever little Ingrid' had identified the divided self. But it was that dangerous L. stuff which enabled her to see this. Nellie felt scorched by Ingrid's Love. After she had walked, by the light of dawn, to Harrow and shoved the note through the door of Ingrid and her mum's house – *Saying goodbye to you will be the hardest thing I do this week* – she realized that she had written a love letter – the first love letter she had ever written in her life. Torrents of fear possessed her. Control, control, that was what had shaped her life hitherto, and Ingrid of the long hair, Ingrid Ashe of the surprisingly fleshy face but nice smile, was going to remove that control and replace it with emotional anarchy. Without control, how could Nellie live? It was control which had won her the Gaisford Greek Verse Prize, control which she found in the confines of the Prayer Book, and the novels of Jane Austen, and the wisdom of Dr Johnson and the music of *Four Quartets*. *Take but degree away, untune that string,/And, hark, what discord follows* . . . People said they wanted love, but did they want a consuming fire? Didn't they really just want companionship? She did not like the phrase 'fuck buddy', it was not her style, but were not young people who sought such a companion perfectly sensible? Were not most married couples fuck buddies? And would you not rather have a nice friendly fuck buddy than be locked in the madness of Tristan and Isolde, Ferdinand and Isabella? And it was the madness of True Love which Ingrid held out. What made the consuming fire so dangerous was that she felt the same about the Girl.

She had to run away from that. If she ran, surely, she would 'get over it'? If she could just 'knock it on the head'? She tried to humiliate the glorious, swirling sensation which it made in her, simply to think of Ingrid Ashe, by slapping it down with commonplace clichés. As soon as she got home, having posted the fateful letter, the emails had begun to stream her way, begging to meet again, explaining that she would never have written that note, still less posted it by hand, if she had not felt the same way, imploring her not to break two hearts quite needlessly, telling her that Aberdeen needed her to save the Cathedral from Dionne and Wong's ravages, praising the Tragedy seminars and beseeching her not to make a tragedy of both their lives. Hundreds of words, thousands, were frenziedly sent from the tear-sploshed iPhone and laptop. Not one of them was answered.

Nellie knew that if she answered by so much as a syllable, it would give encouragement, not simply to the Girl – as she now tried to name her, fearing the three syllables Ingrid Ashe, as if, somehow by using them, she would be empowering them, like some arcane spell or incantation – but to her own anarchic feelings of . . . the unnamed L. thing. The How d'you call which dared not speak its whatsit.

When the first thirty or forty emails teemed into her inbox, she had read them with some fascination. They had such a powerful effect, however, actually making her gasp, lose her breath, choke with emotion, that she grasped, in gestures which recalled her attempts to reach out to the yellow-helmeted fireman-angel in the tower, towards Control. She now deleted the messages unread. Had been doing so for over a week.

They must stop. One day, the Girl would stop writing in this way, stop suffering. She was a frisky, young, impulsive, darling thing. She was a woman of the theatre. She would fall in love with someone else. Begin to play in another drama.

Hours and hours, in her dad's flat, were spent Not Thinking About the Girl, banishing the 'nice smile' from her head, trying not to remember what it was like, during rehearsals, when Nellie had gone among the Trojan Women and repositioned them, as they stood in their statuesque circle. When she slept, the 'rather fleshy' face was next to hers, covering her with kisses.

—Ingrid, if you, perhaps move downstage about . . . now nearer Hecuba! That's lovely.

To make this point, Nellie had put both her hands on those shoulders, and the Girl had reached up with her right hand, and touched the hand which held her. It was as if there were electricity in the touch. They had begun light kissing of one another's cheeks when they met, and when intimacy grew, and Nellie called more frequently at the house in Harrow, she gave smacking great kisses on both cheeks to Cavan Cliffe. But now, she held back, even from a light peck on the Girl's cheek, because to touch her with lips would be to suffer a scalding. It would not be possible to touch her, even lightly, without wanting – EVERYTHING. Once, the Girl had told Nellie how much she liked 'The Laughter of Stafford Girls' High', a sort of short verse novel by Carol Ann Duffy, and Nellie had gone into the reopened bookshop in Howley Street and furtively read it. She liked it a lot, and its overall subject matter, the irrepressible giggles which overcome adolescent girls, had certainly been part of her own experience at grammar schools in the fogbound. But it was for Miss Batt and Miss Fife that she read the poem. Their quiet evenings together 'seemed enough' at first, and before the tale is done, they are in bed together, and in love. Nellie had put the book down. Though the volume's title was one which might have been appropriate reading for the clergy – *Feminine Gospels* – it made her tremble. Later she went back to the shop and bought several of Duffy's books, and read them on the aeroplane back to England.

Already she had developed a Winchester routine, waiting in the flat until eight or so in the evening, and walking as the sun went down. Through the Close, past the old school, and out into the water meadows. The same old thoughts churned. Sometimes her head was filled with the theological preoccupations which had dominated the lunch with old Lesley, sometimes with the poignancy of her father's diaries; but in both cases, they were really only ways of feeling, not thinking, the aftershock of the Girl.

Not long after nine, as she came back across the meadows, there was an atmosphere of dusk, and as she followed the long, crumbling stone of the medieval college walls, the street lamps twinkled into light. Somewhere, a great clock, either in the squat Cathedral tower, or in the college, reverberated through the dusky summer air. And suddenly there she was, with her mousey mane frizzed against the mousey-coloured Winchester stone, and the nice smile frozen with anxiety, and the brown eyes bright with hope.

CHAPTER ELEVEN

That funny little flat! And that funny little bed! Where you had been having such unfunny thoughts. And there we were. I said earlier on somewhere in this book that those conversations you have, when you are both lying there with no clothes on and you have just made love, aren't such a good idea. Because you say too much, and then the other person, next time they are lying with no clothes on, only with someone else, tends to repeat them. But that's not going to happen, my darling, because there can't be another person, my east and west, my only love. Not ever. So, eight years ago, we lay there until I don't know when, talking and talking, and not eating, for hours, telling our stories, and doing what we had both dreamed of doing all our lives and never quite had done before – making love.

—You're laughing.

—I'm not laughing. I'm just – oh, I don't know.

—I do. There you go again. What? What's funny?

—Doug used to say he didn't know who he was in bed with – Eleanor the Priest or Digby the Greek.

Aftershocks

—I know who I'm in bed with.
—Who, Ingrid? Who?
—With Nellie.
—Come here, you.

FINIS

ACKNOWLEDGEMENTS

I have not added acknowledgements to any of my previous novels, but in this case thanks are very much due to Clare Alexander, Karen Duffy, Will Atkinson, Margaret Stead and Frances Wilson, who helped this short book on its way, and to Tamsin Shelton, the copy-editor.